A Step Beyond

A Step Beyond

Marci Archambeault

The Quest
Leominster, MA

The Quest
P.O. Box 1321
Leominster, MA 01453

Editor: Barbara Bell
Cover Art & Design: Jennifer Aldrich

Printed in the United States of America

ISBN 1-888861-07-X

Library of Congress Catalog Card Number: 99-70085

The information contained within this book is not intended as medical or psycholog-
ical advice. For help in these matters, consult a medical practitioner.

This book is dedicated to my friends beyond. The first thing I feel every morning is your love wrapping me in waves of warmth, letting me know that I am never alone. Thank you for all that you bring to my life.

ACKNOWLEDGMENTS

To David. I love you with all my heart and soul. You've touched my life in so many ways. To share my dreams with you makes them so much more complete.

To my mom. You knew this story on a first-hand basis. You lived much of it with me. Thank you for supporting the fact that I needed to follow my own heart even when others told you it was a bad idea. Also for reading over the material and helping me to make this story even clearer. I can fly now.

A special thanks to my editor Barbara Bell. You always seemed to know exactly what I was trying to say, and you made me believe that this book was worth publishing. Your amazing talent shaped this story and gave it the ability to speak to others. That makes you an angel in my life. Thank you from the deepest part of my soul.

To Jennifer Aldrich, my friend, cousin, and graphic artist. The cover of this book is beautiful, and the fact that you are the one who created it makes it even more special. Twist and shout and always make lots of noise while you dance in the rain.

To all of my friends and family. Thank you for all of your support and excitement while I wrote this book. Sharing each step of the way, even the hard parts, made the endeavor so much more exciting.

Lastly, in loving memory of my cat Bingo. You sat on my lap through hours of typing, even doing some of your own here and there, keeping me company. We had sixteen years of friendship and unconditional love that saw me through the best and most trying times of my life. You'll always be a part of me and I love you.

"Life is an adventure; a number of twists, turns, ups, and downs that lead you back to where you started, only much wiser for coming along."

—Marci Archambeault

A Step Beyond

The Beginning
December 19, 1994

David touched my head so sweetly, gently combing my hair with his fingertips. He kissed my cheek lightly, my body melting into his touch. Then he cupped my face in his hands and slowly, ever so softly, kissed my lips. At that moment, I was the most beautiful being in the universe. Through his gentleness, through the power of his love, I could see my soul. Lost in his touch, every part of me — even those I had tried to hide from myself — exploded and lay exposed. Tears of joy rolled down my cheeks. Tenderly, David kissed them away and asked why I was crying. But I couldn't speak; I had no words to describe the beauty I was feeling. Somehow he understood. Silently, he laid me down on the bed and held me, waves of love moving through his soul to mine.

The power inside me began to fight to come to the surface. I shook from head to toe; waves of fire rolled through me. My body heaved. And the tears kept flowing.

I thought I might be dying: All of a sudden there was a light so beautiful, so intense, that I felt it could only be the light of heaven. The light pulled me toward it with such force that I was terrified.

Where had I felt this before? It seemed so familiar.

Suddenly the pulsations stopped, but the light grew stronger. I fought to come back, but a strong sense of love held me there, inside.

And then I heard two voices, one female, one male. They were calling out to me. I knew those voices; I remembered them from somewhere deep inside me. I felt the love in their words, but I couldn't hear what they were saying. All I could do was wait, hoping they would find me. I couldn't go any farther on my own, but I didn't want to turn back. I wanted to feel them by my side. I was longing for something but had no idea what it was. I was desperate to know.

"Show me what I'm looking for. Show me why I feel incomplete," I begged.

Then, with a burst of energy and love, they touched me. I cried again, overwhelmed by the beauty. I knew exactly what they were saying . . .

"Welcome home. Welcome home."

I was finally home.

Õ

I've never felt normal. I used to look at other people and

long to be like them — their world seemed so much simpler than mine.

Not now, though. Yes, a normal life would have been easier. But it also would have been dull. And my life has never been dull.

Those around me thought I was as normal as they were. They didn't see the secrets I kept hidden, hidden so deep that no one — sometimes not even I — could touch them.

While I was growing up, I lived in three very different worlds. One was the world where I lived with my family. I was the daughter who begged for answers, for explanations of the society around me. In that world, I tried my hardest to be perfect: I stayed out of trouble; I got good grades; I tried to fix everyone else's pain.

Then there was the world where I lived with my friends. In that world I tried to fit in, to care about gossip and clothes and saying the right thing. *Cool* meant pretending not to care about anything but being a kid.

Then there was the third world — a dimension of amazement, a space where I touched heaven, where I was loved beyond comprehension.

It's not that I wasn't loved in the other two worlds. I was. But the love I felt in that third world was more intense, miraculous. And I was different in that world: I could see the hearts and minds of others; I could learn the meaning of life, of the universe. I spoke, danced, laughed, and was the truth of my soul.

I liked the Marci of the third world, and I longed to be her in my other worlds. But those worlds were physical, the rules and rea-

sonings there so different from the spiritual world. And I didn't have
the words to explain. That third world was so much more than imagination. It went beyond what the mind could comprehend. Science
couldn't follow me there: That world, where spirits walked, was far
beyond the physical.

As I grew older, a teenager now, I was always aware of my
third world. Every day it spoke to me: Stop hiding. Slowly I began
to talk about my secret world with my mother and my closest
friends. But I couldn't share with them the person I knew I was. I
was afraid that they would never accept the truth of me or that somehow they would destroy it.

Of course the telling wasn't enough. I wanted to give others
the peace I had been graced with. I knew that if I could share the
love, the beauty, of my secret world, I could help others find the
sweetness of their souls and somehow ease the pain I saw around
me.

As the years went by, my need to help others grew stronger.
I had planned to be a lawyer or a schoolteacher. Instead I was drawn
into a fourth world, the New Age world. This was a physical world,
but a world populated by people like me, people who could understand. Yet even in this world I kept certain truths — my soul — hidden. And now I found myself with four separate worlds, none of
them linked to any of the others, facing what seemed the impossible
task of joining them together in some way.

When I was twenty, I founded a company I called The Quest.
I needed a way to reach out to people — to give them the gift of my
third world — without exposing myself. Through the company I
published four meditation tapes. The first packages didn't bear my

last name, never mind my face. My plan was to stay hidden, to keep my secret safe.

Then I met David.

Õ

David is down to earth, left-brained, and conservative. He wears Ralph Lauren. His parents are still together. His friends all work in corporate America or in hospitals. He's a salesman, and he wants to get ahead financially. He loves parties, food, video games, skiing, and having a good time. He's been known to philosophize about life, but only when he's had a few drinks. He is the sweetest, gentlest soul I have ever met.

We met at the company where my mother and David worked. It was late; my mother and I were using the copier to prepare for the health show where I was going to introduce my tapes. As we were working, David came over to talk with us. One smile, and I fell head over heels for him.

I was terrified he would see the papers right in front of him that screamed out, "This girl is nuts!" But he never noticed the papers, only me.

Within a week, we were inseparable. The physical attraction was immediate. David brought out a passion in me: He made me feel sexy, beautiful, and alive. His kisses ignited my body; his voice melted my insides. With him, I felt normal. He didn't know or care that I had four different worlds, and neither did I. Ours was the only world that existed for me.

We had been together a month when I realized I had to tell

him the truth. It was his twenty-seventh birthday, and we were curled up in each other's arms in my bedroom. Candlelight filled the room. As he stroked my hair, I relaxed more deeply than I had ever relaxed in my life. It felt so warm wrapped in his arms, surrounded by his soul.

"This man is taking away all of the pain I've ever experienced," I thought to myself.

I had known for a week that I was in love.

We had promised each other that we wouldn't say those words. I'd warned him not to get too close. I hadn't come right out and told him about me and my worlds, but I had hinted at them. He was so normal, you see. He didn't question how society works; he simply lived by its rules. Life was about making money, securing your future, and having fun. I wanted so badly to be part of that world, but I knew it wasn't possible. Would he love me if he knew who I was? Would he be willing to share my worlds?

It was David who talked first. I don't remember exactly what he said, but it was something about being resigned to my seeing other people again. My heart stopped. No other man had ever given me that freedom — the choice to date other people . . . and the promise not to leave.

I didn't want anyone else though; I only wanted him.

I twisted around, kissed him gently on the lips, and looked into his eyes. There was such gentleness, such timidity there. He looked at me as though I were an angel who had graced his life for a few moments and might now leave him. At that moment, I fell in love with him all over again.

"David, I don't want anyone else," I said. And it seemed as

though I spoke to his soul. "I love you. I love you so much."

I was crying; I couldn't breathe. I had said the words I wasn't supposed to say, words I had longed to say for a week, maybe even since the night we had met. He burst into tears, beautiful tears. "I love you, too. I love you so much, but I couldn't say it first. I love you. God, do I love you."

That night, with candlelight dancing around the room, we laughed, we held each other, and we said the words over and over again. It was a glorious night, but I still didn't know: Would he love the truth inside? Could he accept a woman who spoke to spirits and longed to return to a place beyond this earthly realm?

Several more weeks would pass before I told David about that woman, about me. Again, he gave me an opening, bringing up the supernatural in passing, in a casual conversation. And so I told him everything: about my worlds, about my gift and my need to share it with others, about my vision for The Quest.

And it was fine.

A month later, David joined my business. He brought to it a wealth of knowledge about marketing, packaging, and selling products. He also realized long before I did that one of the products we were selling was me. No more hiding. We rerecorded the tapes and repackaged them, my name and face on every one. David scheduled me, and I went . . . to radio interviews, to seminars, to conferences. And David talked openly about the tapes to everyone, including our families.

I tried to tell myself that this was what I wanted, that I had a gift that should be shared with the world. But the truth is most of the time I just wanted to run away. Of course I knew I couldn't. In the

New Age arena where I now spent almost all my time, I was surrounded by people trying to define a spiritual world that I knew
could never be defined by words alone. I had to get my message out,
and then I could be free. In the meantime, there was no escape, not
even with David. Everything was work.

Fire walking: *The ancient art of placing one's feet to burning coals and walking across them without injury. In ancient times, it was a way for people to dance with fire, to hear its message of love, to experience its power.*

I learned to walk the coals years ago. Since then, I've taught others to dance with the fire. For me, fire walking is a celebration, and that's what I have tried to teach my students.

Power Surges
January 13, 1995

In the midst of that unhappiness, maybe because of it, the most wonderful, incredible, frightening, and confusing thing was happening to me. I began touching a mysterious power.

I had had a taste of what was to come that night in December, when David's touch had caused me to see and hear the man and woman from the other side. I thought then that it was an isolated experience, a moment of love that touched my heart. I had no idea what it would turn into.

It happened a second time on a Friday night in January, right before David and I went into business together. I had planned dinner by candlelight and an evening with David, just the two of us. My mom was going out, and we would have the house to ourselves.

All day I had felt a strange sensation, a shakiness that seemed to be coming from deep within my body. By evening, the feeling was more intense. I could sense that something was going to happen, and it frightened me.

David was supposed to come at five o'clock. At four thirty I called and asked him if we could meet at eight thirty instead. My friend Jess had called; she had something she wanted to talk over. I happily agreed, hoping she would distract me, hoping the sensation would pass.

Jess did come over about ten minutes later, but she didn't stay long, just half an hour. In that time, the feeling didn't go away; it got worse. The trembling grew more intense, and so did a feeling of being overpowered. Although I'd experienced that sensation before, this was different. It was much stronger, and I was scared to be alone. I wanted David with me, but now I couldn't reach him. I ran downstairs and turned on all the lights and the television, hoping the trembling and the feeling would go away.

As I sat down to watch some program or other, the trembling became physical. A wave of nausea came over me, and my abdomen shook. I wondered if I was having a seizure. I was breathing so hard, and now my jaw was shaking too.

In desperation, I called out to the other side and heard the words, "Relax. You are safe. Come to me."

The power was too strong; I couldn't find my way. Thinking that if I could get to the bathroom and take a shower, maybe the shaking would stop, I tried to climb the stairs. But the shaking now was so strong that it dropped me. I grabbed onto the banister to keep from falling. I was choking, barely able to breathe.

I tried to calm down. "This isn't real," I said to myself. "I'm just trying to find excuses for not being alone with David because it's so intense between us." The thought of David and me together sent more shock waves through my body. Their power was almost unbearable. I tried to scream but couldn't.

I had to get to the shower. I was sure the water would wash this all away. Slowly, shaking, I crawled up the stairs. Finally I got to the bathroom and the shower. I turned on the water, but when I tried to stand up, the shaking forced me to the floor.

I knew what I had to do. Bed. I had to lie down and go to the other side. Somehow I knew that the shaking was power, and that if I went to the other side, it couldn't hurt me.

I crawled to my bedroom. I lit a candle and dragged myself into my bed. The moment I lay down, the shaking got worse. It was coming in waves. It started in my abdomen and moved through the rest of my body in spasms. With each spasm the muscles in my neck would contract, lifting my head off the pillow, and my arms and legs would flail. I had no control. My breathing was rapid, and no matter how hard I tried, I couldn't calm down.

I don't know how long the spasms lasted; it seemed like hours. Then everything changed. I saw the candle, its flame licking upward, and felt its familiar call. As I connected to the spirit of the flame, my body grew quiet. A deep sense of relaxation came over me.

I felt a pull to go, but this trip to the spiritual world was different. I had no sense of going to a physical place: There was no ground, no sky. Instead I journeyed to my soul, and there I found the fire. That's all there was. A huge bonfire. It was beautiful, its flames rising to incredible heights, its sparks filling the air with orange fireflies.

The fire pulled me closer. I couldn't resist, but somehow that was all right. As the fire grew, so did my spirit; as the fire reached new heights, so did I. My soul awakened, and I became one with the flames. I felt their power both to destroy and to create change. Yes, a single spark could burn down a house, a forest, an entire town. But the real secret of the fire wasn't its power of destruction; it was the power to change lives. Whatever it touched would never be the same.

The most amazing feeling I was experiencing was love — pure unconditional love. The fire was healing: It had the power to burn away pain, to cleanse the soul. The pieces of myself that had been flung apart by the cruelties of life seemed to fall back into place, and my spirit roared with the vastness of the fire.

The fire had knowledge, an understanding of the world. It showed me that the balance in nature had gone askew. And I understood the source of that imbalance is fear. Instead of revering the fire, people are frightened of it. Instead of celebrating it, they try to conquer it. And I knew that every time the fire is conquered, it must conquer back — not because it's angry, but because that is the wheel of life.

Then I saw the same thing happening with the earth, the water, and the wind. At one time we honored those elements. But for centuries now, instead of respecting them, we have tried to conquer them. We robbed the earth of its metals and its fuel. We broke its ground and suffocated it with our industry. We dammed up the water's flow, crushing its life. We filled the air with pollution, choking the wind. We set aside simple harmony, and the elements were forced to fight back.

I saw the future: Fires destroying what people had built. The earth heaving and cracking, swallowing the signs of industry. The water flooding lands and homes. The wind blowing, clearing away the sources of pollution. And the people running and screaming in confusion, in fear, in anger. They don't understand that nature is simply trying to restore balance. They don't understand that we can't expect the enormous forces around us to be stagnant. Without change, everything dies.

I found myself getting angry. I wanted to scream at people, to tell them that they were taking beauty and destroying it. Then I realized I was no longer with the fire. Now I was one with my rage. Rage was not part of the fire. It understood that change — for good and bad — is part of life. It's people who get angry when faced with something they can't control.

I looked back into the fire, needing to feel its love again. And there I saw the answer: We have to learn to live in balance; we have to learn that we are all one, that no one and nothing is separate. That means we have to recognize our role in nature. It may be easier to rant and rave — to blame God or some other force — when catastrophe strikes. But the reality is that we have to take responsibility for our world.

Õ

With those thoughts, I returned to my body. I was shaking again, waves of energy running up and down my spine. As they slowly stopped, I could hear David downstairs watching television.

"When did he get here?" I wondered.

Finally the twitching stopped, and I lay in bed feeling a deep peace. I desperately wanted to sleep, but instead I got up and showered.

As the water ran down my face and body, I thought about what had happened. I wasn't sure why I had seen the fire. All I knew was the great urgency within me, a sense that the world was on the verge of a very important decision and that people needed knowledge to make that decision. The call I had felt all my life to share the message of the spiritual world burned within my soul.

I got dressed and went downstairs to David. He gathered me in his arms, wrapping me in his love. As he kissed my lips, I trembled one more time.

"What was that?" he asked. I could hear the worry in his voice.

"I'll tell you later."

And I did. I don't know when I realized that I could tell David anything about myself and that he wouldn't judge me. He listened intently as I described the shaking and the fire. He caressed my forehead and my hair, and told me everything would be okay.

Then he said, "Marci, next time this happens, don't push me away. I'll give you all the space you need, but I want you to know that you don't ever have to go through this alone."

I thought I couldn't love him any more than I loved him at that moment. But what did he mean by "next time this happens"? I hoped I would never go through that again.

David was right though. The surges of energy kept coming. Every time he kissed or touched me, the trembling would start. We would lie in bed together, eager to love each other. But as soon as he touched me, I would begin to shake and breathe heavily. Inside I would twist and turn and cry for it to stop. I felt as though I was dying.

David would talk me through it. "It's okay. You need to do this, Marci," he would say. "I'm right here, and I'm not going to let anything happen to you. Don't fight it."

His voice would soothe me and help me feel safe enough to go. As I relaxed, I could hear him speaking but couldn't answer. I was too far away.

Usually it started with drifting. If I'd felt any pain during the surge, it was gone. According to David, I barely breathed. Then, suddenly, I would see the fire. As its power started to overwhelm me, I would race back to my body. And the cycle would repeat once, twice, ten times: The trembling would begin; I would stop fighting and see the fire; and then I would run.

Finally, I would hear David's words and stay. From that point, it was always different. Sometimes I would be with the fire, taking pleasure in the flames while I listened to their message again and again. At other times I would just drift along in the peace. Nothing existed, and that was okay. Most of the time I felt an intense power coursing through my soul. Once I felt what seemed to be a fireball go from my pubic bone up to my sternum.

There was just one constant: I had no idea why it was happening.

I looked everywhere for answers, but no one was able to help. One person made me a crystal amulet that was supposed to discharge the energy. I know that stones hold the energy of the earth, and I had worked with them before, so I accepted it. It broke in half just a few weeks after I started wearing it.

I talked to healers and massage therapists — people who understand the power of energy — but no one knew. Some told me that the energy in my body was out of balance and that they could fix it for me. Usually I said no. And those I allowed to try to help me? They would get one glimpse of what was happening, and then I would never hear from them again.

David was my only real help, but he also seemed to be the source of what we had started to call my "power surges." We'd settled on that name after I'd said the experience felt like standing on a hill holding two metal poles while lightning ran through my body.

Kundalini: *From an Indian yoga philosophy, the energy that is coiled at the base of the spine like a serpent. When a person raises this energy through meditation, yoga, or sexual response, the energy moves in waves through the spine's chakras, six energy centers along the front and back of the body. When the coil unfolds into the seventh chakra, at the top of the head, the person unites with the divine, and the energy is manifested as wisdom and bliss.*

Home
March 18, 1995

One night about two months into the power surges, they changed. It was a Saturday, and I had started my monthly cycle. I had taken massage clients in the morning and early afternoon, but had been in a fog most of the day. I didn't have cramps — which was unusual for me — but I was very tired. I finished up with my clients and went home to call David. I told him I was planning to sleep for a while. He asked if I wanted to go see a movie later that night. I said yes, hung up the phone, and fell sound asleep.

Four hours later I was up and ready to go. I still felt hazy, but I blamed it on my cycle. Besides, haziness was better than cramps any day. Of course, it didn't last. Halfway through the movie, the cramps started, and by the time we got home I didn't feel well at all. I laid down on my bed and instantly started shaking. This time, the shaking seemed stronger than usual: My head was flying from left to right, and it was constant. My body didn't shake in waves; it just shook. I was crying.

David was frightened. "Please Marci, can I get your mom?" He pleaded with me, "I'm too scared to handle this one alone." I nodded yes, and he ran from the room.

In minutes my mother was by my side. She took one look at me — I had told her about the power surges, but this was the first time she actually had seen one — and ran to the kitchen to get me something to drink. She was hoping that all I needed was sugar. She brought back some juice and tried to get me to drink, but I was shaking so badly that I couldn't. By now I was hyperventilating too. David tried to calm me, but my mom told him to let me be, that the breathing probably helped the pain. Then she put a cold compress on my head and tried to give me energy with her hands, but that only made things worse. Her energy felt like a live wire touching my skin. In fact, just her normal energy and David's was too much to bear. The air itself seemed electrified; it burned my skin. I was shaking so hard that my upper body lifted off the bed.

"Why?" I screamed in my head. "What do you want?" But there was no answer.

After a time, my brother walked into the room. I could feel his shock. He knew his sister was "weird," but this was too much.

"She'll be okay. This has been going on for some time," I heard my mother tell him. "It's just energy." She was trying to stay calm, but I could feel her worry growing.

She turned and spoke to David: "If we take her to the hospital, they'll just drug her. I don't think that's a good idea."

David had no intention of bringing me to the hospital, but

everyone in the room felt helpless. There was nothing they could do but sit with me and wait. My brother was on the floor near my bed; David sat beside me, fear and worry in his eyes; my mother sat at my head, praying. I could feel their thoughts. At that moment I knew everything about them; later, when the surge was over, I would forget.

Then, finally, the pain was gone, and I was flying. I heard my mother ask me to breathe, but I couldn't respond. I heard David tell her that my spirit had left my body and that I wouldn't be breathing for a few moments. I knew my mother's fear, and I felt David let go in exhaustion. Their part, they thought, was over. Now they would just have to wait for me to come back.

I moved past feeling them to where there was only peace, but even this space was different. The fire wasn't there. Instead there was a gate made of stone. As I came to it, I saw a magnificent light, magnificent beyond description. The power was so intense, much stronger than anything I had ever felt before. Suddenly I realized that this was the light you see when you die, and that I was about to be within it.

"No," I screamed, "I'm not ready to die." With that, my spirit flew back to my body, and the shaking began again.

I couldn't understand why I had seen the light. Being back in my body didn't help; I could still feel the light calling to me. There was nowhere to hide. I put my hand over my forehead, trying to shut out the vision, but I kept seeing the stone gate and the light just beyond it.

I called to the spirits I had always known, praying for guidance, but they couldn't help. I saw them waiting for me on the other side of the gate.

And then I knew why this experience was so different. I had gone to the other side before, but I had always been aware of my body; I had always been able to feel David or others around me; I had always known that I was still alive. This time I felt no connection to my body. If I left, would I come back?

I heard everything that David, my mother, and my brother were thinking, and I couldn't bear it anymore. In one instant I realized that I was getting tired, that I couldn't hold on much longer. In the next, my spirit let go, and I was facing the light again.

In that moment, I felt the glorious touch of heaven. I became color, billions of colors so beautiful that I was afraid I couldn't bear it.

"This is home," I thought. "Home."

I knew this light. It was the light of everything, the light of creation. All worlds and all knowledge existed in that light. To feel that knowledge was miraculous, a gift. Never again would I be afraid of dying.

With that thought I realized that I wasn't dead, that I could actually see the light — be the light — without dying. My soul cried tears of joy.

I could have stayed, but somehow I knew I had to go back to my body. And suddenly I understood the power surges: They were helping me take on more and more energy within my own body so that I could go to the light whenever I wanted.

With that realization, I was back in my body. I trembled and felt the waves of nausea again. David knew I was back — he'd seen me go and come so many times before. I could hear him tell my mother and brother that it was almost over.

When the trembling finally stopped, I opened my eyes, looked up at David, and said, "Landings suck." A smile of relief filled his face. Of course, I meant it. I hated coming back. Yes, it was a fight to go, but that was my fault. Coming back was worse because this world seemed so harsh compared with the sweetness of life on the other side.

Õ

After that night, the power surges became part of my life. It didn't matter where I was — I might be working or even driving — they would hit with an overpowering force. At times they would take days to manifest, days of feeling moody, the world grating on my nerves. It wasn't anything in particular; it was everything. The energy in everything sent impulses through me. Going dancing was like getting caught in a blizzard. But instead of cold, wind, and wet beating at me, it was people's emotions and my own growing energy.

David began to see the surges coming before I did. I'd be feeling frazzled, and he would know.

"You're going to have a power surge, aren't you?" he'd ask.

"No," I'd say defensively.

He would just smile and say, "You sure?"

"How do you know when I'm going to have one when I don't?" I would ask, annoyed.

"Because you get distant. Everything I say seems to make your skin crawl. If I touch you, you pull away as though your skin is on fire. Even the air around you seems to change."

I would get angry that he knew what was happening before I did. And then I would see how moody I was and would have to acknowledge that he was right: I did change.

Over time I came to understand the differences in the two types of power surges I experienced. The surges that ended with my floating were preparing my body, allowing me to take in more and more energy. The stronger surges would take me to the light, would let me feel the touch of creation on my soul.

Although the world of the light was glorious, the surges themselves were disturbing. I'd be trying to teach a meditation class, and I would have to fight a surge the entire time. Then, for hours afterward, I would be wracked with shaking. I had come to love fire walking, but when I tried to hold a fire walk, the power surges were even worse. The night before, the shaking would keep me up; and the day of the walk, I would have to fight to keep the power down. I didn't want people to see what was happening to me, so I stopped walking the fire.

But most of all, I was angry because the surges interfered with David and me, with our intimacy. Many nights he would stay with me because he didn't want me to face a surge alone. But most of those nights he would end up frustrated. Time and again, I would ask him to leave because I couldn't bear to have his energy near me.

That went on for almost a year before I finally found someone who was able to give me information. David and I had gone away on an annual retreat, the Healing Arts Festival, which I'd been going to for seven years. At the festival, different is normal. That's where I had discovered my love for fire walking.

At one point during the weekend, I went to speak to a beautiful young-old woman who heals people with music. She has long silver hair and blue eyes that twinkle. The cabin where she worked was just one room, made cozy with a bed, a dresser, and a lamp.

It may have been the room; or it may have been knowing her for seven years and taking classes with her. I felt safe.

She had me lie down on the bed and asked me what was bothering me. With tears running down my face, I told her about the power surges. It had been a particularly tough weekend; it seemed that every hour I was having another one more powerful than the last. The woman listened intently, her eyes glowing brighter with every word I said.

"The *kundalini*," she whispered in a soft voice. "And in such a young body. Ooh."

I knew about the *kundalini,* but I had thought that the energy had to be released consciously, that people worked for years to feel its intensity. How could I be experiencing the *kundalini?* The energy I was feeling was releasing itself, and when I tried to be intimate with David it was that much stronger.

I looked into her eyes and said, "I don't know what to do with it."

"Child," she said, "you will learn in time. Patience is all you need. I will call to the spirits and ask them to slow the power down."

With that she turned to her instruments, flutes and crystal bowls. Her voice sang to me as she rippled music from chimes. Every word and sound brought me deeper into the other side. I was calm, and I went easily. With her by my physical side, I wasn't afraid. I let myself go to the light of creation and basked in its glory.

When she finished singing, I drifted back to her soft presence. She looked into my eyes and told me what I didn't want to hear.

"It's going to be hard for some time longer," she said. "The surges actually will get stronger. But I promise you that at some point you will understand."

I thanked her for her help. Although I didn't like hearing what she had to say, I was comforted by the fact that she understood and wasn't afraid. At least I wasn't the only person on this earth who knew the spiritual world; she knew it too.

Õ

The power surges were to change me in many ways. The effect on my abilities was immediate. I had always been very open to and intuitive about people's feelings. Several years before, I had studied massage therapy. During that time, as I worked on people, I had started having their flashbacks. Although that was helpful in my practice, at times it was annoying. Most of the time I couldn't figure out if what I was feeling was me or the person near me. I had finally gotten it under control the year before, but the power surges blew it wide open again. People started asking me to do psychic readings for them. At first I refused. For three years I had tried to share my intuitive ability with others by teaching them to read themselves. But after ten months of power surges, and hoping that doing readings would disperse some of the energy, I decided to take a few clients.

For months people came to me, all of them referrals from people I had worked with or who knew me. I was nervous at first. I didn't want my clients to think I was strange, and I didn't want to scare them. I found that I was able to tell them everything — what frightened them, what was holding them back. Their souls spoke to me; their thoughts helped me tell them the stories of their lives.

Every reading was different. Once this handsome young man came to me. He had never had a reading before, and he was both curious and skeptical. I held his hands and went deeper and deeper into his soul, until I felt as though I had become his story. Then I repeated aloud what his energy already was telling him.

"I'm curious about my girlfriend," he had said shyly.

As he spoke, I saw her — a young woman who talked rapidly, her hands moving all the while; who wore wild colors; and who had a very strong personality. I felt his feelings toward her; I knew what it was like to be in love with this woman. I also knew that their relationship wouldn't last because they were looking for different things in life. He couldn't believe that I knew what he felt inside and had not wanted to admit, even to himself.

He fired off questions, one after another, laughing with amazement when I answered them. After a bit, I sensed his energy closing off; he was winding down. But I felt something deep within him that he needed to know.

"You have one more question," I said.

He shook his head in confusion and said that he was done.

"You're afraid of death," I said.

And in a burst, all of his worries and fears about death came tumbling out. "I've never told anyone about that," he admitted.

"I know," I said, and then went on to tell him there was nothing to fear, that death isn't the dark place he thought it was. And as

I spoke the words "You have a very long life in front of you," I felt the energy between us relax. When I opened my eyes, he was smiling, and he couldn't stop talking about the experience.

The surges also had an effect on the energy that flowed through my hands. Running energy — sharing my energy with others by moving it through my hands to their body — wasn't new to me. When I was nine, the spirits had taught me how to make the energy in my hands tingle. Then, at fourteen, I had taken a course on how to bring that energy up. But this was different: The energy flowing through my hands was tremendous.

My clients loved all of it. And as more and more came to me, I put my teaching and publishing aside two days a week to take them. Then, after ten months, I realized the power surges were slowing down. At first I was ecstatic. The power still grew when I worked on my clients, but it no longer interfered with my life. But then my energy started to dwindle. I had trouble understanding things I read; I was always tired; when I worked out, I'd get dizzy and weak.

I cut back on my clients and kept teaching. It didn't help. My back and neck ached. I was becoming more and more depressed.

Finally, when the pain became unbearable, I went to see my doctor. Dr. Abbas had been one of my teachers at Bancroft, where I'd learned massage therapy; he was trained in everything from Ayurvedic and Chinese medicine, to surgery and chiropractic. He took the first of many blood tests. It showed a weakness in my adrenal glands. It was time to quit everything — work and exercise — for a while, he said.

I did stop seeing clients, but I tried to keep teaching seminars and working on The Quest. Often I couldn't even do that: The world would spin around me, and I would have to lie on the couch for the entire day. I told David over and over again that I needed to get away, but he was worried about money. Then, frightened as I grew weaker, he agreed. We decided to move to Virginia together. Although the move would cost David his steady job, we thought a new place would mean less stress. And for a while I did feel better. Then, one day, I simply couldn't go on. I no longer knew who I was or which world I was in. I had lost my connection, and I had no idea why.

The Game
April 27, 1994

I was at a weeklong training in California to become a fire-walking instructor. I wanted to share the beauty the fire had been giving me since I first danced with the flames when I was fifteen. It had been a wonderful week, filled with love and sharing. That night, in just a couple of hours, a silly game would destroy the warmth.

It was Wednesday night, two hours before our fourth fire walk of the week. The group — there were thirty-four of us — had just finished an Angel Walk. It's an exercise: You walk around a room through two lines of people with your eyes closed while they lightly brush their hands over your face and body. It's like walking into the gates of heaven and being welcomed with love. Everyone was beaming with happiness.

The four instructors asked us to stop hugging and laughing so that we could start the next exercise. We were going to play a game — they called it Black and Red — before we walked the fire that night. They split us into two teams, one Black, the other Red. They gave each team a piece of paper with a grid on it and a point code on the side. The color we put in the square for each round determined whether we would win or lose points. The scoring, they explained, was like bowling, and the point of the game was to win. That's all they told us. Then they sent each team to a different room.

In the room, the men on my team immediately got down to business, arguing with one another about how to win. Gone was the glow of the Angel Walk. Whenever a woman tried to talk, they refused to listen. In time we seemed to be getting ahead of the other team — we had more points. We had figured out early on how to place our colors to gain the advantage. But the men didn't realize that winning this game had nothing to do with the score. They kept fighting over ways to get even more points. As we got further ahead, some of us tried to say that the game might have a deeper meaning than just winning points. At this, the men threw up their hands and said, "Let's wait and see. We'll keep doing what we're doing, but let's stop fighting among ourselves. Let's sing and just enjoy the time we have before the game ends."

When it was over, one of the instructors told us we had won the most points. He went on to say that the way we played the game was the way we lived life. I laughed at that because throughout the game I had tried to tell the men that winning wasn't important, that the game was probably to teach us some lesson. Now I knew that I'd been right.

As soon as we rejoined the other team, the members of that team and the instructors attacked us for not realizing that the point of the game was to end up in a tie so that everyone won. Of course my team got defensive and fought back. Through it all, I was lying down, feeling the sting of the words as they flew back and forth above me.

"Why didn't you help us when we tried to show you what it was all about?"

"You're just angry you lost."

"You're the reason there are wars. All you care about is winning, not what's happening to others. Remember, how you play the game is how you live your life."

"Get over it."

One of the instructors said: "The winning team was the most pathetic team I've ever seen. They fought about how to win, and then, once they were winning, they stopped caring and sang songs. I am sad to see such cruelty in people who are training here."

When I finally couldn't take it anymore, I spoke up: "It was a game. We're here because we want to share something sacred with people. We're friends; we've opened our hearts and souls to one another. Can you throw it all away over a game?"

"Is Sarajevo just a game? It's the same thing. One side just doesn't care about the other."

"But don't you see that what you're doing right now is what feeds war," I said. No one wanted to listen.

"We had you play this game to show you the true nature of people. That in the end, people always fight," said one of the instructors.

That's where it ended . . . without resolution. The instructors sent us out to walk the fire.

I was crying. Several members of the group came up to me and tried to comfort me, but I didn't want their comfort. I didn't trust them anymore; I saw how easily they could turn from love to hate.

As I stood staring at the fire, I felt so alone. Rolf, one of the instructors, came up to me and handed me a rake. "Sister," he said, "turn to the fire, and let it heal your pain."

I walked to the fire and raked the logs away from the coals. As the heat of the flames touched my face, I sobbed.

"Fire," I said, "I need you tonight. All I can see is the anger in the world. I can't look into the eyes of people because everything I see there is false. They pretend to live in sacredness, but when they feel someone is going to take something from them they wage war. They don't really want to live the truth; they just pretend they do. I hurt with the pain of the world. Please, heal this."

And I felt all of the world's pain rushing at my being. I couldn't face it, so I gave it to the fire. That night as I crossed the coals, I danced out my frustration and anger, and I let the fire cleanse my soul. Others in the group, those who had felt as I had, grabbed my hands and made me dance with them through the coals. I let go to the bliss that fire walking is to me. The energy of the fire lifted me up, freeing me from the pain. I reached out to the world I understood — the spirit world. I wanted to shut away the human race.

Anger
November 26, 1996

I was so tired. I would lie in bed, curled in on myself, trying to hide the weakness in my soul. Within me, in that place where I had always found truth and strength, was a darkness. I couldn't feel; no one could touch me there, not even David.

I rested for three months straight. I took all kinds of herbs and supplements to build my strength. I couldn't exercise; I could barely walk. All I could do was sit and read or watch television.

Everyone had suggestions for me: "Change your diet," one would say. "I want you to see my doctor," another insisted. "Get regular massages, go for walks, have some fun. You'll get better," yet another advised. Nothing worked, though, at least nothing physical. How could it when the exhaustion came as much from my soul as my body? I was twenty-three years old, and I was burned out.

Still, no matter how exhausted I was, I never wanted to die.

I wanted my worlds back. I wanted to be with the people I loved. I wanted to teach and walk the fire and reach out to people through The Quest. I wanted to look in the mirror and see the vitality I once saw there. I wanted to climb mountains and dance. And, yes, I wanted to touch heaven again, to feel that near-to-bursting joy and power.

I was overwhelmed by a fatigue so deep that sleep barely touched it. I tried so hard to fight it — that's what David, my mother, my friends were telling me to do — but one day there wasn't any fight left. I remember thinking that nothing else had worked. Maybe it was time to drop into the darkness and let it take me where it would.

And so I let go. A gentle peace washed over me, like a cool breeze on a hot summer's day. I felt a warmth surround me, and then I saw an orange light vibrating around me.

Images of David flashed before me. He had been so kind, so worried. "Work doesn't matter," he would say. "Just get better, and we'll have fun. We'll do wonderful things."

Inside I cried, feeling the sweetness of what he wanted to give me and knowing that at that moment I couldn't accept. I turned him down, telling him I needed to be alone. Time to myself had been impossible since we'd moved to Virginia and started living together. I explained to him that I needed to sleep alone and asked him to let me just be for a while. The tears in his eyes stung my heart. He didn't seem to understand that more than anything in the world, I wanted us back, but that to get us back, I needed to get me back. I had to rebuild the walls he had helped me break down because right now those walls were the only protection I had from the outside world.

His eyes filled with love, he said okay and let me go.

As the memory of our conversation passed, I was sad, but I was also relieved. It felt good not to have to work at our relationship anymore. Maybe it was wrong to feel relief, but I was sure that if our feelings for each other were real, we could be together again. I just couldn't feel badly about being numb anymore; I just couldn't take on his pain each time I pushed him away. I still loved him, that I knew; but for now, I had to learn to love me again.

As I let thoughts of David go, the exhaustion and pain of the past six months overwhelmed me.

"Home," I cried. "I want to go home."

A small spark of happiness flashed into my consciousness. Maybe there was hope. Maybe I would dance again. I kept crying out the word *home* — a mantra that would help me feel alive again.

Then there was only darkness. Visions of David and that flash of happiness disappeared. I was frightened and lonely. I wanted them back.

"I thought I was going to get better," I screamed into the blackness. "It was all just a trick. I'm going to fall forever, alone."

I knew that if I didn't let go, if I didn't stop resisting, I would stay exactly where I was. I ached from the tension; I was so tired.

I let go.

My fear gone, the darkness was peaceful and comforting, like a warm bath after you've been out in the cold skiing all day. At first the cold seems even stronger, and your body tenses. Then, as the water begins to warm your skin, you relax. I floated gently through the emptiness.

That peace didn't last. As I floated, my body began to fill with pain. My stomach ached with sharp, piercing cramps. Knots in my neck pulsed. My back ached. Every nerve in my body stood on edge; every muscle taut, ready for battle. Why was this happening to me? Where was this tension coming from?

Then I saw within me a monstrous rage, a ferocious tiger battering the walls of its cage, trying to get out. I was shocked and frightened. Always when I had gone inside myself I had felt love, laughter, and power; never had I experienced this anger. Had it been there all along? Had I been waging a war against myself?

I knew what I had to do: No more fighting; I had to become my anger.

"The only way out is through," I kept saying to myself. "I need to know why I'm so angry inside."

So I let myself feel my rage. It was horrible, hideous — a fury at those who had made the earth a hell by trading in and using drugs. I raged at their willingness to sell drugs to children; I raged at their willingness to take the lives of others to keep themselves in drugs; I raged at their willingness to violate their own bodies, to suffocate their own souls, with drugs.

I was wracked with anger. My body trembled; my breathing grew harsh. I thought about the souls of children, lost to drugs, lost to the hatred they're taught, lost to the violence they see around them. I felt so cold. I shook violently, convulsively.

I didn't want to feel the anger anymore; I was too tired. But it went on. The rape of babies flashed through my mind. How can fathers rape their children? And where can those children be safe when those charged with their spiritual and physical care — priests and teachers and others in authority — violate that trust?

"I hate this world," I screamed.

Then I thought about the wars fought in the name of freedom. How could freedom come from hatred, pain, and death? Wasn't it really the few in search of power who stood ready to sacrifice the powerless many?

And I saw the forests cut down for money and the animals killed in the name of greed. "You bastards," I screamed and covered my eyes; I didn't want to see any more. It hurt too much.

My own family flashed before my eyes. The wonderful bond we once had now strained by outside influences, each of us caught up in our own hurt. Arguments over dishes left unwashed in the sink because no one could deal with the real issues. Sometimes you can't be the person someone else wants you to be. But isn't that where love comes in? Fine. If something hurts you or you don't agree, you talk about it and go on. Why do people have to keep hurting each other long after a disagreement is over and done? Why is it so much easier to stay in hurt than in love?

At one time, I never shied away from speaking the truth, no matter how painful. But years of taking blame for saying what needed to be said — years of seeing the act of speaking the truth become more important than the truth itself — had taught me not to speak. That didn't change the truth; it only made me angry and hateful inside.

Sick with nausea, my body shaking with tension, my head pounding with pain, I cried out again.

Just as I thought I could no longer bear it, a woman's voice called out to me: "It's okay." The voice was warm, melodic, almost motherly. A hand touched my shoulder, and this time when I cried, I cried tears of relief. Somehow love was penetrating the darkness and telling me I was safe.

"This is cleansing your soul," the voice said. "Let it happen."

"But what happens later?" I called out.

I was so scared. I knew I couldn't go back to my old life; I knew there was nothing left there for me. Sobbing, I asked, "Will I still love David? We've been together for two years. I don't want to change inside and lose him."

"Leave the future to the future," I heard the voice say. "Now is the time to heal. One step at a time, Angel. One step at a time."

I found myself thinking about the night of the training, of the Black and Red game. When I refused the comfort one of my teammates offered that night, he sadly said, "We're only human, Marci. You have to give us time to learn."

Only human. I remember thinking, We call ourselves the most advanced species on earth, but when it comes time to take responsibility, we hide behind our humanness as though it gives us the right to hurt anyone or anything around us.

I suddenly realized that I had lost hope the night of that game and that I had never really found it since. It might have been different if the people had been different. Hadn't my brother been telling me for years that it's human nature for people to hurt one another? But these men and women were supposed to know better. What hope was there if those who want to teach the joy of love and life can hate so easily?

Then I saw it: the wall I had built to keep all of this rage inside me, a wall created with the tension in my body. That's what was stopping me from feeling. And keeping that wall up, that's what was making me so tired.

I flashed back to when I was eighteen years old. I had turned to a psychiatrist for help recovering the memory of a rape that I was starting to sense. As I sat in the doctor's office, she said to me, "Marci, you can never get over being raped. It's something that will affect you for the rest of your life. You can never expect the pain to go away or to really live a life without it, but I can teach you to survive the pain so that you can have some kind of life." I got so angry that I went to a second therapist and then a third. Each said the same thing.

In the office of the last therapist, my silence ended. "You believe that I can only survive, that I can never be whole again. Well, I don't. I was born whole, and when I die I'll be whole. You can't tell me that my soul has been changed because of someone else's mistake. I will never simply survive. I will live the beauty I am inside, and I will thrive." And I walked out of the psychiatrist's office for good.

I did find my way out of the pain, and I reached the highest ecstasy. Then the night of the Black and Red game, I lost hope in the world. All I could see was everything that was wrong with the human race.

And with clarity I saw that since that night I had been doing what I had said I wouldn't do, surviving instead of living. And I saw that I had used The Quest to fuel my survival. When I started the company, I mixed work and pleasure, loving David and playing with him. I went out with friends and enjoyed being with my family. I thought about love and dreamed about the future. But as time passed, the pain I felt the night of the Black and Red game still with me, I began working harder. I pushed David away; I didn't care about romance. And although I still wanted to go out and play, I didn't have the time or the energy. My work had become an obsession.

It wasn't about making money. It was about the pain I saw around me, a pain that felt like razor blades slicing at my soul. I was driven, I think, to save myself by saving others. If I could get the message out — that there is beauty and love inside us if only we can reach them — perhaps I could ease the pain, the world's pain, and then I would be free.

And when I failed . . . when I realized that I couldn't save the world, that I couldn't stop the pain I felt around me every day . . . my body responded with the agony my soul was feeling.

"A huge weight to bear, my child," I heard the voice call to me. "You take on what even the heavens can't stop."

And right then, I wanted to die. I had carried this burden for too long. "I'm tired. I'm so tired," I thought, and I fell asleep.

Õ

I was surrounded by a dark, gray mist. I could see bushes, their flowers closed, and pillars that marked a path through the garden I was standing in. From the distance I could hear music and singing, but I couldn't make out the song.

In a daze I walked toward the music. I heard voices everywhere, a thin, almost childlike chattering. I couldn't see the spirits, yet I felt them touching me with their love.

"What are you saying?" I cried out. Somehow I knew their message was important. "Why can't I hear you?" I was growing tense with listening. "If you want to tell me something, then tell me," I pleaded.

"The truth," whispered something not human. "Become the truth."

"What truth?" I demanded to know.

I could hear the song clearly now. I knew the words, and I didn't want to hear them. The voices were singing the first lines of Madonna's "Live to Tell." The song speaks of a woman who has a secret so deep that she tells "a thousand lies" to keep it hidden. Yet, all the while, the secret is longing to be told.

I fell to the ground, my head down, trying to block out the words and what they meant. But the singing grew louder and louder, and I couldn't stop the feelings the words released within my soul. The song speaks of true beauty. The woman knows the sweetness and warmth of that beauty, but she's locked it away so that no one can take it from her.

The song had always been special to me. I knew that beauty, the beauty you touch when you reach deep within yourself, and the wholeness and freedom that fill your soul when you touch it.

But now I was hearing other parts of the song — the singer asking will she live to tell the secrets that she's learned, and will she have the strength to tell them.

The lie I'd lived as life crashed down around me. All I'd really wanted was to be normal, to see the world and life the way that others saw them, to just be sixteen or twenty.

I didn't want to be strange. And so I ran from telling the world what I know, from exposing myself to people who wouldn't, who couldn't, understand.

"I can't be what you want," I screamed to the spirits I knew were there. "I've already tried. I created The Quest; I've taught seminars. No one wants to hear it. They aren't looking for the truth; they're looking for an easy way around it."

The only answer from the spirits was the song: The woman had run from the truth by hiding it, but she could never run far enough or fast enough to forget it. And the running was killing her; if she kept running, she would never get the chance to speak the truth.

"That's what you're trying to tell me, isn't it?" I cried. "That I can't live a lie? That's what the pain and the exhaustion are all about," I said, tears filling my eyes and anger brewing in my soul. "You don't understand. You're asking too much of me. I can't do it."

Even as I said the words, I knew I no longer had a choice. The lie was too painful, and the truth would never let me be like everyone else.

More memories of David passed before me. When I first met him, we were so in love. When we touched, I could feel the truth inside me so easily. Now, afraid of that truth, afraid of my feelings, I didn't want to be touched.

"I don't know if I have the strength to be my truth," I said to the beings all around me. I knew that if I ever told the truth about the me inside, my life would never be the same. There would be no turning back, no more hiding, no more living a lie. And I knew that many people would call me crazy or ridicule me for what I believe. I had seen it happen to others who had tried to tell their truth.

"For so long, I have kept a secret," I said, picturing all the people of the world in front of me. "My name is Marci, and I see all worlds, all dimensions, all realms. I see the spirits that surround us.

Where you see a tree, I feel its soul and power, the life that flows through its limbs and bursts out into leaves and fruit. Where you see a person's appearance or behavior, I see who that person is meant to be. I feel her heart; I feel the weight of his pain and fear. Where you see one world — the physical world — I see millions of worlds, some incredibly pure and filled with love, others filled with hatred. I see it all, and everything that I see, you can see too."

And I pictured myself saying, "I can't bear to see your pain. I want you to know that you're beautiful, that you don't have to be lonely, afraid, or ashamed anymore. There's a world filled with unconditional love, and it's just a whisper away. I can help you remember it and make it yours again. I can help take you home, to the beauty and the love and the peace."

Could I do it? Could I stand up and speak the truth? I was so afraid.

"Please hear me," I called to the spirits around me. "I want to live my truth, but I don't know how to do it without getting hurt."

The singing grew loud again, and the words of the song spoke about fear and running away. "How will they know?" the woman asks, admitting what her running away might cost the world.

The song was true, every word of it. If I grow old with this secret, what good does it do me? I can't experience the life I've longed for if I hide away. And if I don't tell what I know, who will?

I looked around. Everywhere the darkness was masking beauty. Running away was destroying me.

And then I felt a strength somewhere deep inside me. The mist began to disappear. I could see a light growing in the garden, its beauty beginning to unfold. I was filled with a golden glory.

I called out to the spirits: "If I make it out of this darkness, I swear on the truth that I know that I will tell them." And then I asked for their help: "I ask just one thing of you: Protect me the best you can so that I can live to tell."

Õ

When I woke up, the room was dark and I felt cold. I wondered how long I'd been sleeping. My body still trembled, but I wasn't sure if it was from the cold or from what I had just promised. Was it a dream? It seemed so real; I felt as though I was still there. Did I actually promise to do what I feared most? How would I live in this world without my wall?

In the dark, I crawled out of bed and went to find David.

Letting Go
November 30, 1996

"Within you there's a wellspring of love and beauty, and a power so magnificent that to touch it would bring tears to your eyes. It is the most miraculous power in the universe, and all you have to do to find it is look within your heart. It waits there for you."

It was the morning after the dream, and I woke up to these words ringing in my soul.

"No matter how badly your mind or body has been hurt, no matter what you've done in your life, this power exists. You may not be able to see it now, but I can help you find the way to remember. You will find it — let me show you how."

And the spirit spoke on. "I can show you where it exists. I can lead you to the power, but I can't take the final step. That's up to you. You have to believe in yourself. You have to believe that you have the strength and the courage to take the journey.

"And at times it will take a lot of strength and courage. I know that you've been hurt, that the fear inside you is ferocious. But you can't stay here and hide behind walls of fear and pain. You can't allow your fear of the world's not understanding or being jealous or trying to use your power for selfish ends stop you from touching the beauty of who you are. This I promise: The power within is stronger than any misunderstanding, stronger than any jealousy, stronger than any evil. Once you find it, you'll never fear again."

The words were coming so fast, my mind could barely grasp them, but my soul understood them in an instant.

"We have a long journey ahead. Are you willing to take it? Think hard. Once you step onto this path, you'll never be the same," said the voice, so sweet and strong.

"What must I give up to take this journey?" I asked.

"Everything you believe."

"Why? I've already learned so much. Won't any of it help me?" I cried back in confusion.

"The knowledge that you've learned so far is in your mind. This journey is not about knowledge; it's about truth. The mind can never fully understand truth. Only the heart, the soul, the oldest part of who you are can really experience it. Yes, what you've learned will help you in your worldly travels and in helping others, but this is the journey home. You know in your heart what it will take. Are you willing?"

He was firm, honest. He wouldn't lie or soften the truth. I knew in my heart the extent of what he was asking, to give up all I knew and trusted, and I was very scared. How could I leave behind the walls that made me feel safe in a world where so little felt safe?

But I also knew the ache inside that never seemed to go away, an ache I was sure was the truth. And I knew the need to become my truth was somehow stronger than my fear.

My words sounded strong and confident: "Yes, lead me. Please help me find the way." Inside, I was trembling.

Õ

The darkness that surrounded me this time wasn't peaceful. The nausea and fatigue had somehow heightened. I just wanted to collapse, to sleep forever.

It had been four days since the dream, since I'd agreed to take this journey. Halfway through the fifth, no reprieve was in sight. My days were a blur of exhaustion. When I stood up, I felt dizzy. I could feel the blood moving slowly through my body, pulsing in my head and every joint. The ringing in my ears never seemed to stop. Each night I lay awake for hours.

The world grated on my nerves, on my soul. I couldn't bear being near David: His every touch felt like flames eating my flesh, devouring me. Any confrontation — on television or the radio or in the newspaper was torment, like the sound of fingernails scraping a blackboard. Everything seemed to bring me closer to the edge.

I longed to be healthy again, to be strong, to go out with my friends, to dance. Oh, how I missed dancing. All that power. I would get lost in the rhythm of the music, my body breathing it in. On the dance floor I was free, and it felt wonderful.

And I remembered the days when I wasn't working, when I would go to the woods and dance there to the music of the earth. Oh, the power of that music, how it filled me with knowledge and an awareness of life. And how healthy and strong I was.

Where was that strength now? It was a time when I should have been my happiest and my strongest — my company was growing every day, I spoke at events across the country, I had a beautiful relationship with a man I loved — yet I was sadder and weaker than I had ever been. And I thought back to the time when I was healthy. I had no money, no career, no one special to love, but I was me, I realized sadly. How had I lost myself so completely? And if I found myself again, what would that mean for David?

The sadness brought more exhaustion. I couldn't fight the blackness anymore: I was too tired. I lay down on the bed, and in an instant I began to fall. A thick oozing black slime carried me down into darkness, taking my breath away and filling me with fear.

I reached for some remnant of consciousness, some thought that would bring me back to my life, but none came. I tried harder, wondering why I couldn't remember what I'd just been thinking. Was it David? My mother? But it seemed so far away that I couldn't reach out and grab onto it.

I couldn't feel my body. "Where is my body?" I screamed. A dark thought came to me. What if I never wake up? Oh, God, what have I done? Why didn't I fight harder? Why did I ever go into the darkness?

Then I saw a silver-metal rung, like the step on a ladder. I was falling toward it, and as I slid by, I grabbed hold of it with my left hand. The slime rushed over me. I couldn't see anything, but I hung on. I was sure this was the way out.

Suddenly the slime disappeared, and I could breathe again.

Although it still was dark, I could see around me. The single rung had become a ladder of sorts. There were more rungs below my feet and above my head. I looked up, and I could see the night sky filled with stars. I could smell the grass at the top of the hole and hear the wind blowing. I couldn't wait to place my feet on the earth, to feel the freedom of the wind on my face. When I looked around me, I realized I was in a huge cement pipe. I didn't know how I got there, and I didn't care. I just wanted to get out.

Above my head were several rungs about a foot and a half apart. Still holding on with my left hand, I reached up with my right to grab the rung above me. As I did, I felt a sharp pain cut through me. I released the bar and looked at my hand. There was a deep straight gash in the middle of it. A warm stream of blood ran down my arm.

I looked up and saw that the outside of that rung was a sharp blade and that each rung leading out of the hole was the same. I realized there was no way to climb out without cutting myself. But there had to be a way out. I couldn't bear the thought of falling again.

"Please, someone help me," I called silently in my mind.

At that moment, two people appeared. One was below in the darkness, reaching his hands up toward me. The other was above me, standing outside the hole, only his massive black shadow visible.

"Show yourselves to me," I demanded. "I am in the spirit world. If you're spirits, you must show yourselves to me."

From below an iridescent light began to glow. It spread through the bottom of the hole, growing brighter. Still, I was afraid to look down; I was afraid I would fall. I didn't want to go down; I wanted to go up.

"Why aren't you helping me?" I screamed to the spirit above me.

I shifted my weight, getting ready to pull myself up to the next rung. I didn't care about cutting myself; at least I wouldn't fall into whatever was below me. I pulled with all my might, the razor of the rung tearing through my clothing and my skin. Pain ripped through me. I grabbed the next rung up with my right hand and, using my feet to push my body from the razor I had grabbed as I was falling, brought my left arm up. Now I was standing on the top rung. Hurt and crying, still I breathed a sigh of relief.

Then the shadow from above moved and held out a hand to me. The hand was large and strong, and I knew that if I grabbed it, it would lift me up. I looked up to thank the spirit for its help, but the words froze in my throat. The face was that of the man in my nightmares, the man who had become my symbol of all that was wrong with the physical world, the man who had raped me as a child.

The light from below grew stronger. It seemed to be calling me, telling me to look down and see its face. I turned my head. The light was like a fire, its heat a searing white, orange, and yellow. It danced before my eyes in a sea of radiance. It wasn't reaching up to me; it was a river flowing away from where I hung. And in its center was Rik, his hands outstretched as if to catch me, his presence as always a beautiful and safe softness. How long had we been together, his knowledge and love guiding me?

"Let go, Marci. Let go and fall. I'll catch you," he said.

Rik
March 16, 1983

It had been a cold winter's day. I was on school vacation. My brother's friends had been drinking or doing drugs. They walked into our house and pushed me outside. My brother, always sober, didn't stop them. I had no shoes on my feet, no jacket. For what seemed like hours I stood outside, shaking with cold. And while I stood there I thought about people's cruelty, their willingness to hurt others, even those they love. I was ten years old, and already I was tired of the world and ached for the pain I'd seen around me. And standing there in the cold, shaking, I decided that I would not live in a world so horrible.

In the backyard was an old oak tree I used to play in. It was a thin tree, its growth choked by the pines around it. I was like that oak, I realized, wanting to grow but being held back by others. I climbed to the top of the tree and looked down. There was a drop behind the house, and I saw the tops of the trees below. I was going to jump.

I took a breath, ready to step out of the oak tree, when my dog started barking. Brandy had followed me to the base of the tree and was looking up at me as though to say, "Go ahead. Jump. I'll catch you."

As I looked into the dog's soft eyes, I heard a voice. "Marci," it said, "you're not alone. We will send you a spirit who will guide and protect you. You can still jump if you want, but know that we promise to help you."

Suddenly the air felt warm. I heard my brother and his friends leave the house. Then, in my mind's eye, I saw the ESP board my mother had taught me to use. I could feel the name of a guide. Slowly, in a daze, I climbed down. I went into the house, to my mother's room.

I found the board under her bed. It had a large half-circle, a smaller half-circle, and a square drawn on it. In the square were two lines that crossed each other in the center. One line had the word *yes* painted on it; the other, the word *no*. The smaller semicircle was divided into wedges, each labeled with a number from 0 through 9 at the outer edge. Each wedge was a different color, which made the semicircle look like a multicolored fan. The larger semicircle was laid out the same way, but with all the letters of the alphabet instead of numbers. With the board was a pendulum.

I laid the board on my mother's bed, took a deep breath, and said a prayer: "If this is right for me, please God, send me someone to help me. I need a friend who can teach me to understand this world and protect me from its pain."

I felt a presence all around me, and I was frightened. I thought that as soon as I learned its name, a being would appear before me. The voices I had heard in the tree and throughout my life had never explained that they were ghosts. I thought spirits showed up in white filmy human form, like Casper on television. I thought the spirit would show up in my house, and I had no idea what it would be like. I didn't care though. I needed help.

My hand shaking, I placed the pendulum over the square. I closed my eyes and took a deep breath and asked, "Is it right for me to receive a spirit guide at this time?" I could hear the pendulum moving very slowly, but I didn't look. I wasn't sure which way I wanted it to swing. Then I began to feel the pendulum moving in large arcs back and forth. I opened my eyes slowly. My breath stopped, and my whole body went numb. As I stared down at the pendulum I saw it swinging to the *yes*. I wanted to cry. I wouldn't be alone anymore, not ever again.

I quickly moved the pendulum to the semicircle with the numbers and asked, "When will my guide come to me? Please tell me the month first." The pendulum slowly began to circle the center of the flat line, where all the colors met. Then gently it moved to the number 9.

"September," I thought, "but that's so far away."

Then I realized that September was when I would be starting junior high. As long as the spirit would be there for that, I could wait. I also figured that it had to be hard work for a spirit to materialize, and maybe that's how long it took. This way I would have some time to get used to the idea, to learn not to be afraid.

I asked for the date, and the pendulum swung quickly to the

number 1, then zero, and stopped. I went back to the square and asked whether it would be coming September 10, and it swung yes. Then I asked at what time, and the pendulum swung to 6:00 p.m.

Finally, I moved to the semicircle with the letters. "What is my guide's name?" I asked.

I was on pins and needles as the pendulum slowly began moving. At first I couldn't tell which letter it swung to because the letters are so close together. Then it swung faster and faster, and I could see the letter *R*. I asked the pendulum to stop if *R* was the first letter of the spirit's name, and slowly it did. Two more times the pendulum swung fast and then stopped at a letter — the *I* and then the *K*.

R-I-K. Rik. His name was Rik.

Õ

I lay in bed that night, a frightened ten-year-old. Every creak set me on edge. My thoughts were a jumble: Why did I do this? What if he's mean and I can't get rid of him? What if he tries to hurt me or my family?

"Marci," I heard a voice call to me. In my mind I saw a young man. "Rik wants to come to you the way the rest of us do so that you won't be afraid anymore. Is that okay?" he asked.

"I don't know. Will he hurt me?" My voice sounded timid.

"No, you're safe. Nothing will hurt you," he said.

"But I don't know you. How do I know it's safe?"

"Are you afraid right now, while you're talking to me?" he asked gently.

"No."

"Do you feel I want to harm you?" he asked.

"No."

"Then that's how you know you can trust me. That's how you know you can trust anybody. Let your heart be your guide. Will you meet Rik?" he asked.

I told him yes and waited.

"Howdy, Cowgirl." In my mind stood a young man in an enormous cowboy hat. He wore jeans, a flannel shirt, and boots with spurs. His thumbs were tucked into his belt, and he had a piece of hay sticking out of his mouth. He grabbed the piece of hay and gave me the biggest grin I'd ever seen. He looked so ridiculous that I burst out laughing.

"How did a girl from Massachusetts get a Texas cowboy as a spirit guide?" I wondered.

"My name's Rik," he said in a southern drawl, "and I've come to show you a good time. I figured I'd do a little dance for you."

And suddenly this spirit was dancing around my room, kicking up his heels and making funny faces.

What had I been afraid of, I wondered.

Every night for the next week Rik came to me wearing the same silly outfit and made me laugh. Talking to him was different from talking to God or to the other spirits I would see at night. The other spirits were still there, but Rik was more "there" than the rest of them. The others had no names or faces, and I couldn't see their clothing. I wasn't really connected to them: There were too many of them. But I could feel Rik next to me. When he smiled at me, light filled my heart, and I knew that things were good. He was a gentle soul, and he cared for me deeply.

After that first week, Rik stopped dressing like a cowboy, but his love of fun never went away. He became a part of my life. We talked off and on all day. At night we would talk about the things I had to deal with in school and at home. And we looked forward to September 10, when he would come from my other world into my human world, and I wouldn't be alone anymore.

The night of September 10 arrived, and I was with my family at my grandmother's house. At five minutes to six, I ran into the bathroom; I wanted privacy so that he could appear to me. Six o'clock, one past six, five past six came and went. I walked back into the living room feeling sad and foolish and alone. Everyone was right. The other world was imaginary; it was all make-believe. Rik wasn't coming, and I was alone.

That night in my room, I went to bed shutting out Rik and the others. After all, they weren't real. I felt empty as I cried myself to sleep.

Some time later I woke up. Rik was sitting on the bed beside me, in a pool of golden light. Still half asleep, I wondered if he was real. Then he reached over and smoothed my hair with his hand. At his touch, a warmth flowed through me.

"You are real," I said. He smiled and nodded.

Suddenly I was wide awake. The room was dark. Where was Rik's light? Where was Rik? "Angel, I'm right here," I heard him call in my mind.

"No," I screamed, "that's pretend. I want you with me."

"But I am with you. Your world and mine are separated only by your willingness to go inside," he said.

I didn't understand. Tears rolled down my cheeks. "You promised to come and be with me tonight. You lied."

"No, Marci, I've always been with you."

"Only in my mind," I responded with anger.

"You think that I'm not real because you see me in your mind, but do you just picture me up here?" I felt a tingle in the center of my forehead. "Or do you see me with your mind all around you? Do you feel me with your heart?"

I was silent. He was right: I didn't see him as a picture in my mind; I saw him next to me the way you feel someone next to you when you have your eyes closed. What did it matter? I wanted to see him with my eyes.

"I can't become human and be with you," he explained. "If I were human, I'd have to live a human's life, and I couldn't be with you every moment of yours. I told you I would come to you on this night only so you wouldn't be afraid of me. I told you this night so that we would have time to get to know each other again.

"Marci, I am here with you. Don't keep us apart. I can't enter your world completely, but you can experience as much of mine as you want to."

I felt him so close. I wanted to believe him, but the pain I'd felt that day was still so real. I didn't want to trust again and later find out it was all make-believe.

"Trust me," he whispered, as though I'd spoken my doubts. "Take my hand, and look into my eyes."

I felt the pull of his love and I wanted to believe him, but I couldn't. "I am in your heart and your soul," he said, calling to me. "My world is part of you. Once you touch it, it will always be there for you. I love you, and I will never leave you."

His words, his voice, his love soothed the fear. In my mind, I took his hand and stared into his eyes.

With that, the world I had seen when I first awakened returned. Brilliant colors and white light streamed through my soul. The joy of Rik's being there, of his love, filled every part of me.

And for a moment I thought about the others, the voices I had always heard.

Rik knew my thoughts.

"Marci, we are not what you see on television. We are souls, just like you but with no bodies. You've spoken to us for years. I have been with you all along, but I didn't want to interfere until you were ready to come here. When you thought about killing yourself, I couldn't wait any longer. I am your guide. The church you grew up in would call me your guardian angel. I'm also your teacher; I want to help you understand your world. You have a destiny, and I want to help you fulfill it. I'm also your student, here as much to learn from you as to teach you. And I love you. I love you in a way that your world has forgotten to love, and I will never leave you. You are the most beautiful thing I know."

His words brought me to tears. I felt so safe, so comforted, so right. I fell back to sleep in the warmth of his love.

The Hole
November 30, 1996

"Marci."

Rik's voice brought me out of my daydream, back to the horror of the hole.

"Let go," he called.

"No, I don't want to fall. It doesn't make sense. All this time I've been fighting to stay above, and now you're telling me to fall. It's supposed to be the other way around. The man is supposed to be where you are, and you're supposed to be pulling me up, not taking me down. I don't understand."

"Marci, why are you afraid?" asked Rik.

"I don't know," I answered, but that was a lie. I did know.

The night before I had dreamed about David and me. In the dream, I had told him that I couldn't be with him anymore, that I needed my freedom to go and find my power, that I needed to spread my wings and be a kid again for a while. I wanted to see other people and be the way I'd been when we met two years before.

He was hurt — I could see it in his eyes — but he let me go.

What if I let go? Would I change? I loved David, and I didn't want to lose him.

"Why are you afraid?" Rik asked again.

This time I answered honestly. "I can't see the future. I've been trying to see it for months, but I can't. Always before I could see, but now there are so many possibilities that I don't know what's going to happen. Four days ago, you asked if I would take a journey to remember my truth. I'm afraid that if I take that journey, I will lose David, and I don't want that. I'm so confused."

"Let go," he said. "Trust that the future will be right for both you and David. Remember what the woman taught you."

Õ

It was two months earlier. David and I were driving back to Massachusetts, and it had been a long day in the car. My mind had been racing with thoughts of the tour. I was worried.

I needed this tour to work. David and I had decided to travel around the country running seminars at conference centers. I had been teaching empowerment seminars, but on a small scale. If this series was successful, we'd be set financially. More important, I'd be free to get on with my life.

The Quest was doing well. The tapes were being distributed nationally, and the reviews had been very good. And the seminars seemed to be helping those who came and learned. But it wasn't enough. I felt a need to reach more people, to get the message out, to help ease the pain I saw around me. The process had been so frustrating. Publishers won't talk to someone who hasn't already been published, and getting publicity is no easier than getting published. How was I going to reach more people?

Then I caught myself. Did I really have the answers? My life certainly wasn't perfect; I wasn't walking around happy every minute of every hour. No matter how sure I was of the power within me, my life was still confused.

I was going back and forth in my mind, when suddenly I felt a calm and sensed a soft light around me. My mind relaxed as my soul reached out to touch the warmth of the other side.

It felt so good. I'd forgotten how much I needed that peace, that love.

Then, in my heart, I felt the beautiful woman who used to come to me when I was a child, the same way Rik did. Without words she called to me, and in the language of the spirit world I felt her say that everything I wished for was my destiny to have, that the universe beyond would help me, that I wasn't alone. And, finally, I heard the words, "Marci, let go. Let go of it all."

I knew what she meant. In my mind's eye, I could see all of the worries I was carrying with me: my family, David, my friends, the tour, the business, the tapes, the shows, the traveling, the fire walk next month. There was so much, and I was trying to do it all, to remember all that needed to be done. It was overwhelming.

Then the woman spoke again: "Marci, it's okay to let go. You've done what you need to do for now. Tomorrow's work you'll do tomorrow. Everything that needs to get done will."

"But what if it doesn't? I can't let that happen. I know that this tour is right, but if I leave it up to David he won't deal with it the way I would. What if he forgets something? What if he does something I don't like?" I so badly needed things the way I wanted them to be.

She responded gently, "What's the point of having a business partner if you don't trust him to handle the business? If the tour is right, it will happen. David will take care of it. You have to learn to believe in someone other than yourself."

"But I want my life to be what I choose it to be."

"Everything is your choice. Trusting doesn't mean that you give up what you want in life. It just means that you give up trying to control everyone and everything. You're afraid of what people will do because you're afraid they will hurt you. Life has hurt you so much that you have trouble seeing the good. You're afraid the bad will come back. So you try to control every situation — your work, your body, even your relationships.

"Yes, you choose what you want to happen in your life, but then you have to allow it to happen. All I ask is that you trust in who you are, in your soul. No matter what happens, you don't have to be afraid because life will always lead you back to your truth. If it's your destiny, it will happen. Give your power and the power of the universe a chance."

Over the next month, all of the things I'd been worrying about came to pass. David decided to cancel the tour. The publisher that we hoped would buy the empowerment series turned us down. The fire walk was canceled.

But it had all turned out for the best. I was too tired to do the tour; I simply didn't have the strength. The tapes were selling well as it was. Did we really need a publisher? And the company that was sponsoring the fire walk wanted it done in front of a hotel on a main street in Los Angeles. I would never have felt comfortable with that. Each disappointment had become a blessing.

Õ

I was back in the hole. I could see the man above reaching down to grab me. And I could see Rik below, his arms outstretched to catch me.

The Light
September 26, 1996

I was leading a meditation class. Usually in those classes, I would close my eyes and go with the people, leading them through whatever images I saw, using words to weave the group into my visions. This night was different. My words took the group where they were supposed to go, but my heart and soul began to journey somewhere else.

"Go to a beautiful place of relaxation, a place you would love to be. Let your body relax. You're on vacation," I heard my voice say.

But as I spoke those words, I was keenly aware of a warmth filling my heart. It called to me, to all my senses, and I ached to respond. I couldn't though. I was working with a group of twenty-five people, and I couldn't leave them.

As I slowly wove my words around the group, bringing the

people deeper and deeper into their minds, the call grew stronger and stronger. Torn, I led them to a tunnel through which they would travel into their past. It seemed to take forever to get there, but I had to see them safe before I could set my soul free on its journey.

I opened my eyes. The room was spinning. It seemed hazy and distant, as though it wasn't real. My breathing was growing harsher, more labored, and I could hear myself tripping over my own words. Finally, we reached the tunnel. A brilliant light glowed from its opening. I felt the people go in, some eagerly, others hesitantly. In a short time, everyone had entered.

I was free. I felt an incredible rush of energy through my body, a kind of trembling in every muscle. I felt myself rise up and join the ecstasy. I soared through light that was all the shades of yellow and pink, colors I had never seen before. And there was music, a soft, gentle sound that seemed to fill all the places in my heart that hurt, leaving only happiness. It was bliss.

I'd been flying for some time when a woman's whimpering drew me back to the group. Her face was filled with the pain of some memory. I saw her fight her fear. I wanted to help her, but I couldn't. A part of me was still in the light.

As I drifted back to the peace, I held the vision of the woman in my mind. Then I felt the music flow through me to her. There are no words to describe it. I didn't even know how I was doing it. She stopped crying, and I felt her breathe again.

I turned back to the other world and went to explore. Through the light, I began to see a huge dance floor, floating in space. The most glorious stars sparkled above it, lighting the floor with their reflection. The floor was a polished stone that seemed to pulse with life. Rising from it on two sides were spiral-shaped stone columns. And in the middle of the dance floor stood a young man.

I couldn't see him clearly, but I could feel everything about him, especially his love. I was drawn to him. I knew him; I had known him for eternity. He was the most familiar being I had ever felt. He smiled at me, and the sun kissed my body. I shivered with his love. Then his arms were around me, and we began to dance.

"Dance your soul. Remember who you are," he whispered to me, and in that moment I felt free.

I danced with him, and we laughed together and he shared the touch of heaven with me. I felt the beauty inside me and the power of joy. He knew my every thought, my every feeling. And none of it mattered here. I laughed again with the freedom.

He touched my chin and turned my face to the stars. Within their sparkling dance of light was one much brighter than the others. "Go," he said. "Go find what you are looking for."

Slowly I walked away from him. Freed, my soul rose to the light. My eyes were closed, and I was calm. Whatever was going to happen would happen. I simply let go and trusted.

The light was stronger than any I had ever known on earth. I had been to this light many times, but I had always turned back, afraid of its power. This time, I let it take me. It pulsed through my soul, breaking down the walls I'd built there. Flashes of my ego — the part of me that tried to control my life, my future — seemed to burst away from my being. Gone was the past. Gone was the future. I was free. I shook from the magnificence of the moment. And then it was over. I was back in the room. The people in the group were still journeying, but it was time for them to return. Even as I started to bring them back, the vision shimmered within me.

Õ

I was still in the hole. Above me stood the man; below me, Rik. I hesitated for just a moment, thoughts of David holding me back. What if letting go meant letting go of him too?

Then Rik spoke again: "Marci, I can't promise what will happen in the future. What I can promise is that if you let go, you'll never have to fear hurt again. Where life is lived in truth, honesty, beauty, and love, there can be no evil."

His words touched my heart. I didn't want to fight anymore. It was time to let go. I wanted to feel the way I had felt in the last vision. Slowly, my hands slipped away from the rung. I let go, not in defeat, but in trust.

"This time," I prayed, "there will be no going back."

Safety
November 30, 1996

Rik had seemed so far away, I thought I would fall forever before I reached him. But when my hands finally let go of the rung, I immediately landed in his arms.

The feeling was indescribable. Although Rik held me with so much love, it wasn't love that overwhelmed me. It was safety: For the first time in so long, I felt safe. And I realized that I had stopped fighting. Always before when I had tried to let go to the power, I had set conditions. "I want this," I would say. "This is what matters to me." Or "I'm willing to let go but just for a few weeks. If things don't work out by then, I won't trust you anymore."

Although things always had worked out, I still didn't trust in the power the other side had shown me. The next time, I'd set more conditions. But this time, there were no conditions, no fighting, no time limits. All I wanted was to stay in the safety of Rik's arms.

"Everything is okay, Angel. You're safe now. I'm not going to leave you," he whispered over and over to me in a lullaby of love.

"Where is the light Rik?" I asked, realizing that the light that had surrounded him was gone.

"The light is down there, where I was standing. When you chose to let go, I was able to stop your fall," he answered.

"But why couldn't you have been closer to me when I was hanging up here?" I asked in confusion. "It would have made the choice so much easier. I wouldn't have had to worry about falling."

"Marci, you're always afraid of falling. That's why you never let go. I couldn't be close to you because you hadn't chosen to come with me. You still could have decided to go out the top, to keep fighting the hurt and darkness of the past. Or you could have decided to stay where you were. I couldn't choose for you. I could come only as close as you allowed me to come. This place is nothing more than a reflection of the battle waging within you. You choose how close people get; no one else can choose for you. I could help you only after you let go."

He was quiet for a minute. Then he said: "Remember, I never actually leave you. I'm always by your side, just as close as I am right now. It's only your fear that makes it seem like there is a distance between us. If you could remember that all you have to do is let go, there would be no struggle. You would flow with the power that's within everything; you would never fall again."

I heard Rik's words but not their meaning. I was safe, and that's all that mattered. I wanted to stay in his arms forever.

"Are you ready, Angel," he asked, gently stroking my hair.

"Where are we going?"

"To the light and to understanding," he said.

I wasn't sure how we could go "to understanding," but in my mind I told him I was ready.

Instantly we were bathed in the liquid light. For a moment it felt hot, but then it was cool. It felt like diving into a lake on a hot summer's day.

The liquid light was red, orange, yellow, and a brilliant white. It was thick and oily and seemed to have a life of its own. It rose up in great flames and then splashed down in waves. Together Rik and I rode the waves through deeply tunneled caves of stone. The liquid wrapped around us, and we laughed with the pleasure of the speed at which we traveled. I wasn't afraid. The flames seemed to give me energy I hadn't had in a long time, the energy to laugh and have fun.

Where the tunnel ended, the liquid turned to solid ground. We were standing on a ledge on the side of a mountain, perched high above a sea of liquid light. The mountain, a mass of reddish rock and earth, stretched far above my head into a beautiful sky.

"What everyone else thinks is hell doesn't seem so bad now, does it?" Rik leaned over and whispered in my ear. His arms still were wrapped around me, but he no longer carried me; I was standing on my own.

As I started to move forward, Rik let me go. The beauty and power of the sea left me breathless. I had never believed in the church's vision of hell — a pit of fire and brimstone burning sinners for eternity. Although the sea burned, and it was below the earth, it certainly was not hell. It was magnificent. I breathed in its essence and trembled at its power.

The liquid churned like the open ocean before a storm. It was a deep red and orange — lava, the earth's blood. It had been here since the beginning of time. It knew the secrets of creation and of destruction, and it seemed to tell me they were the same. It pulled at something ancient in my soul. I felt it call to me, not in words but in simple knowing, as though we were of a kind, sharing the fabric of our being.

I looked up. The sky was filled with soft, pale colors and light, as though the sun had just set. It seemed to reach forever. And somehow its size made me feel larger. Within that sky I could see all of the magical experiences I'd had in my physical life, all the experiences that had brought me to the other side. They weren't so much pictures as swirls of dark purple light: I would look at a swirl, and I would feel the memory in my heart. They all came at once and touched me deeply.

I wanted to understand. I wanted to see and feel what this place was trying to teach me. I knew that something in me was awakening, and for a moment I was afraid I couldn't do it. A small voice inside was asking those same questions: "What will happen to David and me? What will happen to my business? Will I be able to live in the world if I know this truth?" But I realized I couldn't let those questions stop me. I couldn't walk away from something this beautiful. I had searched too long to come to this point; I had to feel the truth.

In the sky I saw two faces — one female, one male. But even as I thought of them that way, I realized how little those labels meant. These faces were so much more than simply female or male. I knew them. I had seen them before in this world, and I had ached when I couldn't see them in the physical world. They were the spirits that had called to me in my first power surge. They looked at me without judgment, without fear, without the need for definition. They had such power — a power that doesn't draw its strength from control but from love. And in their love I felt my own beauty and strength. I was home.

Õ

Rik softly touched my shoulder. "It's time, Marci. It's time to know again who you are," he said.

I felt surrounded by magic. Even the air was alive. How different this world was from the place where my body lived. This was home, and when I wasn't here, I missed it terribly.

Already I was dreading going back to the physical world, although I knew at some point I would have to. The fear was there again. Knowing this beauty, this peace, how could I go back to a world of ugliness and pain? How could I live in that world knowing what I knew of this one. It hurt too much.

I turned to Rik, and he saw my fear. "I can't Rik. I want to so badly, but I can't," I cried to him. "Help me. I'm so confused."

His eyes shifted. He was looking over my shoulder. I turned to see what he was looking at. At the edge of the rock where we stood was a huge glass barrier. In the center were two enormous doors, their handles wrapped with heavy chains and locks.

"I put that up, didn't I," I said to Rik — a statement, not a question. He looked at me with understanding, making no judgment, just acknowledging what I already knew. "I want to do this, and I know I need to trust, but I can't. I can't stop shutting myself out from the world I want so much to be in."

"Marci," Rik said, "the walls you create don't just keep people and the world from hurting you. They also keep the power in you contained. The walls aren't about your hurt. You've healed that hurt through your empowerment program. There's nothing left to hurt you outside; you can't stop fearing what's inside."

"You ask too much, Rik. I'm too angry at the world. Every time I feel my power, every time I try to use it to help people, someone hurts me or tries to take it away. That's how it works in my world."

"You know that people are afraid of love and truth," Rik answered. "Think about Christ. Those who feared his power needed to destroy him. And those who believed his words chose to make him a god. He wanted to teach them about the places and things he could see, but they didn't want to learn; they wanted him to do it for them.

"Of course, the fault also lies with those who have touched the power even slightly, those who at first wanted only to help others but then grew egotistical with the power. They fell deep into a hole, never realizing what placed them there. Now these people with no heart preach to others about living life to the fullest. Surely you're not afraid of them.

"No. What you really fear is giving up life."

He was right. I didn't want to give up David. I didn't want to give up enjoying the physical world, and I was afraid that would happen, that the beauty of this world would destroy any pleasure I had in the other.

"Marci, let me help you with your fears. Let me show you that everything will be okay. This I can do for you." Rik spoke gently. He wasn't angry with my hesitation. Hearing my thoughts, he laughed and said, "Hey, I chose to take care of you. You think I want to be out of a job?" He picked me up in his arms and hugged me. "Everything is going to be okay. We knew this would happen. That you doubt, that you think about where you're going means you have reverence for yourself and for the power. That's not a bad thing."

I thanked him. "I don't know what I would do without you, and I never want to find out," I said, giving him a playful punch on the arm to say "Don't ever leave me."

"You'll never have to. It's not like you're an assignment. I'm not going to go away after I finish teaching you. You're my teacher as well, and you're stuck with me," he said, trying to reassure me.

"But you said that your job would be over," I responded, pouting like a child whose parents were about to head off for the weekend without her.

"Just a joke. Don't be so serious," Rik said. "That's something strange about humans. You think that worshipping God or a higher power is supposed to be serious. When I look at some of your churches, people seem miserable and bored. That's not what it's all about. Worshipping isn't about rules; it's about living your truth. Standing up and doing a jig would be better. Laughing and telling jokes would be more reverent. Talking about how bad you are, to me, that's blasphemy."

He had done it again. Somehow Rik always managed to ease my fears, to relax me. And he seldom missed the opportunity to throw in a lesson at the same time. Of course, he made sense. That was one of my problems. This world always made sense; it was the physical world that didn't.

"So," I asked, "how do I get over this?"

"We talk and we remember. We take our time, and I try not to frighten you." He took my hand in his, and I knew I would be okay. I wanted to feel better and know my truth. With him by my side, I could do that. "Let's start with your fear of not being able to be with David," he said.

"I'm not sure that I want to hear this," I answered with a sigh. "I don't want to lose him."

Rik took my hands and led me away from the edge of the mountain. He sat down and motioned for me to join him. Then he took my hands again and looked into my eyes. In his eyes, I could see his soul, but I didn't want to look right then. My guard was up.

Thoughts of David washed over me. He was the only man I had ever made a real commitment to. He was my partner in every way — in business and in love. But ever since we had moved to Virginia, I had felt myself pulling away from him. I had felt my destiny calling me to something more, and I knew I couldn't take him with me. So I had begun to close myself off from his love. Sensing that rejection, he'd grown distant. We had never fought; now the tension between us was constant. And there was an emptiness in us that had never been there before.

"Why do you fear losing him?" Rik asked gently, trying to coax me into feeling what I didn't want to feel.

I slid my hands away from his, stood up, and walked toward the glass walls. I looked at them and at what lay beyond, wondering how to explain the way I felt. Finally, I turned back to Rik and answered, "If I go there," I said pointing to the sky, "I can't take him with me. I'm afraid that I will change so much that I won't be able to love him anymore . . . at least not the way I love him now." I paused for a moment, looking at Rik but seeing only my situation with David. "I know what love is like when you touch power. You don't want just one person. You don't want to feel limited by a relationship. You love everything and everyone because they're all a part of you."

Rik nodded, understanding. "This isn't something new. I remember your last serious relationship and the strain of him wanting to marry you and you knowing that you couldn't. You loved him for who he was and who the two of you were together, but you didn't want to marry him. You wanted to go and be your truth. And I remember how other people thought the two of you were perfect, that you were crazy to let him go. The same thing is happening with David. Because the two of you work so well together and obviously care about each other, everyone thinks you should get married."

"Exactly. But I don't want to hurt him," I said in frustration.

"Marci, that last relationship was different from the one you have with David. David doesn't care about getting married. He's not trying to keep you all for himself. He wants you to carry out the life that you were meant to live," Rik said.

I didn't say anything. Rik was right. David didn't want to cage me; he wanted me to do what was right for me.

"You think that David is so different from you; you think that he can't come with you. Well, you're wrong. No, he can't take the same journey you take. No one's journey to the self is the same as anyone else's. But David is also very powerful. Right now, your des-

tinies are diverging a bit. You need to go out into the world. David
needs to be in a stable place so that he can grow the business. But
David's destiny is very tied to yours. His power is in bringing the
message — through your products — that people aren't alone, that
our love is here waiting for them to accept it.

"You each have a part to play. He's the ground crew; you're
the flight crew. He can't fly and do his part; you can't stay grounded and do yours. But he's right beside you going at his own pace in
his own way."

As Rik was talking, I thought about the ways David and I
had tried to change each other. When I needed to move away from
home I hadn't wanted to leave him, so I had tried to take him with
me. He had agreed wholeheartedly on the outside, but inside he had-
n't wanted to move. He'd done it for me, to help me get away from
all the stress. Now instead of going ahead with our plans for the
business, he was holding me back. I wanted to go explore the world,
and he was angry at me for that. Even worse, he wasn't sure he
would be there for me when I came back.

"It's time for that to change," Rik said. "Neither of you has
stopped loving the other. In fact it is wanting to be together that has
led each of you to try changing the other's destiny. What you both
have to realize is that you can't rely on each other for your security
and happiness. Those things come only from within and only then
can be shared."

"So what do we do? I love him so much, and I hate being
apart from him." I hoped Rik would say some magic words, and
David and I would have our beautiful relationship back.

"You let each other go. You stop worrying about the future

and trying to make it perfect between the two of you. You realize that you don't have to take care of each other. Maybe you should try to see David for who he truly is. You have a gift of seeing people's hearts and minds and souls. Look at David. See what we see in him. See why he was the one chosen to help you. What he's been showing you is his fear. Look deeper. See his truth."

"I can't," I said. "When we first met, it bothered him that I could "feel" people, and he made me promise I would never do it to him, that he would always have his privacy. He's given me permission since, but I could never do it. I guess I'm afraid to, and I don't know why."

"Because he brings out your power," Rik said. He was right again. Since I met David it had been hard to deny the power within me. "Why don't you start there?"

I thought for some time about what Rik had said. I realized that I had started to blame David for everything. I blamed him for not knowing more about the business, for not letting me go away, for keeping me from healing. The truth was he hadn't kept me from anything; I could have gone at any time. And it wasn't his fault that he didn't know the business when he came on board. He'd never even worked for himself before. It had taken me time to get organized. Why did I expect more from David? He not only had the business to contend with, he had been laid off from his job when we first became partners; he was learning all kinds of strange things about a world he'd never known existed before he met me. His whole belief system was changing. And then there were the stresses — the financial worries and his concern about me and our life together.

Suddenly I knew that I had blamed David so that I wouldn't

have to face the truth: I was the only person in my way.

The walls I had built to keep David away began to fall. I turned to Rik. "Why is it so hard for me to let David into my life again? Why am I so terrified?" I asked.

He didn't answer; he simply looked at me, his eyes asking me the same question. Then I noticed that the world around me was different, that everything had changed. The colors were duller; the air was cooler; a wind was blowing my hair.

In my mind I tried to see it all beautiful again. But as soon as I tried to change everything back to the way it was before, the ledge that Rik and I were on began to crumble. The mountain was falling apart. The sky around me was melting.

"No," I screamed as I started to fall. "No. It can't go away."

"Why?" Rik asked. We were falling, he and I, but he didn't seem to notice. "Why don't you want this world to change?"

The noise was deafening: waves churning, wind whipping, rocks falling everywhere. "I'm not ready," I screamed. "I'm not finished."

I no sooner spoke, and the world was as beautiful as it had been.

Rik looked up at me with a proud grin and asked, "What aren't you finished with?"

"I'm not finished healing," I said. I was shaking. I kept checking myself with my hands to be sure I was in one piece.

"That's right," he said looking at me with his bright blue eyes. They sparkled and drew me into his soul. "You're afraid to break down the walls because your soul is still tired. You haven't gained back all of your strength yet. You're afraid that if the walls come down, you'll lose yourself in your relationship with David and stop caring about your own destiny. You've done that before, but you're not willing to do that now."

Then he added: "Remember that it's okay to be an individual. It doesn't mean that you and David have to be separated; it simply means that your relationship won't be everything that exists in your lives. When you're ready, the walls will disappear."

Suddenly everything from the past two years made sense. When David came into my life, I wasn't fully healed from a battle I had gone through years before. There'd been no time. I started the business. When I met David, I was still an empty shell. Yes, my body was stronger, but I hadn't dealt with my fears of the physical world, the need to be normal. David was so normal, he helped me feel that way too. Then he helped me touch the other side again. He seemed to bring out my power, and I grew to rely on him. He did everything for me, and I expected more and more. I was angry with him when I didn't feel right. I was hurt and sad when he didn't spend all of his time with me. I was pushy when he couldn't grow the business as fast as I wanted him to. I depended on him to drive me places, to make the physical and emotional pain go away, to make me happy, to help me feel connected, and to help me achieve my destiny. And for a long time, he did all that . . . and more . . . without complaining.

The move to Virginia changed things. He felt we were making a mistake, and he was angry. But when his needs surfaced, I wasn't able to help him. I was too angry at his withdrawal from me, and I was too tired. There were walls between us, and this time they were David's.

When we went to visit our families, the walls came down. David was happier, safer, and ready to protect me again, to do for me. But by now I knew my dependence on him wasn't good. I couldn't even sleep without him next to me. I was terrified at the loss of me, and I hated myself for my weakness. Instead of talking with him and trying to explain, I began to build my own walls. Poor David. He thought I was falling out of love with him, and he thought that if I needed him — needed his strength — everything would be all right again. He needed me to need him. We had become too dependent on each other. It all made so much sense.

The fear was gone. My walls were still there, but I felt a freedom I hadn't felt in ages. I wasn't angry anymore; I was elated. I shouted a cry of happiness and freedom, and jumped and danced around the ledge. I called to the sky, "I'm coming. Soon." I felt the beings there waiting for me, smiling and laughing with me.

I understood now that the walls wouldn't come down until I was ready to stand on my own two feet. The walls weren't very different from the eating disorders I had grown up with. There was no easy cure for them. Over a period of years, I had tried determination and what seemed like a million programs, but the addictions didn't go away until I stopped focusing on them and started focusing on their cause. I had been trying to break down the barrier between David and me for months. Now I realized it would fall when the time was right.

Of course the walls between David and me weren't the only walls I'd erected in the physical world. In the past year I had let hurt with my family and friends turn to anger and then hatred. I'd been afraid that they, too, would hold me back. The emotional barriers I'd built were the first step in a physical separation I had thought necessary to living my destiny. Now I realized I could love others — David, my family, my friends — and still be me. I just had to remember who I was and not get caught up in who they were. I had to be my truth.

This was a new day, the day of my dawning. Whatever fears I might have, I was ready. I turned to Rik, determination in my voice, and asked, "Where do we go from here?"

David
November 30, 1996

Rik laughed with the joy of my joy. "It's good to see the spirit inside you again," he said. "Think about how you feel right now."

I did as he asked. "I'm not tired," I said, dancing again with my newfound energy. "And the sense of falling and the darkness are gone."

Rik nodded. "Beware of the dragon that waits inside. The high you're feeling comes from knowledge, from understanding. But that feeling is fleeting, like the rush of a drug. Look deeper, Marci. What do you actually feel inside?"

So I looked deeper within my soul. A crashing wave of fatigue washed over me. The fatigue was my darkness. It was a huge spiral in the deepest part of my existence. As I let myself go into it, I realized that Rik was right. The energy I had felt was fleeting; it would go away, leaving me angry at David, at the world, even at the other side for taking it away.

This, too, was a pattern with me: flying high and then crash-ing to the ground, flying and crashing. I remembered my mother's being so frustrated by my highs and lows, not understanding why I couldn't just stay on middle ground. Now I realized that even a strong soul has ups and downs. But if I was my truth, the ups would be a celebration, not just bursts of energy, and the downs would be lessons leading me forward, not the feeling that life was no longer worth living.

This time, without Rik's prompting, I looked inside again. Just beyond the darkness was a light, the light of creation within me. It seemed far away, but it was there. Even the darkness seemed dif-ferent, lightened somehow by my happiness. And I understood that each high wasn't the answer in itself, just a small step. I was on my way.

Rik nodded his head with understanding. "Good," he said. "It's time to move on. It's time to *see* David."

I was puzzled and frightened again. "I thought the walls were supposed to stay up until I take them down," I said.

"I didn't say to take the walls down; I only said that it's time to see him. You've always had the power to see the good in people; but you've tucked that power away because you're afraid that while you're focusing on the good, the bad will somehow hurt you. You think that looking at the bad can help you avoid the traps people set, but it only keeps you trapped inside. It makes you just like them. Just because you see David doesn't mean you have to run back to your relationship with him. All it means is that you won't be holding yourself back because of fear."

I sighed and looked down at the ground. Why did every step have to be so hard?

"Because you're afraid," Rik said, his voice answering my thoughts. "On this journey, you have to put fear aside. It won't help you. Trust me. I will help you." He reached out his hand to me, and I realized that at some point we had traded places. I was sitting on the ground, and he was standing up.

"I can do this," I thought. "Just trust Rik. He's always been right before."

I took his hand, and I felt his energy enter my consciousness. I closed my eyes and felt his strength: He would protect me.

"See David in his everyday life," Rik said.

His voice rang through my soul. I felt the darkness swirl around me, and I breathed deeply trying to feel my way through it. At first I focused on Rik's strength; then I began to feel my happiness wrapping itself around me like a soft mist. But in moments the fear was back and with it the anger I held toward David for leaving me emotionally. A hole opened in the blackness.

Õ

David standing in our living room. I could see his dark hair, his beautiful smile, his broad shoulders. He was wearing jeans and a sweatshirt.

"*Feel* him," Rik said, telling me to see beyond the physical.

I looked into the first layer of David's being. In that space I felt his warmth. He was like a puppy, eager to love and to show his affection, playful, wanting attention and approval, wanting to please. He was also curious and adventurous, which made him hard to hold down and train. So many people had tried to make David into what they thought he should be. Even I had tried to do it. I wished with all my heart that I hadn't, and I was sad at the thought that in a way I had succeeded. I hadn't meant to change him; I just needed him to stay focused on the business. But I had changed him. I had taken away his playfulness.

"Marci, look deeper," Rik said. "You didn't change him: The warmth, the playfulness, they're still there. You just forced out another part of him. Don't get lost in your own emotions. See the truth of his soul."

I didn't want to leave this sweet playful David, but Rik was urging me on. Sadly, I let this David go and found a very different David, a part of him I had only glimpsed before. This David was strong and fiercely determined. "Am I making this up?" I wondered. But I could feel his determination, his strong need to succeed.

Suddenly the determined David was gone, replaced by the sensual David, the man I had fallen in love with. Here was the flame that ignited my soul, making me beautiful and soft and powerful all at once. Here was the strong confident man who wouldn't allow me to hide within myself, who loved taking control, who brought me to heights I never thought possible. Although fire roared within him, he was gentle and sweet and so beautiful. I remembered this David with longing, and I missed him. Yet even as I asked myself where this man had gone, I knew the answer. Like all the other parts of David, this part was still there; I just hadn't seen it for a while.

The anger came back. Oh, how I missed the power of this David. How dare he take it away from me? I wanted to hurt him as

I was hurt.

Then I softened. I also wanted to feel David's soul again — the real David, strong and brave, not the hurt and uncertain David of the world's creating.

Rik's voice brought me back. "Marci, everyone has the power within them. You recognized that power in David from the start, and he sensed that power in you. You were magic together, you two, and you can be again. But right now, each of you has a journey to take, and each of you must choose your own way to make that journey. You didn't make The Quest David's destiny. He did. You simply tried to push him along because you saw it was right for him and you wanted it to happen quickly. The thing is, My Angel, although you created the company and its products, The Quest isn't your destiny.'"

Rik answered my unspoken question. "I didn't say that you wouldn't be a part of it; I just said it wasn't your destiny. Yes, you were supposed to start the company. And you'll always have a part in it because you are the company's product. But it's David's vision that will grow The Quest. See the part of him you haven't seen before.'"

I tried to focus again on David's determination, but I was angry at what Rik had said. If The Quest wasn't my destiny, why had I given so much to the business? My anger turned to rage. I wanted to throw something.

Rik wasn't impressed. "Marci, let it go," he said.

I took a deep breath and returned to David's soul, but not happily. I wanted answers to my questions.

I saw a huge white house, the structure and the grounds filled with pools and fancy cars and hot tubs and a dance studio. Everything was of the finest quality. One wing housed an office. David was standing behind a beautiful mahogany desk, a phone to his ear. He was king of this castle, not because he had things, but because he had built an empire. He had taken my ideas and his, and built a kingdom. The Quest had become everything he had envisioned.

I realized what Rik meant about the business not being my destiny. The company had always held me back, tying me to a place and taking more time and commitment than I wanted to give. But David loved it, the wheeling and the dealing and the power. This was a new power — not the power of his beautiful fiery soul, but the power to build an empire. This was David's destiny, David's dream. It wasn't mine.

I thought about my dream and realized it had very little to do with The Quest. Yes, I wanted to help people, but to do that I needed to go out into the world and learn as much as I could. The person who was really committed to The Quest was David. And right now that commitment meant long hours at work and little time for me. I hadn't pushed David away; the drive to work was pulling him from me.

"Why does there always have to be this pull in relationships?" I asked Rik.

"When two people who know each other's souls come together, there's an immediate connection. The newness of the relationship reminds them who they are inside, and the high is incredible. They can love each other fully and unconditionally because their joy blocks out the world and all of the day-to-day stresses of living in that world. Later, as they feel more comfortable with their love, they also feel secure enough with each other to let the world back in, and with it their individual plans and dreams for living in that world. With that reality comes a letdown. There's a void where the high has been. Longing for what was — but unable to give up their individual dreams — each blames the other and tries to change the other back to the way he or she was in the beginning. They get so caught up in the struggle that they can't see the love anymore.

"It's not that commitment is bad; it's the restriction it imposes that's bad. If two people can give each other the freedom to do what they need to do in life, trusting that their bond won't be destroyed, they can love freely without sacrificing their own truth."

And Rik went on: "When people look only for the high of a new relationship, they rob themselves of the beauty of growing together. But if a relationship is meant to be, knowing who you are inside is the only commitment you need to make. That's what brings the individual true happiness and peace. And it's that individual peace that allows a relationship to grow over time. Only when David seeks the truth of his soul will the pull between the two of you go away.

"Now see the ancient part of him," Rik said, guiding me further into David's soul.

And I saw brilliant light emanating from David in bursts of white and soft color, the light I'd come to know whenever I'd come home to the spiritual world. It was his love for me, and it was unconditional. I was free to be myself; all he wanted was for me to be happy. The power of that love enveloped me. His soul was the ancient dragon, knowing and wise.

I looked at Rik and saw in him what I had seen in David. His soul beamed love and hope and strength toward me. I knew that if I asked, he would heal my soul. But I chose not to ask. I needed to find peace on my own; I needed to find it within me. Rik had known, of course, what I would choose. But he showed me his beauty so that I would know that he would be there for me if I fell. That knowledge helped me face what I knew was next, the biggest challenge yet: I had to stop fearing the physical world.

Truth
November 30, 1996

The rock beneath me began to quake, the tremors vibrating through my body. This time I didn't fight; I accepted whatever was going to happen. I wanted freedom; I wanted my soul to thrive; I wanted to live the life I knew I was meant to live. I lost sight of Rik as I fell through an opening in the rock. I felt him letting me go, and I felt his blessing.

The rock was cold. The space was so tight that I didn't fall very fast, yet it took only a few seconds to move through the twenty feet of stone. At the bottom were two rungs like those in the concrete hole, but, to my relief, they weren't razor-sharp. I grabbed them and held on. I was hanging a few yards above the sea of color. I could feel its heat and see small splashes of color below my feet. I wondered what was going to happen next, but I wasn't afraid.

"Hey, you," I heard a voice say. "Over here."

Twenty feet to my left was a young man hanging, much like I was. The only difference: He was swinging and flipping off his rungs; I was holding on tightly.

"So, do you have the guts?" The challenge was made with a laugh. Where Rik was a strong but gentle, almost fatherlike, spirit, this spirit was more like me. In his smile was a touch of the devil and a love of adventure.

"That depends," I answered. My words were cool, my smile mischievous.

"Do you have the guts to see the world from a different view? You think it's all wrong. Do you have the guts to see what's right?"

"I'd love to see the good. I've been trying to do that my whole life," I said, annoyed that this spirit thought he knew more than I did.

He wouldn't back down: "You haven't tried anything. You're afraid to see the good. You don't want to be tied to the world by your love for it."

"That's not true," I insisted, insulted by what he had said.

"You're afraid to see their souls, just like Rik said. So, I want to know if you're going to chicken out." Then he did a backflip and caught the rungs. He didn't seem to care whether I was going to go any farther.

"This conversation is ridiculous," I said with confidence and a challenge in my voice. "I may get scared, but I've never actually backed away from anything."

"Good. Don't start now. Where we're going, a person could lose her mind." With that, he let go of the rungs and jumped into the liquid sea.

I wasn't sure what he meant about losing my mind, but I didn't care. If I could face letting go of David, nothing could hold me back now.

I looked at the sea. I was so close to it, I could feel its heartbeat. It seemed to hold all the knowledge of the world. I wanted to understand; I wanted to know the goodness of the physical world. "Please, help me love them," I called to the sea as I let go of the rungs and plunged in after him.

I expected to find myself swimming in the molten liquid. Instead I was sitting next to the spirit on a small stone ledge right above the sea. "What are we doing here?" I asked. "I saw you dive into the liquid. I thought I dove in after you."

"I thought we would do something a little different. Everything you've been through has been so serious. I figured we would have a little fun." With those words, he pulled me to him and kissed me full on the mouth.

At first I laughed and moved away, but he didn't stop. When I tried to pull away, he wrapped my mind in his and wouldn't let go. My mind and body wanted him, but my heart and soul were screaming no.

As his kisses became more forceful, I felt as though I was drowning. He made me want him, or maybe it was his desire I was feeling. I couldn't fight it. His energy was so strong, and I was so open that I couldn't tell which thoughts were mine and which were his. Something felt so wrong about this, but I didn't have the strength to stop him.

"You know you want me," he said, and immediately the

word *rape* screamed through my mind. The shame and pain that I thought had disappeared for good when I healed the hurt of my childhood came rushing back. I felt disgusting.

I cried out for Rik, but instantly the scene changed. The spirit had stopped attacking me. He was beside me now in a dark ugly place. All around were trash and sludge. A man was sitting in a corner, a tourniquet around his arm, a needle sticking out of his forearm. He radiated a darkness that made me cry out in sadness. Behind me a woman was giving her body to a man, not because she cared for him but because she couldn't feel anything anymore. I heard a small child cry out in the night, another victim of brutality. To my right was a door, and I knew that beyond it were more people in pain.

"I believe the song calls it 'comfortably numb,'" the spirit said.

I couldn't answer. I was thinking about a Pink Floyd concert I had gone to two years before. I remembered not being able to feel anything while I was there. I had been surrounded by thousands of people, many of them high on drugs, all of them high on the music. I remembered my numbness and the terror it had made me feel.

"Feel their souls," the young spirit said.

At that moment, I hated him. He had brought me here, and I wanted out. I couldn't bear the horror.

I reached out for the memory of Rik and David, and found myself clutching a rock in the fiery world, an anchor in the molten ocean. "I did go down under the sea, after all," I thought to myself. Before I could catch my breath, the spirit was beside me again.

"You okay?" he asked. He was different now, more like the

soul I had seen hanging from the ledge. "I'm sorry about that. Okay?"

He read the fear in my eyes.

"Look, it was the only way to bring you to the hell you already fear. I had to bring down your energy level. Because you had experienced rape, I figured it was the easiest way. I didn't mean to hurt you."

"What was that place?" I asked.

"You know what it was: hell. Anyone who has ever been raped or addicted to alcohol or drugs or who has stopped feeling simply because it's too painful has been there. There are more people alive in hell than dead. That's why you're afraid to show yourself in the physical world. You're afraid that the living hell will destroy your truth."

He paused for a moment, letting his words sink in. Then he went on quietly: "I asked you if you were scared, didn't I?" He seemed to be trying to get me to trust him again.

"No," I said angrily. "You asked me if I had the guts. You didn't say anything about going to hell. I could go back to my body, turn on the television, and see what I just saw. I don't need your help."

He nodded. "I just knew how tough it would be, so I tried to get you riled up. I had to do what I did; it was the only way to bring you down to that level. Okay? I'm sorry I freaked you out and made you doubt the healing. But I had to make you feel 'dirty' so that you could feel what those people feel. I said I was sorry."

I knew he was telling the truth: I could see it in his eyes.

"I forgive you," I finally said. "I know that you were just trying to help me, but I'm pretty sure I could have dug up the feeling on my own, thank you very much."

He looked at me expectantly. I knew what he wanted to hear. "Yes, I'm going back with you. Just don't leave me, and don't push me this time. I'll feel their souls when I'm damn well ready to."

"Deal. Just don't get stuck in their stuff. Rise above it. I don't want to have to wait ten years while you figure out how to come back."

He smiled and went on: "I guess you know now what I meant by 'a person could lose her mind'?"

I did, and I prayed it wouldn't happen.

I took his hand, and we jumped into the molten sea. We were back in the same place, and again I was feeling the horror of what those people felt.

"When a person is raped, she hides her true self away," the spirit explained. "Sex is supposed to unite two souls in truth. Rape exposes the rapist's hell to his victim. Even though that victim can hide her truth from the rapist, she can't help but see the rapist's hell. The pain of that hell is so great that she comes to believe in her own shame, just as you did.

"If victims could only know there is nothing wrong with them. . . . But most never again feel safe enough to let their true selves shine. So, many of them end up here. In fact all of the people who come to this place are here because they're running away from some horror, because they've forgotten that they are worth something. Of course, that's not really surprising, given that the world looks at them with pity or disgust or even fear. So no one helps them."

I listened to his words; I could have spoken them. As I looked around, I still felt the pain, but it was different somehow. The terror was gone. My truth was shielding me.

I turned toward the man with the needle in his arm. He was sitting against a wall, his body slumped over his knees. I knelt in front of him and gently nudged him. There was no response; at first I wasn't sure he was breathing.

I felt enormously sad for him, but I also understood that he had come here for a reason and that I couldn't interfere with that. I, too, had come for a reason — to learn. So I placed a hand on his knee and entered his consciousness.

Immediately I felt the numbness and then heard a deep howl of fear, fear that he would never be free again. He longed to be rid of his addiction, but he also was resigned to it.

"If only he knew," I thought, "how beautiful he really is." I knew. At the same time that I felt the chilling cold of his despair, I had felt his soul.

He had been married; he had a daughter; he'd been an executive in a corporation. He was well liked and respected, but he couldn't see what others saw. Blinded by feelings that he was somehow inadequate and by an anger he couldn't explain, he couldn't see the affection and the respect. His doubt and shame and anger made him suspicious, and his suspicion destroyed his relationships with his family and his co-workers.

He didn't understand the source of his shame and anger; he didn't even remember the incident that had destroyed his life. He was a child, five or six at most. He'd done something his parents didn't like, and they had beaten him, fractured his skull. But when they took him to the hospital, his mother and father cried over his injuries and told the doctor he had fallen from a swing.

The anger began to grow in him then, along with the realization that the only way never to be beaten again was to become the one who beats. But the child he once was — the truth of his soul — was still there. He was meant to be gentle and caring; he was curious and loved nature. His destiny had been to work with animals, but he had forgotten it the day he was hurt. Years later, he had turned to drugs to block out the confusion and pain.

At first the drugs took away the pain and let him feel his truth. He thought he had touched heaven. He had forgotten what it felt like to be happy, and that wonderful substance brought it back. Then the crash came, and he couldn't find it anymore. He was haunted by the sweetness of what he had felt. If only he could have it back for just a moment, if only he could feel his truth again, he thought, he would be okay. So again and again he went searching for it. In time the drugs failed him: The high was gone, leaving just a numbness. Nothing else existed. He had entered hell; and although he wanted to leave it, he no longer believed there was someplace better.

I took my hands away. I wanted to cry. I wanted to take him in my arms and give him the love he needed to come back. He was a beautiful soul, but no one saw that anymore. He'd become a thief to support his habit; he would kill if he had to. He simply couldn't feel the pain of hurting someone else. There was no pain. There was nothing.

I hated drugs and alcohol. I watched them destroy one beautiful person after another. I'd lost friends because I wouldn't try drugs, but I couldn't understand the attraction. I looked at that man and realized I couldn't hate the drugs anymore. It wasn't the drugs that brought people to this place. Drugs, alcohol, rape — they were just paths, not causes.

Behind me the man and woman were having sex. I could hear them. No, I could feel them; I could feel their energy. Their desire was so strong, the passion almost crushing. But there was no love there, no caring for each other or even for themselves. All they wanted was to satisfy their bodies' needs, to reach that high for just a moment.

And then I sensed something else. Their passion was actually anger. They were using sex and each other to express the violence they felt within them.

I looked deeper into their souls. The woman felt worthless and ugly, a legacy from the men in her life. For her, sex had become a way to feel valued and beautiful: "See. This man wants me." But as soon as it was over, she felt empty again.

She wanted love, but she was afraid. As long as her relationship with men centered around the physical act of sex, she could tell herself that they really didn't know her and that their harsh words were not true. What if she opened herself to a man and he, too, told her she was ugly? What if all those men had been right? How could she go on? Where would she hide? She couldn't take that chance, so she stayed numb inside. She longed for someone to know her inner beauty, to understand her and share her joy. And her fear that she would never find someone to love her brought her to this hell.

It was different for the man. For him, sex was about power. He liked controlling her responses — one moment ecstasy, the next pain. That she was angry at men only made him want her more. He used her body like a drug; the moment of release, his high. But that release wasn't really sexual; it was a letting go of all his anger.

"Those bastards," he was thinking, remembering being beaten and raped as a child. He would get back at them with every woman he touched. *Love* and *trust* weren't in his vocabulary. He had loved and trusted when he was young, and he'd been hurt. Now he wanted to hurt back, nothing else. Feelings were a sign of weakness, and weakness left you vulnerable to hurt.

I wanted to look deeper, beyond their pain, at something beautiful. Threatened, the man stopped me. "Get out!" he screamed in deep throaty anger.

I stepped back and apologized, but I already had seen enough. His soul was magnificent, his heart filled with love that he couldn't share. What he really wanted was to lay a woman down in a huge bed of feathers and roses, and to embrace her gently and love her. But his fear was too great.

It was so sad. Here were two people who had everything they wanted in their arms, but instead they chose hell.

I looked around me again, into the darkness and beyond, and I saw the numbness everywhere. There, walking down the street, was a well-dressed woman. She was beautiful but thin. And when I looked at her I knew that she was starving herself and that more than her self-image was at fault. It was about control: She could control what she ate; she had no control over all the other forces in her life.

Layer by layer, I uncovered her truth. I saw her self-loathing, then her pain, and finally her shining spirit — smiling, loving, free, every part of her singing in joy. She was a whirlwind, wanting to meet everyone and do everything. Where had that destiny gone?

And then the scene changed. I saw the wars that had taken place in the name of a god. I saw people, millions of them, brought to their knees and forced to accept something that wasn't their truth because they wanted their children to live. I saw eyes that at one time had glowed with defiance now dulled by torture. They were all there, the Native Americans, the blacks, the Armenians, the Jews. I felt their pain, not just the physical pain but the agony of losing what they loved most — their freedom. I shook with rage as I turned to look at the people who had caused this suffering over the ages in the name of some belief or the other. And the brutality was still going on, not just in Northern Ireland and Kosovo, but in societies all over the world, every day.

I knew that whatever article of faith they hid behind, the real issue was power. I found myself screaming at them, and as I screamed, I saw their horror. These people who brutalized others knew nothing else. I wanted to believe that they were cruel and hungry for power, but the truth was that many of them didn't even know they had done wrong. Their need for power was grounded in fear. For some it was just the fear of people who were different; for others, the fear that their beliefs might not be true, and they needed those beliefs to feel good about themselves. But they were all afraid.

My anger was gone. These people weren't monsters. None of them wanted to be in this hell, but whenever they tried to leave, the fear and pain came back. Like me, they had stopped believing in the good. Drugs, alcohol, sex, food, religion — they were just ways to escape.

I turned to the young spirit. "The world is okay, isn't it," I said. I wasn't asking; I was telling.

He nodded yes.

I went on: "It never felt okay; it all felt wrong. But I can see now that there are no bad people; they're all just learning. I have no right to judge them. Inside, they're all beautiful, and I can choose to see that beauty."

In my mind I saw all of the horrible things people had done to one another, and I could see what had driven those people to such cruelty. If I could see the beauty that lies beyond people's fear, perhaps I could live in this world.

Again the spirit nodded, as though he had heard my thoughts. "This world is a place to learn. That's why you're here, to learn all that exists within the miracle of creation, both good and bad. The people in this world have done a very good job of finding the bad, of creating hell. If you choose to look only at that hell, you'll be dragged down into it.

"Remember that we are all one: You can't hate the pain and not hate yourself," the spirit said, repeating what the fire had once taught me.

"But it's so hard," I said. "It's so hard not to hate someone who murders or rapes or brutalizes others." Immediately, thoughts of Jeffrey Dahmer filled my mind. I shivered.

The spirit saw and understood. "Yes, there are people who act like monsters, but very few. Most of the horror that you fear in people like Dahmer doesn't exist in physical form. It's in the minds of those who create your entertainment. They give it form in movies, television shows, books, and video games. The mind doesn't know the difference between reality and make-believe; it absorbs it all. I'm not saying that there is no horror in your world; I'm saying that it's not nearly as bad as you believe it is."

The scene changed again. I was looking at a huge, dark, swirling mass of energy. "Where is the soul in this?" I wondered.

My guide didn't answer.

Nervous but determined, I opened myself and went in. I couldn't see anything, but I could hear it — horrible screaming. All the hate, the anger, the numbness, the despair were there, so much worse than what I had felt in the individual people.

"This is what grows in people's minds," the spirit said.

"What do you mean?" I asked.

"We share one energy. This is the energy of the darkness."

I could feel the truth in his words. In that massive noise was every horrible thought people were capable of, every bit of hatred they had ever felt. Even the numbness had sound.

I thought about the spirit's words, that so much of the horror is fantasy. But the numbness it creates in us is very real. When we watch a murder on a television show, we think no one is being hurt, but the truth is *we* are being hurt, and the source of that hurt is separation. It's the willingness to accept an us-versus-them mentality. We're the good guys, and they're the bad guys, and as long as the bad guys are the dead ones, it's okay.

All of a sudden, I could see the soul of hell. The pain and the horror weren't real; they existed in our minds. We believed hell into existence, but it was all just energy. There, in the middle of that ugly swirling mass, I could see the truth of creation, and I wasn't frightened anymore.

I saw Dahmer's face again, this time with no sense of horror. This was a man who did what he did because he had no other way to cope with the absence of the miracle. Evil was not truth. I had always known that, I think, even when the man who raped me gave me a reason to believe that it was. Everything came from the same light. Evil was simply the absence of the miracle; it was what came of forgetting the truth. It had no form of its own. The world was okay.

I looked at that swirling mass and understood. "It's all good," I said, "even what seems bad. The horror, the pain, the tragedies, they're just different faces of good, signposts marking the way home."

I thought back to what the church had tried to teach me, that God was good and that He created everything. But I could never understand how a good god could have created the bad I saw around me. Now I understood. "Evil," I said aloud, "is just the truth hidden away."

With those words, the darkness was gone. The spirit and I were floating in the molten sea.

"You have no idea how hard it is going to be to live in the world knowing this," I said to him.

"I would think it would make it easier," he answered, flipping onto his back.

"You don't understand," I said. "When something bad happens, everyone gets upset. And if you don't, they think you're inconsiderate, uncaring. When people are upset, you're supposed to get upset with them."

He understood better than I thought. "Yes," he said, "and when someone hurts you, you're supposed to play the game and hurt them back. You're right. It is going to be hard to live with this knowledge, particularly knowing how people in this world try to impose their truth on others."

Now he was blowing a fountain of lava out of his mouth. I tried not to laugh.

"Yes, that's part of it, but there's more. If I were to tell people what I just learned, most of them would get defensive. I don't want to fight anymore. But if I keep my mouth shut — and that's not easy to do when people are trying to push their beliefs on me — they'll think I'm cold and unfeeling. They expect people to care, and they call us on it. Confrontation is part of my world."

"So change," he said. "You don't have to play that game anymore. You know the truth, and when something is truth, it doesn't ever go away . . . no matter how many people believe in something else. You don't have to fight for truth's sake, and you don't have to help people who don't want to change."

He thought for a minute, and then said: "I do have one question. I understand that people are afraid to let go of their own beliefs, but why would they care what you believe?"

"Well, my world believes that people who are bad should be punished, that that's the only way to keep order in the world. If I were to go around saying that criminals are good and that we shouldn't punish them, in their eyes I'd be advocating chaos."

The spirit looked at me in amazement.

"I know what you're thinking, but let me finish," I said. "My world believes in original sin. We've been told that we are all sinners and that the only way to get to heaven is through sacrifice and being good. But inside, people are afraid they can never be good enough. That fear drives them to punish those who break the rules

— the 'really bad' people — and gives them hope that maybe they aren't so bad themselves after all."

"Strange way of thinking," the spirit interrupted. "And I can see how that brings them down to the lowest level of energy."

"Let me *finish*," I said again, a little louder than before.

He nodded and laughed.

"The spiritual realm knows that all people are part of love, and that it's only the bad things that happen to them that make them feel disconnected from who they are. That's why I was able to feel the darkness, because something bad happened to me. From the spiritual point of view, when people do something horrible, they do it because they're hurting. Punishing those people doesn't make the problem go away; it makes it worse. If we could love them instead, they would have to face what they've done and learn from it. And if they could return to love, they would never hurt others again. Do you see what I'm saying? The spiritual world believes that it is those who harm others who need more love because they hurt the most.

"The people in my world don't understand that. They need to keep hating. That's their choice; it isn't mine to judge or to change. But if I can hold onto that thought — that all people, no matter what they've done, are beautiful — I can accept the physical world and live there."

I stopped for a minute, struck by the realization that this was something I had always known. "In a way, I think I've always known that," I continued. "That's what helped me overcome the pain of the rape and even forgive. But I couldn't let go of my belief that evil exists or of my anger, and I just couldn't feel safe."

I stopped again, suddenly frightened. "What if it happens

again?" I asked. "What if someone hurts me or I see cruelty around me, will this understanding go away?"

"That's easy," the spirit said. "Just return to your truth. Nothing can take that away."

With a twinkle in his eye, he disappeared under a wave. He resurfaced a minute later and said, "You told Rik the world holds no magic for you anymore. I think it's time to show you what you've been missing."

Ancient Knowledge
October 31, 1996

I was in California, standing on a hill at the edge of the ocean, the wind blowing through my hair. The water below me was so blue, so powerful. I realized as I stood there that the ocean had the power to take the land I was standing on and destroy it. But it didn't. It simply lapped against the rocks, needing only to exist.

The wind grew stronger and seemed to lift me up and carry me along. In my heart I was flying. I felt so free. The city around me was filled with cars and pollution, with crime and violence, but none of it mattered. All I could feel was the power of the sea, and it was magnificent.

Four days later, David and I went hiking. As the sun was setting, we reached a forest of giant sequoias, some of the oldest and largest trees on earth. It was very still — there was no one else around — and the trees glowed in the twilight.

At first I was struck by the size of the trees — I read someplace that it would take twenty-five people holding hands to encircle one of the larger trunks. But then I found myself thinking of their age, of all the knowledge they held of creation and how the world evolved.

"If only this forest could speak, would people remember who they are inside?" I wondered. How can we believe we know so much more than anything else when here stands a life form so much older than we are? And for a moment I was sad. I was living in a world that had forgotten how to see the magic in everything. Yes, people would come and look at the trees, but just to say that they had seen them, not to feel their magic or learn from them.

Then, in my mind, I heard one of the trees speak. "We don't mind. It's okay that people have forgotten as long as they keep coming. Someday they will remember."

I was standing in front of the largest and oldest tree, over 2,000 years old the sign said. I couldn't see the top; it was too far above me. But its base was huge and gnarled: A single knot where it reached down into the earth was as big as I was. Breaking a rule, I stepped over the fence around the tree. I was longing to touch its trunk, to feel its beauty. The wood was so soft and polished, a shine applied by centuries of wind and snow and rain. In places I could see where fire had touched it. Here was a tree that had survived so much . . . even mankind. It was glorious.

I felt something great in my heart. This tree was a miracle of life. The memory of who I was, the oneness and light of creation were inside this tree. It was so ancient, a great-great-grandmother. I wanted to lay down my heart on this tree; I wanted to feel it around me, embracing me, sharing its energy.

David was calling me; I wasn't supposed to be there. I gently kissed the tree, and it seemed to kiss me back, sharing its soul with me. People had told me that standing next to the giant trees was humbling. I felt no humility. Instead there was an awakening, an awareness and an amazement at being part of life.

I didn't want to leave; I wanted to stay within the warmth of this tree. Then I saw another tree, not as large but just as wonderful. This one, like many of the trees around it, had no fence. It drew me, and as I walked toward it I felt a deep longing for the other side; at the same time I felt what had become my constant companions, the fatigue and the darkness.

I moved around the tree and saw an opening that had been burned out of its trunk. I went inside. A warm womb of wood surrounded me, embraced me.

David was off in the distance, asking how to speak to the trees.

"Just stop and listen," I said. "Shut off your mind, open your heart, and feel them call to you."

He left me, and in that warm place I leaned my face, hands, and body against the tree. For a moment I felt how tired my soul really was, so tired of fighting. Then I was lost in the wonder of the tree, filled with its love. Suddenly I was able to touch again what I had forgotten how to touch. I remembered who I was inside, the ancient part of me. And I found myself in that long-ago world, where trees and people were one. *Home, home, home.*

The tree brought back memories of me: my spirit of adventure, my need to know everything about the universe, my tendency to tease, my eyes filled with laughter. Remembering made me feel alive and happy. I wanted that life back — I wanted to be that person again — but I wasn't sure that was possible.

And suddenly I knew why I'd been so exhausted. It wasn't about vitamins or food or sleep. The darkness I was feeling didn't have a physical source; it came from losing who I was. And the cure? I knew I wouldn't find it just in the spiritual world. To heal, I would have to look to the earth itself and to its ancient knowledge.

I didn't want to leave; I never wanted to leave. I wanted to stay in that tree and be healed. I wanted the pain to stop. I wanted to be strong again. I wanted to be home.

With that thought, my body trembled and I felt the flames of the fire around me. It had been months since I had seen the fire. I had turned away from it because I couldn't bear living in the physical world without it. I didn't understand what I was supposed to do with all it had shown me. But in turning away from the fire, I had forgotten the way home. The sequoia helped me remember, and remembering had made everything clear: To find me, I needed to go.

Lava Sea
November 30, 1996

"Look at the sea," the spirit said. "It is the blood of the earth; it holds all the memories that exist in the past, present, and future of your world. See how vast this ocean of knowledge is. The darkness of your world is only a small part of this ocean. That means that the rest of it is lighter, higher, more beautiful. It's time to feel it and to know its truth.'"

As he spoke, I felt the sea grow around me. I looked at the churning liquid, the wonderful reds, oranges, and yellows. It lifted me up, and I felt its power surround me. I bathed in its essence, drifting in waves of fiery light. For so long, I had been unable to see any good in the physical world. I wanted the sea to show me that good, to prove me wrong. I let the waves take me. Drifting on the fiery softness, I became one with the sea, sharing its knowledge.

I remembered the time in California a month before, standing on that hill watching and glorying in the ocean. I let myself feel the wonder of that day, a new life unfolding, the ocean's power drawing it out of my soul, every wave a celebration of me. And then I thought about the forest of giant trees and what I'd learned there: To remember who I was, I would have to turn to the ancient knowledge of the earth.

The ocean had turned to pinks, purples, and blues, colors that reminded me of the sunset in the forest. In another place, Rik and I had watched a sunset together.

"Nature has such a beautiful way of showing off," Rik said. "It never hides its beauty from the world. It knows only truth, and it's never ashamed of that."

I thought of it again as I floated on the lava sea. Why can't we show the most incredible parts of ourselves to the world? Why do we feel we have to hide?

Waterfall
November 1, 1996

The day after our trip to see the sequoias, David took me to Yosemite. As we drove out of a tunnel, I looked up and saw the sun hit El Capitain and Half Dome. We were in the most beautiful valley. I kept thinking, "God's country, this is God's country." David parked the car at a turnoff, and we got out and stood staring out at what I thought must be the most beautiful place I had ever seen in my life. With each breath, my spirit soared.

From there we drove to a waterfall. I began climbing the hundred and fifty feet of steep rock that led up to the base of the falls. I wanted to listen to the water crashing, but all I could hear were the shouts of people around me, yelling to one another how they had climbed to the top. And so I climbed higher, until, finally, all I could hear was the song of the water as it touched the stone of the earth. Its soothing voice helped me forget the world below. I looked up and saw a rainbow arcing across the deep blue sky. As I watched the bands of color join and dance within the water's mist, I realized that some of the most beautiful things in life come from something that is half in this world and half in the other. The rainbow is always there; I just had to be open to experiencing it.

Fire is like that too, I thought, always there. Create a spark, feed it, and it would keep you warm and fill your soul with light. Maybe the ability to feel beauty is also right there just waiting for the right spark.

As I looked out over the valley, I felt as I had the night before. Something inside me was healing, being renewed. I felt so pure and clean and honest. There was no way I could live a lie here; there was no way I would ever have to. This too was home.

I climbed higher and higher, my only companions the birds and the wind. When I reached the pool at the base of the falls, I watched the water dance with the rocks, the mist reaching me where I stood. The rainbow was still overhead, and once again I heard the words *home, home, home,* like the beating of my heart. Energy rushed through me in waves of happiness.

I felt alive. There was magic here. I could feel it in the water, in every rock, in every tree, in the sky. And I could sense the life thriving beneath the surface of the water. I looked again at the waterfall and how it had carved the earth; together the water and the earth had made a masterpiece. Like an artist who creates a painting to help people understand what he's feeling, the heavens had created this gift to remind people of both the world's beauty and their own.

I was a part of this masterpiece. I was also the light of creation. I felt one with everything around me — the trees, the water, all the colors of the rainbow. A smile spread across my face, and I started to laugh. My laughter grew stronger and stronger as happiness bubbled up from deep inside me. I felt my soul shake free the darkness and soar with life. I had felt this way before. There was a time I knew this feeling well, but then it went away.

Õ

I had my first experience of God the night I walked the fire for the third time. I was eighteen years old. It had been a night of magic. I had come back to the fire to thank it for the courage it had given me. I had come to ask it to lead me to my next adventure; I had no idea where it would take me.

That afternoon, before the walk, I was dancing in the woods by myself. I was excited; I couldn't wait for night to come. I was running and leaping, when I looked up at the sky. There I saw one cloud in the shape of a feather, a perfect feather. As I stared at it, I felt a warm, loving touch on my shoulder. It filled me with peace. At that moment I saw the fire in my mind, and I knew that something wonderful was about to happen.

Õ

What is God? Who made God? If God made all of us, then how was He created? All my life I had been asking questions like these.

I had gone everywhere for answers. The church didn't seem to know. My mother had always just accepted. Even science had no answers for me.

I had spent my seventeenth year learning massage therapy. I had the time that year to explore my questions. Working with Rik and writing in a journal, I came to know what creation is all about. That year I uncovered ancient memories deep within my soul that helped me understand.

I learned that everything is and always has been energy. I learned that everything is one, a whole beautiful beyond imagining. And I learned that life demands we leave the whole so that we can learn about and come to understand its beauty.

The process of tearing ourselves away from the whole is difficult in itself. It is made more difficult by the loss of energy. Think of the whole as heaven, the source of all energy and light. The farther we travel from that energy and light, the bleaker life seems. We call the absence of heaven *hell*. The farther we travel from heaven, the closer we are to hell. Yet we have to travel to understand the beauty of the whole. It is our experience of hell that allows us to experience heaven more fully.

Õ

Later, when it grew dark, we lit the fire. The group formed a circle, holding hands and singing a song called "Oh, Great Spirit." I felt the warmth of my friend the fire. Its strength and mystery called to me. As before when I walked the fire, I was awed by its size, its ability to grow from just a spark to great flames, its energy, and its power to bring about change.

I would have stayed by the fire all night, but the leader, Ed, called us inside. Once there, he made us close our eyes, and then walked around the room and asked each of us our reasons for walking the fire. He chose me first.

"Last year I decided to walk the fire to get in touch with the fire element," I said, "but in the process I also got in touch with the water element through my tears. The fire changed my life. It brought me through so much last year, and it gave me life. Every time I needed a friend, all I had to do was light a candle, and there it was for me. This year I've come to dance with my friend and to thank it for the life it's given me, and to let it lead me wherever I need to go."

When each person had shared, we opened our eyes and sang and danced together. The fire tender came into the room and told us that the Northern Lights were visible, right above the fire. We all walked outside and watched the magical beams of light that seemed to rise out of the earth.

Touched by that beauty, my friend Danny started crying. I put my arms around him and held him close while the group began to sing "Amazing Grace." Never before or since have I heard it sung so beautifully. That night the veil between heaven and earth was very thin. That night, I knew, I finally would understand.

As we sang and danced some more, the power I was feeling grew stronger and stronger.

After a while, Ed began to talk about the heat of the fire. He told us that at 500 degrees, skin melts in half a second. The coals were about 1,500 degrees, he said, and it would take from three to five seconds to get across. Then he asked if there was anyone who was not afraid. I was the only one who raised a hand.

Ed was puzzled: "You said all those beautiful things earlier.

How can you not understand that fear is what you're supposed to be feeling now? I thought that you of all people would know the true essence of the fire walk."

But I wasn't afraid anymore. The fire had become my friend. Besides, I knew that whatever was going to happen was going to happen . . . no matter how much I feared it or fought it. I explained that I couldn't wait for the fire to bring me where I was meant to go. I wanted it to lead me on because I knew that the me inside could never be harmed or changed.

The room fell silent. Finally Ed spoke again: "What if we never feared again? What if we never once feared what life might bring us? Would a world without fear frighten us? Because without fear or hate, we would live in peace."

The room exploded with cheers. We began dancing and singing "When the Saints Go Marching In." Soon we had created our own lyrics:

> *When the flames go burning up.*
> *Oh, when the flames go burning up.*
> *Oh I want to be in that fire,*
> *When the flames go burning up.*

Most of us were excited, but a few still were scared. Three came into the middle of our circle, and we hugged them tightly. The first was a beautiful woman. When the group had met that afternoon, she had said she wasn't planning on walking the fire but had come to see what it was all about. We had laughed because she was dressed completely in red. When we told her that, she'd been surprised and then embarrassed. But when she went to take off the red jacket she was wearing, underneath it she had on a red sweater and a red turtleneck. Now we comforted her, knowing that she was destined to walk with the fire.

The next woman talked about a need to stomp: She wanted to stomp out everything inside of her. For her we did another round of "When the Flames Go Burning Up," all the while stomping incredibly hard.

The third person was also a woman. I had seen her and wondered why she had come to the festival. The only time she smiled was when she was with the children; otherwise she looked unhappy and out of place. Now, as she tried to explain her fear, she was shaking so that it was difficult for her to speak.

Finally the words came out: "This is so hard," she said, "I've only been sober and clean for two months."

We were stunned. For someone who had only been sober two months to think about crossing a bed of hot coals was incredible; it took so much courage. We stood there, tears running down our faces, in awe of her strength. We held her until it was time to do our practice run.

We laid out mats to the length of what the fire would be. Then we held hands again and started singing. People walked up to the mats and faced their fears, and when they walked across them we cheered their victory.

When the woman who wanted to stomp stood before the mats, I could feel her fear. It wasn't just the fear of crossing the fire; it was the fear that by walking the fire her life would change, there would be no going back. I began to stomp; I stomped to give her the strength she needed to get across. Then the others began to stomp too, and the room shook with our energy.

"I can't do it," she screamed.

"Yes, you can," we answered her. "You can do it. You can do it."

And with one more scream, she did.

The rest of us went through the practice run, and then it was time. We took off our shoes and socks, and together went out and circled the fire. Somewhere music was playing softly. People started walking. Ed crossed first. Then I saw others crossing, but for some reason I held back. I kept thinking that I should just go, but my feet were cold and I wanted them to warm up — I wanted to feel the heat.

I watched Danny walk across. "Why can't I just do it?" I wondered, but something inside said this fire walk should not be rushed. I talked to the fire. I heard it tell me it would protect me. I said that this year I didn't want any blisters. It told me not to fear, that what would be would be, and that it would guide me. Then it asked me to join it.

I stood there before the fire and cried out, "I am one with everything." And then I walked across. My friends were waiting for me; they hugged me and cried. I cried too with joy and a sense of freedom. I had made it.

When the woman who had stomped out her fears came to the fire, again we stomped and cheered her on. I pictured her stomping her way through life, never letting anything get in her way again.

Suddenly Ed called for silence. He asked if there was anyone who hadn't crossed yet. No one answered; we all had walked the fire. That seldom happens, at least not as quickly as it had tonight. For a moment we stood quietly together, drinking in the beauty of the night.

After a bit I walked the coals again. This time Rik was with me. As I walked, the most incredible feeling came over me. Suddenly I was the grass, the earth, the trees, the stars; even the people around the fire were a part of me. Together, we were the universe. Nothing was separate. Heaven was earth, and earth was heaven. I was the wind and the moon.

It was in that second — in that moment where my me became the whole — I knew God. It was just a moment, but my life had changed forever. I knew now that I was not me, that everyone was me and I was everyone. I knew now that what an individual experiences, we all experience. And I understood that when one person frees herself, she also frees that part of her that is in everyone else.

Õ

I was back in Yosemite. Night came, and we had to leave the valley. As we drove along, the landscape changed. Gone were the trees and the rivers. Power lines and neon lights marked the sky.

As I looked around at the symbols of a society that had come to measure life in dollars earned and time saved, I was struck again by the beauty of the valley we had just left, of the giant trees we'd touched the day before. And I realized that these places are signposts. When we forget the beauty, they remind us, they help us find our way home.

Majesty
November 30, 1996

The lava splashed over me again, but I couldn't feel it. I looked at my guide and reached for his hand.

" I don't want to forget anymore," I said sadly. "I think I remember — and in my head and heart and soul I do — but when I go back to the world, I can't seem to live it."

"In time, you will know, Marci," he said. "We'll help you. And once it's ingrained in your being, you'll never forget again. It has taken thousands of years for you to lose sight of the beauty. Every lesson you've had since you began to live your lifetimes was in part to make you forget so that you could learn from another point of view. But now every lesson will teach you how glorious it is to remember. Every soul takes this journey, and every journey is perfect.

"And if it takes time — and it will — that's okay too. You

have eternity to come back. Don't rush it. Besides," he said with a twinkle in his eye, "your world is kind of fun when you allow it to be."

I thought about his words. A part of me wanted to believe. He said there was no rush, that I had all eternity to go back. But I wanted to go back soon. I looked into his eyes and realized that that was okay too, that no soul was ever barred from heaven. You simply have to want to go home, and your life becomes the journey there. The choice is ours.

"There is something else you should know," my guide said, his love and light piercing my heart. "Feel the lava," he said. "Feel the blood of the earth. Let it tell you its story." Then he squeezed my hand.

At first the lava was hard to feel. I had experienced so much, I just wanted to rest for a while. But at the same time I was curious: I wanted to know what the lava had to tell me. I wanted to feel its majesty. Majesty. That was what I was seeing in my young guide's eyes.

Very slowly, I breathed in. As my lungs filled with the heated air, I saw the light get stronger and brighter all around me. I couldn't see my guide. I began to breathe faster, and with each breath the light grew more brilliant. It wasn't any hotter, but the energy felt so much more intense. Suddenly, without warning, the lava seemed to burst through my heart. It melted its way through my chest and then exploded out my back. I could feel it pulsing through my body, becoming my blood. Every vein, every artery beamed orange and yellow and red as it danced through me.

Then I heard it, so softly at first that I couldn't tell what the sound was. Slowly it grew louder, its heartbeat one with mine: *thump, thump, thump.* And through the beat, the words came: *home, home, home.*

The lava carried me into the air. I could see mountains and rolling fields, the beauty of the earth all around me. I called out in joy. The power of all that existed pulsed in my soul, and I was one with it.

The lava was the blood of the earth, and I moved with it. I felt the lava meet the water and become the land. I felt the touch of the air as it caressed us, giving everything life. There was a power in each — water, land, air, fire — so different but yet so similar, the same source taking different forms. And as I touched each element, the pulse grew stronger. Alone, each element had life, gave life. Together, they were life itself.

And so we traveled, the lava and I. With it I became the ocean. I was the rise of the land, the mountains. I became the valleys, filled with a richness that fed life and all of its mysteries. I was the grass growing. And everywhere, in everything, I saw the beauty of the earth. I felt more alive than I had ever felt before.

Then it was gone. I was standing above the lava, on the land. Everything around me was burned and charred. In the distance were buildings, their windows broken, their doors hanging off, their walls damaged and crumbling. There was no life, and I could feel the earth's pain.

Here was another lesson. Life is joy and beauty and magic. When we lose those things, we die. Oh, maybe not physically, at least not right away. But emotionally and spiritually we die.

I looked around me at the emptiness. Where once I would

have felt anger at a world that had cut itself off from all that is good, I felt something else, something miraculous. Slowly it began to take form, to find its voice. When it finally spoke, I heard the call of hope.

It spoke to me of something so strong that no amount of neglect and abuse could weaken it. It was there, in the water blackened by pollution, in the land scarred by waste, in the fire made an enemy, and in the air befouled by smoke and soot. I knew now that the earth has its own power. In time it would heal, all of its elements in balance, working together. And I knew that we were one with those elements, that we too had a place in that balance.

A single tear rolled down my cheek. I knew now that I too could heal. Like the fire and the water and the land and the air, I had an amazing power. I shared their energy. I could feel the truth inside me welling up. I had become like the charred earth, barren and empty. But somewhere deep inside me was the power I needed to live again.

As I looked at the broken world around me, I felt the stirring of life. As I watched, the fire burned brightly in the sky, bringing light. The water turned blue again. Flowers were sprouting and blooming. The air smelled fresh and clean.

A light within me flickered and then began to shine. Like the fire, water, land, and air, I felt new life. I felt the magic of my truth: I could love unconditionally; I could take pleasure in dancing and playing; I could hear the fire and know the peace of the water; I could love adventure and look at life as the best adventure of all.

Again I heard the beat of the earth, but this time it was joined by another sound, the voices of people everywhere. Drums were beating all over the world. A wondrous thought came to me. What if all the voices all over the world were joined together for just one moment? Would people remember their truth? Would they remember their soul? I was stunned by the possibility, the idea that we could put aside our differences, our arguments, our pain, and join voices in an explosive burst of energy and love.

Visions of the world connecting flashed through my mind. I could see it, the people in each country connected to the next by satellite. I shivered at the thought. For one moment, no killing, no hatred, just love. And for that moment, no matter who you are or what you've done or how badly you feel about yourself, all would be forgiven. Just like heaven, I thought. We have it in our power to create heaven here.

I found myself back in the warmth of the lava. The world was still a beautiful and magical place. Why hadn't I seen that? For the first time in my life, I was at peace with the world. I didn't have to heal it or change it. It was its destiny to be miraculous.

Õ

"Where did you go when you were young and you journeyed to the other side?" the spirit asked.

With his words, the vision disappeared, but the feeling was still with me.

"There are so many different realms. Which one did you choose?" he asked again.

We had been through so much together, I thought of him as a friend, someone with whom I could share anything. So I opened up my soul and showed him my special world.

There are beautiful lawns there, and trees and sparkling rivers, and the air smells so sweet. When I was little, I would journey to a building there. Although it looked as though it was made of stone and wood, it was made of energy. To me it seemed an enchanted palace. On the walls were beautiful paintings and tapestries that seemed to speak to me as I walked by.

I had a room there, in that palace, a magnificent room with a fireplace and a marble hearth. The bed was no ordinary bed; it didn't have a mattress or a pillow. When I would lie down on it, it would wrap its energy around me, a soft cocoon for sleeping. And someone or something would sing me to sleep. I never heard music or words, but I could feel them.

In that world there was nothing to fear; I felt so safe there. Always with me was the woman who had helped me learn to let go. She never left my side. She mothered me, taught me, and watched over my soul.

Each night, in my mind, I would journey to that place. It was a refuge and a source of strength to face the next day.

Sometimes there would be dancing, and I would join the souls of that world in laughter and play. We would wear crowns of flowers in our hair and beautiful gowns. The gowns looked as though they were made of fabric, but like the palace and the bed, they were made of something more alive.

In that world I could feel my true self and the truth of everyone around me. There was never a reason to lie or hide or feel ashamed. All there was was truth.

As the memories of that place flowed through me, I could

feel myself twirling round and round. Sometimes we danced in pairs, one hand in the air, the other resting on a partner's waist. Other times we danced side by side or in a line, weaving in and out until we had tied ourselves into huge knots and fell down laughing. I never saw musicians, yet there was music, wonderful music for dancing.

I opened my eyes, back in the lava sea. It had been years since I'd gone to my special world, much too long. I ached to return.

"Are you in there?" I heard the spirit from the lava ask. I jumped at the sound of his voice.

"Sorry. I got lost in my own thoughts," I said, still dazed.

"I could see your world so vividly, and then you shut the door on me." He was pouting.

I laughed. "Sorry, just a temporary interruption in programming."

I opened my soul again to the spirit. We were back in my special world, but in a different place. Off in the distance I could see an old castle. I walked up to it and went inside. Everywhere books and more books were stacked. There was so much knowledge there, not just in the books but everywhere.

I would go to the castle to visit a wise ancient soul, my friend and teacher. Wherever I found him in the castle, we would always go to the roof, and there he would teach me.

From the roof you could see a fairytale world, filled with color and life. It had seemed so different from the world I lived in, but now I wasn't sure. Hadn't I just learned that the physical world was brilliant and alive, that all I had to do to see the beauty there was look deeper?

My teacher and I would sit there on the roof and look out at the castle gardens. There were stairs along the back of the castle's walls that led down to the gardens, to pathways of greenery and flowers that brought you to a pool of water. One day the spirit took me there and told me to look into the water.

"What do you see?" he asked.

I turned my head and looked up at him. "I see myself, of course," I said in confusion.

"But what self do you see?" His voice was wise.

I looked again. I was beautiful. "I see me," I said.

"What part of you? Are you in the physical world by yourself? Or are you off with your friends? Are you talking to Rik in your world? Or are you in this world?"

I looked down. I was embarrassed. I felt as though I had done something wrong, that I had failed him in some way.

He knelt down beside me and gently, with such love, lifted my chin and said, "You have not failed me. You can never fail me. I just wish you knew which self you are tonight."

"I don't know," I said. "I just don't know."

"Are you not all of them?" he asked.

"I don't know," I said again in frustration.

"Yes, you do. You know in your heart. Which one are you?"

He spoke so lovingly. I wanted so much to answer him. I took a deep breath, closed my eyes, and tried to look within myself, but I still didn't know the answer.

When I opened my eyes, we were back on the roof of the castle and Rik had joined us. He handed me a sphere made of very thin, delicate glass. Inside it was a butterfly, its wings fluttering. The butterfly was beautiful, but I felt sorry for it. It wasn't free.

"Why is it inside the glass?" I asked.

"We ask you the same thing," my teacher said. "This is a symbol of you as you are now, locked inside yourself. To be free, you have to know who you are. You have to bring all of the pieces of yourself together."

"I don't know if I can," I said, frustration rising in my voice. "I don't know how to be the real me in the world."

"Your life will lead you," he answered. "It will always lead you back to the truth. You just have to watch for the places where the road twists, and trust."

"But how will I know?"

"There will always be signs. But you must know which way you want to go, which part of you you want to be."

"I have only wanted one thing in my entire life," I said with conviction. "I want to be who I am here, in this world."

"And who is that?" he would ask.

I never answered. I always fell asleep as he would ask the question, and then it would be morning.

Time and time again I would go back and look at the butterfly in the glass.

"I want to free the butterfly," I would say to them.

"Then free it," my ancient teacher would say to me. "Break the glass."

But I realized that if I broke the glass, the pressure or a shard could kill the butterfly.

"You see," he would say, "freeing your soul is a dangerous task. You must be very sure how you go about it, or you can destroy yourself."

"But why?" I would ask.

"Because if it happens too quickly, you may not be able to withstand the force," he answered. Then he would look at me intently, as though the answers I searched for were in me if I only looked deep enough.

"Can't you see? The love the universe holds is so powerful that if you're not prepared for it, it could destroy you or make you mad. Be patient."

Õ

"What's wrong?" the young spirit asked me. "You've just shown me the most beautiful world, and now you look so sad."

"You don't understand," I said, shaking my head and staring at the orange glow of the lava all around me.

"Maybe I can if you give me a chance," he said. Then he took my hand. I could feel his love and acceptance flowing into my body.

"It is so easy in this world," I said. "You always know when you're here that the universe is filled with love. In my world, it's not that easy. So many times I have reached this point, feeling as though my life has been changed forever, and so many times I have just fallen back into the old ways."

"I'm not sure what you mean. I'm sorry because I know that right now you just need someone to understand you." He sounded so sincere.

I tried to explain. "It's like what Rik said to me before,

'Beware of the dragon.' Even though I know that everything I've felt here is real and true, that knowledge seems so fleeting. I have learned these things before, but I have never had the courage to change my life forever. I have never had the courage to be me in the world I live in. It is so easy to forget," I said, despair in my voice.

"To forget what?" he asked.

"To forget everything I've learned: that everything is good and beautiful; that everything is love, and that love does protect and guide you. Most of all, it's so easy to forget who you really are inside." I shook my head and sighed.

As I said those words I realized that forgetting really wasn't my problem. I always remembered the truth of my soul; it gnawed at me day and night. My problem was that I couldn't become it.

"But life always leads you to your truth." The words came from behind me. Rik was speaking, his voice loving, touching the deepest parts of me. I turned, and there he was, handsome and strong.

"Life will never let you hide once you've made the decision that you want to be your truth," he said.

I looked deep into his eyes and asked, "Then why does it always seem to lead me backwards, away from my truth?"

He laughed. "Child, there is something you need to see. It will explain everything."

"What is it?" I asked, hope and longing in my voice.

"Crossroads."

"What?" I had no idea what he meant.

"You need to see how everything in your life has led you to this day, that there were never any mistakes, no backtracking. Come with me, and you'll understand so much more." He held out his hand to me.

I let go of the young spirit's hand. I thanked him, not with words, but with a simple look and the feeling in my heart. Then I turned back to Rik, took his hand, and let go to wherever he was leading me.

Õ

I was in a tunnel; it was dimly lit, like a subway tunnel. I still could see the lava ocean and sense the ledge where the glass wall kept me from reaching the man and the woman.

The sky just outside the tunnel was filled with swirling clouds that held the memories of my life. Those clouds had come together and formed two roads of golden light, alive and pulsing. I trembled; I didn't know why.

The sky was fiery and much darker than it had been when I entered the world of lava. The darkness made the roads glow more brightly.

The roads themselves were narrow, not much larger than sidewalks. One led straight ahead into the distance. The other crossed the straight road about five feet from the tunnel. Although it ran horizontally, I knew that it turned back on itself, crossing the first road here and there but never actually going anywhere.

"You say that you've always ended up back where you started," said Rik. "Well, it's time to take a really good look at your twenty-three years. There's so much you need to understand. You once asked for a map. Here it is." He pointed to the roads.

"Should I walk these roads? Is that what they're here for?" I asked, uncertain what to do.

"No," he answered. "What you're looking at right now are crossroads. Everyone has them. In the world you live in, there are so many choices. Even here, in this world, there are choices. These are the maps of our lives. They chart the choices you've made, turning where you turned, going straight where you kept straight. Go back. Look at your life. Then and only then will you be able to understand the roads that lie before you."

"But where do I start?" I asked.

He took my hand and smiled. "At the beginning, of course," he said.

The world tilted and shook, and everything went black. I held tightly onto Rik's hand. I didn't really want to go back and face my life; I didn't want to go back and face myself.

As quickly as it had tilted, the world righted itself. I saw the road of my life in front of me, but it had changed. Gone were the circles and the bends; it was very straight and narrow. Then it was gone.

Before me was a little girl with blond hair down to her knees and big blue eyes. She was sitting in a room, its walls covered with pink and yellow flowered wallpaper, writing in her diary. She was seven years old.

"When I grow up," she wrote, "God wants me . . ."

"No," I said, stopping the picture. "No."

"Why?" Rik asked. "What's wrong?"

I shook my head back and forth, staring at the little girl. The motion had stopped, but I still could see myself sitting there.

"I don't . . . I mean . . . I can't. Oh, damn, I don't know. I just can't do this right now," I cried, tears streaming down my face. "I'm sorry Rik. Please don't be disappointed in me."

He looked at me with so much love in his eyes. "I could never be disappointed in you. Never. Go back to your world. There are things there that you need to deal with and learn before you move on. Go. It will be okay."

Dr. Abbas
February 10, 1997

"You have a serious chemical imbalance in your blood," Dr. Abbas said.

I was sitting in his office. It had been two and a half months since I had gone to the lava world. Since then, my life had been turned upside-down. David wasn't happy in Virginia, so we had decided to come back to Massachusetts.

We weren't living together anymore. David wanted to move back home with his parents for a while, until he felt on solid ground. I didn't mind; I knew that I needed some distance from him, some time to focus on me. And I hoped that this separation would bring us back to what we originally felt for each other.

But the move hadn't changed anything. We had been fighting constantly. I had felt safe in our home in Virginia, and I was angry with him for forcing me to leave. And I couldn't find an apartment. Everything I looked at was dingy or too expensive or out of the way. I would sit in my room at my mother's and look at the newspaper and cry. I didn't know where I was supposed to be or what I was supposed to do. I didn't seem to belong anywhere.

Then there was the stress of dealing with my mom. Her fiancé had had a bad accident and was still in the hospital with a severe head injury. She was worried and frightened, and although I tried to be there for her, to help her be strong, I had nothing left to give.

I tried to go away. A friend of David's told me about a condo on the ocean in Myrtle Beach. He would handle all the reservations. It sounded heavenly — a place on the beach, a rent I could afford, and time to work and get back to myself. I got in my car and took off for South Carolina. But when I got there, I learned that David's friend hadn't made the reservation, and the condo was taken.

I felt so alone. I didn't have a place to live or put my things. And I blamed David. He was safe now, and I wasn't. I needed him, and he wasn't there for me.

I left the beach, not really knowing where I would end up. "A grand adventure," I told myself. "I can go anywhere. If I just keep driving, I'll end up where I'm supposed to be." But I was tired and sick, and just couldn't go on. Crying, I turned the car north and drove home.

And the whole time, I thought about David and me, wondering what had happened to the two of us. I thought about the way we were when we first met. I thought about how he would whisper in my ear, and no matter how much I wanted to run from him — run from the intensity of his passion, the intensity of who we were together — I couldn't. Just his voice had the power to hold me to him.

We used to laugh all the time, wrestling and playing. We would stare into each other's eyes for hours, and I could see his love for me, the honesty of that love. We were happy just to hold each other, just to be together. And our lovemaking was so beautiful.

Somehow, we had gone from being lovers to being business partners. I didn't understand why we couldn't do it all, why our relationship wasn't working anymore. I wanted it to work again. That was the key, I thought. If we could rebuild our relationship, everything else would be okay. I was determined to make things right.

But by the time I got home, I didn't have the energy to make things right between us. I thought I was dying, and I didn't know why . . . and I didn't know how to stop it.

No part of me remembered what Rik had said about David and me, how we had to follow our separate destinies.

Two weeks went by, and I was back at the doctor's office. My stomach had begun to ache so badly that I couldn't eat.

Abbas had decided to do more blood tests. As I sat there in his office staring at the piece of paper with the results, I realized why I'd grown so weak. My calcium level was 60 percent lower than normal. My red blood cell count was 40 percent lower than it should have been. The levels of cholesterol, potassium, sodium, iron, magnesium, and B12 in my blood were all depleted. I was running on empty.

"You see this vitamin right here?" Abbas asked. I didn't really look. "This allows you to think and make decisions. And you see this one right here? This is what allows your muscles to move and to hold tone. This is what allows you to get out of bed in the morning." He kept pointing to things, repeating over and over that I had nothing left.

"But I can change it with diet. I just need to eat better," I said.

"Marci, you can't change it with food alone. You need to take supplements. You have no sodium, no potassium. Without them and the balance between them, your body can't exchange nutrients through the cell walls. You're starving. The only reason you're still standing is because you're twenty-three years old and stubborn as a mule. You should be in the hospital."

"But how did this happen?" I asked, confusion and anger growing in my voice.

"I don't know," he said. "Probably lots of stress for too many years. If you keep going this way, you're going to cause permanent damage to your nervous system and other parts of your body, or you'll die."

Then he went on to describe a program — a diet and twelve supplements. "If you start now, in four months you'll feel better than you've felt in years. I promise you," he said.

I left his office without saying another word.

Õ

"Marci, talk to me, please." We were in David's room when he finally tried to break the wall of silence.

The words spilled out, hateful and hurtful. "You don't understand, you can't understand, what I've been going through," I screamed at him. "You don't know how scared I've been. I've been sick for a year and a half. I knew I was burning out, but I had to keep going because I needed the money, because we needed the money. I loved my work, and I had so many clients. I loved exercise. All of that's gone because I'm just too weak to do it. For a year and half, I've been failing."

I stopped. I was standing in front of the mirror, and I saw myself, pale and tired and heavier than I had ever been.

"Look at me," I screamed. "I'm ugly, and I've been gaining weight and I don't know why."

"But the doctor told you why," David said, trying to reassure me. "He explained that the weight isn't fat, that you're carrying around thirty percent more water than normal."

I didn't want to be pacified. "It doesn't really matter why it's happening when none of your clothes fit anymore, when you're fourteen pounds heavier than you used to be," I said.

"But you still look beautiful. You don't look fat, you look gorgeous," he said, trying to make me see myself through his eyes.

"I look in the mirror, and I don't see myself anymore. I see this pale person with dark circles under her eyes," I said in disgust.

"Because you need to rest," he said.

"Resting doesn't get me anywhere. All I do is spin and spin when I lie down." I couldn't look at him. Just then, I needed a full measure of self-pity.

"What do you mean?" he asked. I could hear the concern in his voice.

"When I lie down, I feel as though I'm falling," I said, turning to him. Tears ran down my face as I realized how scared I was.

"In Virginia, you were getting better," he said. "You were journeying again, and you seemed to be more like your old self."

"I was, but now I've lost it." I hadn't been able to reach my special worlds since we'd moved back. But the loss I was feeling had more to do with the loss of what I had learned in those worlds. I couldn't remember anything that had happened in the world of lava. I had described the experience in a journal, but it was packed away in a box somewhere. It didn't matter, though; I didn't really want to look at it. Those experiences hadn't changed anything permanently.

I tried to explain the frustration to David: "How many times can you make a connection and then lose it? It's as though I can't be in this world. When I'm on the other side, I'm okay. But when I'm here, I just fall apart. I don't know what's wrong with me.

"I can't even think straight. You don't know how scary it is. I drive around and somehow I miss exits. I'll look at the exit and I'll know that it's the one I'm supposed to take, but I go right past it and don't even realize I've missed it until ten minutes later, when my brain catches up. I go to the store, and all I need are two or three things, and it's too complicated. I'm holding the products in my hand, but I can't figure out how to go to the register and use my credit card. So I end up putting everything down and walking out."

Sobbing now, my words gave the fear form: "I thought I was going crazy," I whispered.

"I did too, Marci," David said in a sad voice. "I was scared because you were so depressed and crying all the time. I thought it was because I had brought you back here, and I blamed myself for your pain. That's why I've been so distant. I was wrapped up in my own guilt. But don't you see? Now we know why you've been feeling so badly, and we can make it better. You have to let your body heal. I'll help you. I'll take care of you as much as I can. We'll get you those supplements, and we'll find you an apartment."

"The supplements are so expensive, and so are the apartments, and there are the car payments to make. How are we going to afford all of it?" I asked.

"It's okay. You've said it yourself so many times. Whatever you need will be there for you. Rik and the others will take care of us the way they always have."

I know he was trying to comfort me, but I wasn't ready. I was still too angry and hurt.

"I found a place to live, and then I lost it," I said, talking about an apartment I had moved into for two weeks, until I discovered the heating system was broken. "I still don't have a place to live, and I don't have the strength to find one. I don't even know if I want to be in this area. I don't know where to go or what to do."

"You're confused," David said, "and that means you shouldn't make any decisions right now. Stay put until you know what you want to do, and then do it. I won't hold you back or ask you to stay. You can go anywhere in this world that you want to go, but right now you have to get better.

"I love you. You have to trust me," he said. "You have to let go of the business, and put it in my hands. You have to concentrate on you. Do you understand?"

I nodded with more confidence than I felt. Then I remembered my conversation with Rik. "What must I give up to take this journey?" I had asked.

"Everything you believe," he had answered.

In my heart I called to him: "Rik, I agreed to take this journey, but it has only led to heartache. I'm not better; I'm worse. Why should I go on?"

"The only way out is through," he said. That was all.

That night, by the time I went to bed, I could barely move. Exhausted, I fell asleep. I dreamed I was in a world of darkness. I felt so tired, yet I was running. I was searching for a place to build a health center, a place where people could come and find their magic. I would live there, in a safe and loving environment, and David and I would run it together. In the dream I went from town to town, looking for a place to build my center. But whenever I found a site I thought might work, I couldn't seem to make a decision. I'd say to myself, "This could work. It's not exactly what I wanted, but it would do . . . at least for now." Then I would run to the next property. I didn't want to make the wrong choice.

I felt a hand pulling me, stopping me. I turned around and saw my great-grandmother. In life she had been the most beautiful woman I had ever known. She had soft white curly hair and big blue eyes. Her face was round and beautiful, her skin like peaches and cream. Her body was soft and plump, and wonderful to hug.

She died when I was fourteen, but she is still with me. At times when I miss her or I'm scared, I smell lilacs, and I know she's there. She loved lilacs.

In the dream I felt myself let go. Memère took my hands and held them tightly in one of hers. Then, with the gentlest touch, she caressed my cheek. A tear rolled down my face.

"I miss you Memère. I miss you so much," I cried.

She whispered the words "*Je t'aime,*" "I love you." And as she spoke, I remembered how upset I'd been right before she died. I had wanted to see her, to say good-bye, to tell her that I loved her. But the family had said no. They thought I was too young; they didn't want me to remember her "that way." Now here she was, at a time when I was afraid and weak, her hand on my face, saying those words to me: "*Je t'aime,* My Pretty Face. All your dreams will come true. I'm here for you." I felt so safe and loved.

I was crying as I reached for her and hugged her close. "I love you, Memère. I love you so much." She was guiding me, and I knew that everything would be okay.

I felt another touch. I turned and saw the face of an angel, my friend Jay. He opened his arms wide, and I fell into them, crying. I had met Jay in school, when I was studying massage therapy at Bancroft. We sat next to each other the first day of classes and became fast friends. We studied together and practiced the massage.

In time, Jay told me his story. He had been an addict, using drugs, alcohol, even sex to reach what he called "the ultimate high." One day, he just stopped doing all of it and started focusing on healing and learning how to bring out what was deep within his soul.

Jay was the greatest healer I had ever known. With a touch, he could make pain go away. Yet, despite a good diet and health regimen, he never looked well. There was always a grayish tint to his skin and dark circles under his eyes. Two months after we graduated, he told me he had AIDS. At that time, his T-cell count was so low he shouldn't have been standing. He lived for five more years.

At times he would call me from a hospital and say that it was pneumonia again and that the doctors were sending him home to die. I would run to see him, and he would reassure me that he wasn't going anywhere. Then two months later, he would call and tell me that he had just climbed a mountain, or that he was in Maui and could I join him.

In the months before he died, he began to talk about dying and being at peace with death. He seemed to be making the choice to die. I couldn't accept it, though. I kept telling him that he was going to beat the sickness, that AIDS wasn't going to kill him, that he was too young and too powerful a healer to die. A card came from him at Christmas; it was the last time I heard from him.

A few weeks later I was driving, listening to the radio, when I heard a song about a friend's death. A strange sensation raced through my body. I knew that someone I loved had died, but that it had been a good thing. I thought immediately of Jay but brushed the thought away. A week later I ran into a teacher from Bancroft who told me Jay had died the week before. I hadn't known Jay's family, and it would be months before they found my number and called to say he was gone.

In my dream, it made sense for Jay to be there. When he was alive, we had talked about opening a health center together. I believed he had come to me to show me where the health center should be. I remember feeling so grateful that he and my great-grandmother were with me. Now everything would be okay. I would find a site for the center; the center's success would fund The Quest; I would get well; and David and I would see all of our dreams come true.

Jay knew what I was thinking. He looked at me and gently

said, "I'm not here to talk about The Quest, Marci, or to help you with a health center. All the things you want and dream about will come true in the right time and place."

"They will?" I asked.

"Haven't they already?"

I hesitated, thinking about what he was saying. "Well, yes, to a degree. It does seem like all the things I saw as a child are coming true, but . . ."

"That's not why I'm here. Listen to me," he said so forcefully that I knew he was trying to tell me something very important. "Think about my life. I was looking for the ultimate high. I looked for it in drugs, in alcohol, in sex, in fast cars and rich foods."

As he spoke he seemed to grow larger, his energy boring into my soul. "I did those things because I was looking for something more. What I found was death. One day I was with a friend who was trying to shoot up. She was so weak, I had to help her. As I watched her shake and get sick, I suddenly knew that this was not the ultimate high, that it was nothing. But it wasn't until I was told that I was HIV-positive and I was going to die that I changed my life. You see, the sickness saved me. I was destroying myself; I didn't know who I was. But when I realized I was going to die, I found a reason to live. I wanted to live.

"So I ran around trying to find a cure. This person had the right therapy, and that person had the perfect solution. Each course I took, each program I started, gave me another high because I was sure that this was the answer, that this would save my life. But I still didn't have the answer. In the end, I learned that only I could save myself. I realized too late that the greatest high of all was letting go and just being me. Whatever my tragedy, whatever my pain, I was my truth. My body might die, but I — my soul — would live forever."

The dream changed, and Rik was there. "People get sick when they deny who they are inside. Sickness brings them back to themselves; it forces them to face who they are. You, of all people, should know that," he said.

Rik paused for a moment and then asked, "Why did you start The Quest?"

The answer came quickly to my lips: "I started it because I wanted people to know what I had found on the other side."

As I said the words, I looked away and took a deep breath. It had been so long since I had thought about the work I was doing and why I was doing it. I had gotten so caught up in the mechanics of getting the message out that I had forgotten the message itself.

I looked back at Rik and tried again: "I started The Quest because I wanted people to know that they are perfect and beautiful — that no matter what happens in life or how much shame and hatred and anger they feel, they are love and that alone is their truth. I wanted them to know that nothing — not age, not sickness, not addiction, not even death — can tarnish or destroy that truth.

"And I wanted to show them how to find you, the world beyond the earth. I wanted to tell them that when their souls touch that world, it's like being born again. I wanted to help them remember the beauty.

"Was that wrong? Is that what's made me sick?"

Rik stepped forward and touched my face. I sensed my great-grandmother and Jay beside me. The darkness disappeared, and spirit upon spirit wrapped around me. In a single soft voice they said, "In trying to help others, you've taken on their pain. You've been running up an escalator that's going down. It's not your job to change the world."

"But I always thought . . ."

"No," they stopped me. "We know what you always thought. You have power, so you thought you owed it to the world to be its truth. Because you can see what would make people happy, you thought it was your job to bring it to them. But you can't fix everything. That's not your job. Your destiny is just to be who you are. You can help more people by simply living your truth than by telling them about living their truth. Remember what the lava taught you: There is nothing wrong with the world; everything is as it is for a reason."

I was angry and confused. I had never felt I had choices. My life had always seemed a series of experiences, each leading me in one direction or the other, always in response to that gnawing in my soul. If I was here, it was because the spiritual world had led me here.

"But you said when I began this journey that I had a destiny to fulfill," I cried out. "I never asked for the power. I don't want to be my truth or anyone else's truth. I just want to be normal. I never chose to save the world, a world that doesn't want to be saved. The call inside me forced that choice on me, and now it's forcing another choice on me: Become my truth or never get well. It's not fair. The world will never accept the real me."

In an instant, I felt the sweetness of my great-grandmother's touch and Rik's love, and I could feel Jay apologizing for what he had said. But suddenly I knew they had nothing to apologize for. I was a prisoner of my own truth. The last thing I remember was Rik crooning to me, "Let go, Angel, let go. Everything is going to be okay."

Normalcy
February 11, 1997

I awoke before dawn. For the first time since I had left the world of lava, I felt that everything would be okay. I would get well. I would find a place to live. David and I would make peace. The spirits' words and love had given me hope. I knew they were with me, guiding me.

Unfortunately, over the next few days, my health didn't improve. I wanted my life back so desperately: I wanted to go out dancing and to spend time with my friends; I longed to be the way I used to be. But I had no strength. Each night I would collapse on the couch. No matter how much sleep I got, I always needed more.

Fatigue ruled my life. The power surges were gone; so was the energy that used to pulse through my body and hands, healing and soothing. My back and neck were tight, and my head ached. I tried to remember who I was inside, but I couldn't. Just beyond the exhaustion I could sense an energy that I knew would heal me, but I couldn't reach it. There, just beyond my grasp, were peace and health and financial success and a magical future with David.

And gone were the lessons I had learned on my journeys.

There seemed to be a huge wall keeping me from the other side, and I couldn't remember how to get around it.

I remember lying in bed and calling to the spirits for help. And the spirits would answer, "Who are you?" They weren't asking me my name; they were asking me my truth, trying to touch something inside me. "Who are you?" they would say, their hands out, their palms facing me. I tried to touch my palms to theirs, but I couldn't do it. I didn't want to feel my truth.

Some nights David would hold me and place his hands on my body, trying to help the energy flow through me. At those moments, I could glimpse the other side . . . a white light or a beautiful tree. But when I would reach out to join the vision, I couldn't. I was too much in my own way.

Then, early one morning, I woke up with the feeling that Rik was near. The warmth of his love was so intense that it seemed to me that he must have taken physical form, that he must be sitting right beside me. He was so close I didn't have to open up to the other side to be with him. I felt him with my heart.

"Why?" he asked. "Why can't you just let go? Why are you so insistent on denying who you are? Why do you refuse to accept it?"

I felt his sadness for the pain that filled me.

"Because I don't know how to be my truth in this world. My life here can never become what I believe it should be," I said.

"Look at your life," he said. "Look at how much it's changed since you were in high school. Then, you had to be three people, but now you can just be you. David accepts you for who you are, and so do others."

I started to speak, but he stopped me.

"I know," he said. "What if you change, and he doesn't love you anymore? That's what you've been afraid of since the power surges started. That's why you stopped them. I know. We've gone through this time and again. Angel, you can't keep questioning David's love. He's told you so many times that it's okay for you to be who you are. All he wants is for you to be better. David isn't your reason for not letting go; he's just your excuse."

"Maybe David's not loving me anymore is an excuse, but whatever the reason, I'm scared, and you can't comprehend that."

"Then explain it to me," he said. "Maybe I can understand."

How could I explain fear to a spirit? How could Rik understand the pain of being different? But I was determined to try. If he wanted to hear it, he would.

"You know how much I love your world," I started. "When I'm there, I'm free to be my truth, to feel my beauty, and that's glorious. But our worlds are very different. The physical world is about conforming. Society teaches us to be alike. When I talk about being normal, I just mean that I don't want to be different. I want to fit in. I want to have fun. I don't want to think about who I am.

"And yet all my life, I have been different. When I was little, other kids would be fighting over candy or deciding where they were going to play; I was wondering who made God or how I could save the world from a nuclear holocaust. I was so serious. Even in high school, when everybody else wanted to talk about what they were going to wear to a dance, I wanted to talk about philosophy. I tried to be like them, but it felt like a lie. I was just so different. Yet if I wanted to be with my friends, I had no choice.

"Other people look at a tree and see a tree. I see its past and present and future; I see its energy. Other people worry about money and what they're going to eat tonight. I think about those things, too, but differently. It's not about me and my needs; it's about the world and its needs. It's about energy and how it works and how it connects all of us.

"In this world, people are threatened by those who see things differently. I think back to when I met David. He used to go out drinking with his friends. Oh, I went along happily. But I don't drink, and I made his friends uncomfortable. They were sure I thought I was 'better' than they were. But I wasn't judging them; it was just my choice.

"And the truth is, I'm not sure I wanted to be there or anywhere people were drinking. When people drink, the walls they've built come down, freeing all of their emotions. They don't see it; they don't even realize it. But I do. I get lost in all their energy; I'm consumed by it, unable to think my own thoughts. That scares me.

"And there were lots of other times when my gift seemed more like a curse. Can you understand how frightening it is for a child to feel dark spirits in her room at night? Can you understand how hard it is when you can't tell your grandparents or your godfather what you're thinking because you're afraid they won't accept you?

"I cherish my power to see the other side. I know it's the

most wonderful gift anyone could ever have. But it doesn't make life in the physical world easy. Sure, some of that has to do with being different; but a lot of it has to do with me and my expectations of myself.

"If I could see the future, how could I explain my failures, even the temporary ones? Why couldn't I protect the people I loved? If I knew the dangers of drugs, why couldn't I make other people understand? And each time I had to admit that I couldn't change something, I felt as though I'd let you down, all of you. Sometimes the responsibility is just so enormous.

"You know, I can't even go dancing. I get on the dance floor and suddenly I feel the power inside the music. Then I feel the fire, together with the earth, and the beat, and I become the me inside, lost in the intensity of the sound. But when I look up, people are staring at me, and all I feel is strange.

"It's no different in the New Age world. When I look at the fire, people stare at me and then demand to know what I'm seeing and how they can see it too."

I stopped for a second and then slowly started again. "I remember my twelfth birthday. I had asked some friends to sleep over. We were telling ghost stories. I always had good ghost stories because, of course, I always had ghosts. I was describing one visit from the spirit world, when a friend interrupted and asked me, 'Are you sure these stories are real? Maybe someone was just playing a trick on you.' The words were barely out of her mouth when the music box across the room started playing, the curtains on my windows began moving, and a mirror fell off the bedroom wall. All my friends were screaming and wanting to go home; they were convinced the house was haunted. It was months before anyone came back."

I could see Rik now, and he was smiling, trying not to laugh at the picture of a house full of screaming girls.

"Okay," I said, laughing myself, "I guess it was kind of funny, but it didn't feel funny then. It really hurt to be different."

"I know," Rik said, and I sensed that he did.

I was quiet again for a minute, saddened by another realization. "It's hard when you have to live three lives," I said. "From the moment you came into my life, I wanted to be with you. If I had to die to do that, I didn't care. I wanted to die, but you wouldn't let me.

"I love all of you more than anything in this world. I love you, Rik, most of all. You've been my teacher, my friend, my father, my guide, my haven, and I want to be with you. It's so hard to be living in a different world from you.

"David is wonderful. He's made me feel safe. With him, I can be my truth. But David and the other people who say they understand and accept me aren't like me. Even those who can open up to the other side, who've seen the spirit world, don't see it all the time. They can choose a time and place. I can't; it's always with me. That's why it's so hard to accept: It separates me from everyone.

"The reality is that when I met David, for the first time in my life, I wasn't afraid of the world I live in. And for the first time in my life, I thought I could be like everyone else — fall in love, get married, have kids.

"I remember when David and I were first together, a friend of mine said to me, 'It's okay that you're in love with him, but don't put away who you are. You can't run from your destiny.' I told him

I wasn't sure my destiny was even real. I explained that I was in love with David and that I was happy just being with him and having fun. Do you remember? That was when I told you that I didn't want to teach anymore or to learn about anything else, that I just wanted two years off."

"I remember, Marci," Rik said. "I remember. But you didn't really get those two years, did you?"

"What I got was two years of denial. Once David started working with me, everything was New Age, and he wasn't an escape anymore. That was when I started burning out. I couldn't stop feeling the other side, so I tried to get lost in building our business. I figured if I could focus on The Quest, I might be able to stop the visions. Except when power surges forced me to, I stopped journeying to the other side. I stopped dancing. I stopped going for walks in the woods. I broke away from everything that connected me to the spirit world," I said wearily. I was tired of talking.

"I know," Rik said, "and that's why you're having a problem being with David right now. You blame him for how you feel because he's the first person who made you feel safe. When you aren't with him, you want to find your truth. When you're in his arms, all you want is to stay safe."

I nodded yes. "When I first met David, I told him that I had this gift and that it was my destiny to share it with the world. I explained that I couldn't control the need to help others, and that that meant I couldn't promise to be with him forever. He turned to me and touched my hair and face. Then he looked into my eyes and asked, 'Can't you just forget all of this and let me take care of you?'

"Being with him was so wonderful. We would go up to my

room, the lights low, and stand in front of the mirror, his arms around me. He was so handsome and so much taller than I, and I felt so safe in his arms. He would caress my shoulders, and I would watch him kiss my neck. I could see in his face how much he adored me. When he touched me, he brought the magic and beauty of the other side into my flesh-and-blood world.

"For the first time, I wasn't afraid to be with somebody in this world and share my truth. I knew he would never try to take it away from me or use it for his own purpose. I felt whole and beautiful and normal." I laughed, "Well, except for the occasional power surge, of course."

Then, very quietly, I said, "I love him, Rik."

"I know you do. But I also know that David doesn't really have anything to do with why you've closed down inside. You have to look at the real reason."

He looked at me intently and then went on: "Loneliness and hurt have a lot to do with your refusal to be your truth. You always believed there were others like you in your world — you used to dream about them — but you've never found them. You feel alone and overwhelmed with the burden of helping the world all by yourself. That's why you deny your truth."

I knew Rik was right, at least in part. My gifts made me different. Each time I'd go to a festival or a fair or a workshop, I would search the people there, looking for a soul like mine, just one. I never found it. At times I felt so alone.

Rik understood my loneliness, but he was adamant. "We've told you before," he said, "no one is asking you to take on responsibility for the world. Just remember who you are, that's all. We would never ask more of you than that. Never. If you're not your truth, you're not really alive. By denying your truth, you're allowing yourself to die. It takes more energy to deny something than it does to become it."

Time
March 15, 1997

Two weeks went by, and I found a beautiful place to live —
a house, not an apartment. It had everything I wanted: It was fur-
nished, and it came with a dishwasher and a washer and dryer. There
were three rooms on the first floor and a huge loft on the second.
Sunlight streamed through massive windows that looked out onto a
lake. It had a fireplace and a deck. For the first time in months, I
relaxed. I had a home.

My life seemed to be going more smoothly. The supplements
were beginning to give me more strength, and the fog in my head
seemed to be clearing. It still was hard to drive sometimes, or even
to think, but I was beginning to function again. I was beginning to
come back to life.

I had given up the idea of building a health center, at least for
now. I realized that it was just another excuse to ignore what was

happening inside me. I was beginning to understand the lesson that Rik and the other spirits had tried to teach me: No matter what happens in life, everything turns out for the best. There isn't any point in worrying; things always work out.

That lesson had helped me find a place to live. It also helped David and me find each other again. We had been so distant and edgy, each of us afraid of being rejected by the other. One night I thought to myself, "The hell with it," and kissed him passionately. Together, our bodies ignited. The affection, the tenderness, the passion were all there.

Two nights later, David and I built a fire at my house. Through the window we could see Mars shining brightly and a comet shooting through the sky. In time, the fire died down, and the coals slowly dropped their ashes. We sat a few feet away, watching the light dance.

Now that David and I were together again, I thought my problems were over. But something wasn't right. As I watched the coals and felt their heat I was amazed that I had walked on them, put my bare feet on them. Where had that confidence gone? I started to cry.

David pulled me into his arms. When I told him what was wrong, he said, "Maybe you can't do it now, but you will. You will dance with the fire again."

But when, I wondered. It seemed so far away, so unreal.

After David left, I put more wood on the fire. I wanted to feel the dance again; I wanted to feel the fire's love. I wanted so badly to reach out and hold the fire in my hands, to touch the power for just a moment, to feel the other side again.

"Why can't I cross this line? Why can't I do it?" I asked myself. Then I called to Rik: "Rik, I hear everything you've been saying. I do. I see how much this journey already has changed my life, how it's leading me back to myself."

And I did. And I also saw how being with David was keeping me from that journey. When I was with him, I wanted to lose myself in his touch; loving him was all that mattered. Life was so much easier in the safety of his arms.

It was the intensity; I was so tired of the intensity. Normal was easy and safe, even beautiful in David's arms. No wonder I wanted normal.

"I just can't face this," I said to the fire and all the spirits around me. "I know that I have to remember the truth, that it lies within my secret world. I don't want to deny who I am inside anymore. I'm trying to do what you asked in the world of lava. I'm trying to forget everything I thought I knew about this world. I know that diet doesn't necessarily make you healthy, that being thin doesn't make you happy, that a successful business doesn't make life perfect. I realize that I can make decisions about where I want to go, but that I can't control the path that takes me there. I know that I have to let go and let my energy guide me."

And then I realized one more thing, the hardest thing in the world to admit: "I love who I am inside," I cried. "I love my special world."

Tears poured down my face, and suddenly I felt the brilliant light of that world and heard the call of a million spirits whispering to my soul. I felt their hands touch my back, and their energy break through to my heart. I sobbed for all the times I couldn't feel this love, for the heartache and pain of trying to deny.

"I have to be me," I cried out to them, "and I know that's what you want. Help me. Help me, please. Help me be who I'm supposed to be. I want to die and be reborn. Fill me with new life. I need your love and wisdom."

I could feel the warmth of the fire and the spirits all around me. I could feel the walls around my heart start to fall.

"Don't you see," I cried from the bottom of my soul, "I just wanted a break. I just wanted to be normal. It's been so hard to journey alone. But I can't fight anymore; I'm too tired. I want to feel beautiful again, and I want to know who I am."

Then, after months of feeling lost, I finally heard the sweet mantra: *home, home, home.*

Still I hesitated. "I'm not ready yet," I said. "As much as I love the highs of heaven, I can't bear the coming down. I've done it so many times."

The mantra didn't go away. I couldn't deny anymore that I could feel my truth. An image flashed through my mind. I saw myself at the Healing Arts Festival when I was fifteen. I was dancing, looking into my partners' eyes, singing to them. Through the power of my love, many of them saw their truth, and I had felt such joy being my truth and showing them theirs. No one, nothing, could stop me. I danced and I sang, and I didn't care who watched. I was flying on the wings of heaven.

Now as I stared into the fire, I felt the same power rise within me, the feeling that all is one and that I am part of it — the feeling of God. In a second, it was gone. But I knew that was all right, that there was so much more to see and that in time I would see it all. I felt the spirits' hands touch me, and Rik's heart reaching out to mine. And then a great weight lifted. My shoulders dropped, and all my muscles relaxed as I let go the burden of the world. I felt young and free, a child again. Yes, I knew how to change the world; but I also knew, finally, that it wasn't mine to change.

I turned away from the fire. The woman spirit who had come to me so many times before was standing there. She wore a black cloak, a black created from all the colors of the rainbow. She seemed to be carrying something heavy. As I watched, she lifted it above her head and seemed to hand it to someone. I laughed at the thought that she was returning responsibility for the world to its rightful owner, a much higher power than I.

I could feel myself starting to heal. The words *home, home, home* filled me with joy and peace. I could breathe again; I could feel the energy racing through me.

Then I felt Rik stroke my hair and heard him whisper, "There's plenty of time."

Time. I kept hearing the word over and over as the fire danced itself to sleep. There was time because in the spirit world time is different: Today, tomorrow, eternity, they're all the same.

The fire was out. I lifted myself up and looked outside, staring at the lake, the trees, the stars. It was cold outside, but I knew I needed to walk. The night was still, the air crisp. A slight breeze kissed my face. The moon was just a sliver. Usually I would feel a need to call to it, but not tonight. I knew now there was time. Whenever I was ready to feel the energy again, it would be there. It always would be there for me. I was home.

Pieces
March 15, 1997

I lay down on my bed and closed my eyes. I found myself standing in a field, the moon full above me, my arms raised over my head. It was raining, but the drops weren't water. It was power raining down on me. As I felt it flow into me, I started to laugh, a laugh from deep within my soul, a "Hello, I'm back" laugh.

Suddenly I was afraid. I had been here so many times before and then had to turn back. I didn't want it to happen again.

I felt the woman spirit nearby. She was wearing a beautiful blue robe, shimmering with jewels of every color. She carried a pillow of purple velvet, trimmed with gold and tassels. As she walked toward me, she seemed to float.

I looked down at myself and realized I was wearing a red dress. The fabric was very sheer and plain. Around my neck I wore a gift the spirit had given me when I was sixteen. It was a necklace with a gold ring, a symbol of the circle of life. She had told me then that anything I wanted came from that circle of life, that it was the gateway to many different worlds. She had taught me how all of life is connected. She showed me different worlds and species and how — despite different languages and cultures — they were all one.

That was just the first lesson. I knew there was so much more to understand about the circle of life. I knew it could teach me how to heal and how to change the rhythm of life within those who had lost their way. Some of it I had learned but couldn't remember. Some of it I couldn't yet comprehend. It would take time to remember and to understand.

The spirit's voice broke into my thoughts. "Marci, you have to trust. Let go, and everything around you will be your guide. You're the only one who can stop you from following your path. If you say you can't choose the truth right now, then that's the path you'll take. It's your choice."

She held the velvet pillow up to my heart and said, "On this pillow is your power. If you want it, take it back."

I looked at the pillow in confusion. "But there's nothing on the pillow," I said.

"Exactly. You can't see power with your eyes. It isn't an object; it has no form. It doesn't come from a stone or a scepter or a book or a piece of jewelry. Power isn't in material things, that's why material things can't bring you back to who you are inside. Even I can't give you power. Only you can do that. All I can do is help lead you back to the truth once you choose to find it."

I understood what she was saying, yet somehow I felt that my power *was* there on that pillow. As it filled me, I could once again see the beauty of the trees around me, feel the wind blowing through me, and sense a happiness in my soul. I was the power; my body and everything around me were manifestations of that power. Slowly I stopped struggling. Almost asleep, I whispered a prayer: "Please let it be here tomorrow morning. Let this feeling grow and live within me. I love all of you."

Õ

The next morning I opened myself to the worlds beyond. I could hear the lava world calling to me. I could feel the beauty of the gardens beyond the castle where Rik and my ancient teacher had shown me the butterfly. I could feel the vastness of heaven pulsing in my soul.

I was lying on the floor in my loft. I closed my eyes and breathed deeply. The sun streamed through the skylight; I could feel it dancing on my face. I felt tension in my back, my shoulders, and my neck. I made myself relax, meditating, going deeper and deeper into my subconscious. The physical world no longer existed.

It was dark, but off in the distance I could see a large door framed in light. I felt the light pull me through the darkness.

"It's time to remember," the woman spirit called softly to me from the other side of the doorway. "It's time to remember how to heal." A sense of home filled my heart and my soul. As I stepped through the door, I felt no fear, no pain. I finally had accepted.

I began to fly, my soul growing and expanding until every part of me was a part of the light. It was as though the essence of me had become one with the universe, as though I was the light of heaven. I didn't have to think or make decisions about where I was going. I had no form; I simply was.

I looked back at my body, and I could see the pain I had been going through, the exhaustion. I could see the walls I had built to shut out love. In an instant I broke them down, and in the same instant I felt the energy in my soul flowing into my body.

My poor body. How I had abused it over the years, and how it had struggled to survive. My soul had created this vessel, this miracle, and instead of honoring it and loving it, I had criticized it and mistreated it and hated it. And with those thoughts, I returned to my body but still was connected to the spirit world.

As I sat there looking out at the sky, a hawk flew into sight and began circling right above the skylight. It was so close that I could see its claws, the down of its feathers. Over the past few months, every time I drove, I had seen a hawk. Sometimes the bird would fly across the road in front of me. Other times, I would see one or two of them perched in a tree.

In Native American lore the hawk represents the messenger. What message did the birds have for me? What were the spirits trying to tell me? This morning when I heard the cry of the hawk, I understood. I was the messenger; I would bring the message of the other worlds to this one. That was my destiny. I could either accept it or fight it.

Slowly the memory of my truth began to unwind from all my tangled memories. Finally I saw them, the friends I used to dream about, six boys and six girls. In my dreams, we would come together and talk about our lives — not our everyday lives but other lives we'd lived and our future in this life. In those dreams, I was the person I always wanted to be. I loved life. I wasn't afraid; I didn't hide. There was no shame in being different. With my friends, I was safe to be whomever I wanted to be, to dance and fly and laugh with joy . . . and to dream. I loved them, and more than anything I wanted them to be real, to be with me.

But a part of me never believed they could be real. By the time I was thirteen, the world had convinced me they were make-believe. I still dreamed about them, but I began to plan a future that didn't include them. I was going to go to an Ivy League school and become a teacher, a lawyer, or a therapist. Then, when I was sixteen, my plans changed. I left school to learn more about me and my powers. And the hope that my friends did exist, that I wasn't alone, that somehow I would find them and that we would be together, came back.

For a year, I looked for them everywhere, but I never found them. Once again I went on with my own plans. But the longing to find them grew stronger, more painful, each day. So again I told myself it was all make-believe. It took time to forget; it was years before I stopped dreaming about them.

I took a deep breath. One of the dreams I had tried to forget was playing itself out in my mind.

Õ

I am in a Native American village. My father, the chief, touches my arm and points to a handsome warrior, the greatest warrior in our tribe. Although he's young, all of the people in the village respect him — not just for his skill with weapons but also for his kindness. I hear my father say, "He is the one I have chosen for you to marry." I am elated, excited.

The dream changes. The young medicine man of the tribe — the shaman — is standing before me. His eyes are deep and wise, and I know that I love and honor him. "Will you meet with me later in my lodge to take a journey?" he asks.

We have journeyed together before. I love traveling to other realms with him and the knowledge he has given me. I nod my head, yes, I'll meet him. He nods too and asks me to bring a bucket of water with me.

I carry the bucket into his hut and sit down across from him. I am full with the news of my marriage and the promise of a journey.

The shaman takes my hands in his and looks into my eyes. "Are you happy about marrying him?" he asks.

"Of course," I say. "Why wouldn't I be?" I'm surprised that he would question my happiness. "He is a strong man, a good provider, and he treats me well. I know that he loves me by the way he looks at me. Why should I ask for more?"

"Maybe, you are meant for more," the shaman says, as he begins to stir the water in the bucket. I watch the rainbow spiral he's creating, and instantly my reality changes. I am back in my bedroom. The shaman is with me, but his name now is Todd. Suddenly I realize that I know this man from somewhere else, that he has been with me and in the dreams I had of my friends.

I am frantically rummaging though my drawers and my closet. I'm searching for glass beads I bought years ago at a powwow. I can't find them, and I start to cry. For some reason, I think the beads are my connection to the other side.

Todd smiles at me and says, "You may forget your connection at times, but you can never lose it."

His words bring me back to the shaman's lodge. I am lying
on the ground looking up at him. I have so many questions to ask,
but there isn't time. He is about to take the tribe on a journey. As we
walk out to the ceremonial grounds, I look for the man I am supposed to marry. I want to journey with him, to see our future as husband and wife. The shaman places his hands on my shoulders and
turns me toward the young warrior. I see him talking and laughing
with another woman.

"But we love each other," I say.

"Yes, you do. But tonight, you and I will be partners on the
journey."

I don't understand why the shaman wants me to journey with
him. I get angry. If I hadn't stayed so long in his lodge, I would be
standing with the warrior. I don't want to lose my future husband.

The drums start beating, and the shaman takes me in his
arms. He whispers three ancient words to me, and instantly I am
somewhere else.

I am in my future, in my present lifetime. I am standing
before a crowd of people, touching them with my words as I bring
them to worlds beyond. Todd is with me, and so are the other friends
of my dreams. We aren't lecturing or preaching; we choose to teach
with laughter and caring. It feels wonderful and so right. There is a
balance here between work and life: the time to nurture not only others but myself — time to travel, to study, to dance, to play.

I am back in the village. I look at the shaman, realization
dawning. "It's you," I say. "You're the one who comes to me at

night. You're my soulmate."

Then he kisses me, a tender kiss that makes my soul tremble with life and hope and love.

I never forgot that kiss. No one had ever kissed me as he did in that dream. No one had ever made me feel the way he did.

Memories came flooding back. It was Todd who saved me from the shame of rape. It was Todd who reminded me that sexuality is beautiful and that love is meant to be shared. His was my first kiss; he was the first man to hold me in his arms while I fell asleep. I was eight years old, and I knew what it was to be deeply in love.

I first met Todd in the beautiful world where I danced at the castle. In time we would meet with our other friends. Sometimes just the two of us would go to a special place, a pool of water in a forest of ancient trees. We would dance there in the moonlight, kissing and laughing and making promises about the future.

I could only be with his spirit, but he was so real to me. I could feel him; I could curl into his warmth. Sometimes we would talk about our lives on earth. He would tell me about his girlfriends, and I would tell him about the boys I dated. And sometimes, when the world was too hard to bear, we would hold each other and cry.

I dated and thought I loved lots of young men, but I never made love with any of them. I loved Todd, and I wanted the first time to be with him.

Then I met David. My feelings for him were so strong that I knew it was right to share my body and soul with him. I wanted to be with him; I wanted to give him everything I was. But to do that, I had to push Todd away, so far away that there wouldn't be any traces of him left.

Õ

I could feel my body tingling. I was back in the loft. I lay there, staring up at the skylight, thinking about all that I had just seen. David. David had been in my dreams for years, long before I met him. He was the warrior I was supposed to marry. I knew now that we would never be separated.

Then I realized how torn I had been. I had wanted to become my truth, but I was afraid that if I did, that if I found my friends and lived life with them, I would lose David. I also understood so much more about The Quest, why I both loved and hated it. It was the future I had created for me, a way to help people; but it also represented the loss of that other future, the one I'd seen in my dreams. I wanted The Quest to succeed, but I also wanted to be my truth.

I felt the call again to go within myself and rest. I breathed deeply, but nothing happened. There was no pull from the other side.

"Tell me what I need to do to get better," I said to the spirits I could feel all around me. "I'm beginning to remember who I am, but it's going to take time. How can I help myself here and now?"

I could feel their hands touching me, their warmth penetrating my body. A brilliant white light shimmered around me, a shell protecting me, and I could see the spirits in it and breathe their essence. The light sparkled with brilliant flashes of orange, yellow, purple, green, and colors I had never seen before.

As the shell of light grew brighter, I could see every cell in my body, all the atoms and molecules of my being. Everything was moving and changing, and that thought pleased me. I liked the idea of death and rebirth; I liked thinking of the past as a building block of the present, and of the present as the foundation of the future. In that moment I loved my body, its balance and the systems maintaining that balance.

Then I saw a tiny crack in the shell. In seconds it grew larger. The light poured out into my body in waves. I breathed in that shimmering flowing light, feeling it in every part of me.

I was lying still, and yet I was moving. Everything inside me was moving. I was liquid. I felt my belly open, and the pain I had been carrying for so long flooded my body. I screamed in agony. Then two hands touched me there, and the pain was gone. A second later, I saw a flash of blue leave my body.

The healing went on. There would be an ache in my thigh or a sharp pain in my knee, and each time the hands would touch me and the pain would disappear. And each time, a flash of a different color would leave my body.

Now the pain had moved to my forehead, where intuition is said to be. I felt the woman spirit touch me there. "You must learn," she said, "that this is not your enemy. This is where your power lies. It isn't about seeing the future; it's about knowing the truth of what lies beneath the surface." The pain began to ease. "It's time to open up, Angel. Let yourself be open and free," she said.

Another spirit touched my heart, and I felt a deep green. "You are a healer," I heard a male voice say. "Your ability to feel what others are feeling is your greatest gift."

I felt delicate hands on my upper abdomen. "Here is your power," the spirit said. "This is where your voice comes from. This is where your gold lives."

Lower, around my navel, I felt a blockage, a huge wall separating the halves of my body. I realized it was an energy block, something I had created to distance myself from the physical world. It was breaking down, and hands were starting to take away the pieces. Then a voice asked if I wanted it back.

"No," I said. "I want to be free. I want to be open."

I felt as though I was flying. I could see myself traveling, happy, vibrant, and full of energy. I was as free as the clouds, shifting and changing. There was no place I couldn't go, no height I couldn't reach. What a glorious feeling it was.

I remembered a conversation I had when I was fourteen with my brother's girlfriend, Kori. I told her that I wouldn't get married until I was at least twenty-seven years old. I said that I wanted to travel and see the world before I settled down. She asked me what would happen if I met the person I was supposed to be with for the rest of my life before I was twenty-seven. Would I travel with him? I said I would love to travel with someone I cared for, but that when I was twenty-four I wanted to travel alone. I needed time, I said, to be on my own.

I hadn't thought about that conversation in years. Now, here I was, just months away from my twenty-fourth birthday, facing the decisions I had known all my life I would have to face.

As I lay there, feeling the energy flow through my body, my mind was racing with questions. Should I stay? Was it time to go away and travel? Was I ready to share my knowledge of the other side? Did I even have the strength to go? Did I have a choice? Which way would lead me to my truth?

Beauty
April 4, 1997

The next few weeks brought beautiful weather, and I felt my strength returning. I knew that I wasn't out of the woods yet. There still were times when I couldn't get up off the couch without everything spinning and bright lights flashing in my head. I knew I still was exhausted, but at least there seemed to be hope. David was taking care of the business, and I was staying home and taking care of me.

I was finding happiness again, and it wasn't coming from the outside world. My truth was emerging from within me, and it was healing me.

I began to go for long walks in the woods near my house. One day I walked to a place where I could sit and look out over the lake. I felt the breeze on my cheek and the cold of the rock I was sitting on. I breathed deeply, but I couldn't relax. Something was bothering me. A call had come today — "If you just didn't answer the stupid phone," I said to myself — someone from a television program asking me to do an interview on New Age. I'd put the woman off; I just wasn't ready to deal with the world.

After a while, the trees, the water, and the blue of the sky calmed me. The calendar had announced spring two weeks before, but this was the first day that really felt and smelled of the season. I took another deep breath, and this time my diaphragm relaxed. Air flowed into my lungs and seemed to fill my body. I closed my eyes and opened my hands. As the breeze touched my palms, I felt a tingling of energy. It was good to be open again to the energy around me.

And I could feel a symphony of energy around me: The breeze rustling through the trees, birds calling to one another in a hundred different notes, squirrels chattering, the sun's rays beating down, strength and knowledge flowing up through the rock I was sitting on — all came together in a wondrous song of life. I felt myself expand with joy.

Against the rock was a pile of leaves the wind had left there late in the fall. I thought about how in time they would feed the earth that had given them life. There was such beauty in that cycle, and only humans failed to see it. We pump our dead full of chemicals and place them in boxes, trying to preserve what cannot be preserved — breaking the circle of life.

"Enough," I thought. I wasn't going to spoil the day trying to understand human frailty. I was gloriously happy, and I laughed a deep laugh. Just a few weeks before, I had been so tired and worn out that I would have walked through those woods and not felt anything. Today, open to my truth, the message was clear: "No matter how dark and cold the winter, spring comes." And I understood: No matter how sick or sad or hurt I'd been, I would heal. No matter how tarnished or abandoned the soul, it would be reborn. I laughed again in the pleasure of hope.

In my mind, I left my body. I was a sprite, dancing on the sunlight, exploring the leaves just starting to sprout on the trees around me, the bark, the soft moss. I was so tiny that it all seemed massive; but I wasn't frightened. It was a grand adventure, and I laughed and jumped and played.

Suddenly I heard a voice calling me, a voice I recognized from my childhood. Instantly I left the forest of my body and entered the world beyond. I followed the voice to an enormous old oak tree. Standing next to the tree was a small round woman. I laughed with the pleasure of seeing her. She laughed too, although she tried to look stern as she asked, "Where have you been?"

"I don't know," I said shyly.

"It has been a long time, my child." Then, her voice soft and welcoming, she said, "Come join me, and feel the trees. Feel the forest all around you, and remember your soul."

I went to her and hugged her. I could feel her rounded breasts and plump belly as she held me tightly to her. Then she pulled back and looked closely at me, taking inventory with eyes that seemed to pierce my soul.

"You have become as beautiful as the sparkle of the water." I knew she wasn't talking about my physical being; she never looked at the surface of a person. She took my hands and placed our palms together. "See what I see, my child," she went on. "See your soul.

You're not sick or tired; you're simply hiding away from the world."

I looked into her eyes and saw the love there. Then I saw her soul and all that she had seen. There was no pain there, no sense of what I'd been suffering in the physical world. She didn't see pain because she knew it wasn't real. She understood that the truth of the soul — love — is all that exists.

She took my hands in hers, and the vision ended. We scattered leaves as she danced me round and round. I scooped her up in my arms and swung her around, and she, suddenly grown taller, picked me up and swung me around as well.

With one leap, we landed in a hammock high in the old oak tree. Lying there, staring at the stars, I could feel the universe, its massive size, the greatness of all that existed. I thought how lucky I was to witness this. In this world, it didn't matter how long I'd been gone; all that mattered was that I had found my way back, that here I could become my truth.

The scene changed. The woman was gone. I wasn't up in the tree anymore; I was in a narrow room. Along the walls of the room were tiny windows. I looked out and knew that I was in the roots of the tree.

When I looked up, I saw an ugly old man. Like the woman, he was small, but his nose was huge, his face a mass of wrinkles and scars. He was stooped over, and as he walked toward me he limped.

"I remember you," I said. "I remember you from a dream I had a long time ago."

"Of course you remember me." His words were matter-of-fact, but he spoke them softly, almost like a lullaby. "I came to you many times, and we played in the woods."

But it was his soul I remembered, not this ugly form. "You were beautiful," I said. "What happened to you? Have you been sick?"

"What does it matter?" he asked. He was challenging me, and his eyes twinkled as he waited to hear my answer.

"It doesn't, I guess, but you look as though you're in pain."

"There is no pain, not really," he said, his eyes fixed on mine. "Oh, yes, there is physical pain, but when the soul is alive and free, nothing can get in your way." He smiled at me and then asked: "You've had some problems lately feeling you're not beautiful, haven't you?"

I breathed in deeply. In this world I knew my beauty; I felt it in every part of my being. Physical appearance didn't matter here: Everyone, everything was beautiful.

"In your world, you have forgotten to see the beauty that is you," he said.

"That's true," I said.

I sensed the walls of the room around me. They were cool yet warm and comforting.

"So?" he said, breaking into my thoughts.

I tried to explain. "You're right. There was a time in my life when I felt beautiful. Now I look in the mirror, and my face is all swollen and puffy; my skin is broken out; I have deep circles under my eyes; and my hair never does what I want it to do. And this can't be my body: It doesn't feel like me. My clothes don't fit, and I'm . . ."

I stopped midsentence. The man was laughing at me. He fell to the ground, slapping his leg with a hand.

"Why are you laughing at me?" I tried to be angry, but I had started to giggle. In seconds, I was laughing with him.

"You," he said, trying to keep a straight face, "*you* are worried about being ugly?"

"I didn't say I was ugly. I just said I don't feel beautiful."

He laughed harder. "Look at me. I'm twisted and deformed," he said, gasping for breath.

"But I see your soul. I see how wise and strong you are, how beautiful you are. It doesn't matter that you're disfigured; I see who you are inside," I said.

"Your world says that beauty is in the eyes of the beholder, but what I see is a world trapped in image. Whose house is bigger, whose car is faster, whose clothes are fancier, and whose hair is done just so," he said.

"That's true, and I have the hardest time living up to it all. Sometimes, no matter how hard I try to create a 'look,' I end up feeling frumpy," I said in frustration.

"Why do you think that you can't live up to it?" he asked. "Maybe you know that the whole thing is foolish."

"I *do* know that, and I really want people to see the beauty inside me. But when I don't look beautiful, I feel as though everybody is disappointed in me. It's kind of crazy."

"In a world where looks matter so much, that's not crazy — that's survival. Play the game if you want, but don't forget that physical beauty isn't what's important. Your soul is beautiful, Marci."

Then he went on: "There's something else you should remember. It's okay to show your beauty. Does the peacock keep its tail down because it doesn't want anyone to see how beautiful it is?

No. It's just being itself. You can't help being beautiful because you are — inside and out. Be proud of that beauty. Don't hide it."

He was very serious now. "I know that you have to live in your world and that appearance is important there. But you can live in your world and be your soul," he said.

Õ

As the troll spoke, I thought of a young man named Rich. I had met him at the Healing Arts Festival when I was sixteen. I saw him from a distance the first night of the festival. He was the most beautiful man I had ever seen. His body was hard, strong, and sleek, a golden shade of tan. His hair was dark and full, and his eyes were gloriously deep. Even from a distance, I could see the beauty in them.

I don't know what made him turn toward me — perhaps he felt me staring — but when he looked in my direction, I could see that one side of his face was disfigured. My first thought was to turn away. I didn't want him to think I was staring at his scars. But I couldn't help myself; I did stare. After a second or two, he smiled at me from across the room, a smile that filled my heart.

I met him the next evening, when I joined a group of people who were dancing. I was having so much fun that I didn't even notice that Rich was my new partner. When I looked into his eyes, I saw such beauty there that I couldn't help but let my truth show in my eyes. Our connection was immediate and deep. I felt as though I had known him my entire life. Later, I met up with him again by the fire. We sat together and talked about crystals and how we loved them. He asked me what my favorite crystal was, and I told him rose quartz. He smiled and said that was his favorite, too, because it symbolizes unconditional love.

The next morning he presented me with a beautiful piece of rose quartz. He put it in my hand, wrapped my fingers around it, and said, "This stone has gotten me through so much, and I have a feeling that you are destined for quite a bit as well. Let it help you. I will see you again. I promise."

But I never saw him in this world again.

Õ

I knew what the little man had been trying to tell me. Even though Rich's face was disfigured, he was the best-looking man I had ever known. The lesson: It didn't matter what I looked like on the outside; my soul was the source of my beauty.

I was back in the room inside the tree, and the little man was speaking: "Search for people's souls," he said. "When they seem dark and angry, search for their souls, and you will not fear them. Remember that people are cruel only because they don't feel the pain they cause. If you can see their truth — and by doing that, remind them of their beauty — they won't be able to hurt you.

"You have a gift, a great gift. You can see inside. Let yourself see. Look beyond the trees and the birds. Let yourself see all of your world, all of its energy. You're frustrated because you understand the world's problems, but you can't fix them. Don't look at the problems. If you choose to see only the beauty in the troll that is your world, you'll also see the hope."

Memories of my journey into the lava world came flooding back. I hadn't wanted to think about that journey. The months since I'd moved back from Virginia had been so hard. But I was ready now, not only to look at the world with different eyes but also to let go of my anger. I had begun to understand that it wasn't just the world holding me back. I was holding me back by refusing to see the beauty in me.

A bird flew by. The room in the tree disappeared, and with it the little man. Back in the woods, with the energy of the sun pulsing through me, I started running and dancing, jumping from fallen branches to stones. I sang loudly, pushing away all unhappy thoughts of the world. I was finding peace.

I walked back to my rock and lay down. A calm enveloped me. In the distance, I could hear the lake lapping at the shore. I was open to every sound, every feeling, every sensation, and I was happy.

After a bit, Rik came and sat beside me. He hugged me and rocked me back and forth. "It's good to see *you* again," he said. "It's been too long since I've seen you running like a child through the woods. The businesswoman was getting kind of boring, you know."

"Thanks," I said, sarcastically. "Thanks, so much."

"I'm just teasing. It is nice to see you at peace again," he said.

"It's nice to be at peace. I love the woods and the water. Do you remember the house I grew up in? It was a lot like this one — by a lake, nestled in the trees. I missed living in the woods. After we moved into the city, I tried to get out into the woods as often as I could, but there always were other people around. There was no peace. Or I would see buildings off in the distance. I think buildings make you lose yourself."

"I wouldn't know," he laughed. "Spirits don't tend to be anywhere, so I've never gotten lost in a building."

"Cute," I said, "real cute."

"Oh, Marci, it feels good to be joking with you again. I don't like being serious all the time. You know, for a spirit, I'm kind of funny. And you were making me seem so boring. All that teaching, it was driving me crazy," Rik said. He was definitely in a playful mood.

"Sorry you had to do your job," I said, teasing him back. "I've really missed walking through the woods with you, laughing and talking about anything and everything."

"I missed it, too," he said with a smile. "But look at us: We've still got it."

"I remember one year at the Healing Arts Festival. We had gone for a walk in the woods together. You said something funny, and I was still laughing about it when we came out of the woods. I didn't realize there was anyone there until this man came up and asked me what I was laughing about. I told him that something had struck me funny, but he didn't believe me. He looked at me very seriously and asked if I could talk to spirits. When I said yes, he got all flustered and said, 'You mean they can be funny?' He didn't seem to think you could possibly be fun." I was laughing now, remembering the man's confusion.

"Sometimes we make you laugh because it's the best way to get through to you," Rik said. "Of course, sometimes it doesn't work. That's when I simply hold you or wipe away your tears. It's all in a day's work."

I was serious now. "Thanks," I said, "for everything."

Rik shook his head. "No need for thanks." Then he looked closely at my eyes. "There's something bothering you, isn't there?"

"No," I said, trying to turn away.

"Want to talk about it?"

"It's just so beautiful out here, and I'm trying to stay focused on seeing the good in the world." I didn't want to deal with anything else.

"Ah, but that doesn't mean you can ignore all that's going on," Rik said. "You still see it; you just don't get caught up in it. We see everything that happens."

"I guess you would," I said. I hesitated. "Thirty-nine people just died," I finally said, my heart heavy. "They were members of a cult." The news had been full of stories about the Heaven's Gate cult.

"And they chose to do that," he said. "It isn't yours to be sad about."

"I know, Rik. But it's the idea of the cult that's bothering me. I look out at the world, and I see a place that teaches you to conform, a breeding ground for cults. But the people around me don't see it; they don't understand. Last night on television, all of these 'experts' were asking how this could have happened. They were so shocked.

"But they shouldn't be. The world's history is filled with cults. Didn't they learn anything from Hitler? The Nazis were a cult. People were down; they had no money, no future. Along comes Hitler, and he tells them they're special, they're better than others, and he gives them hope. So what if their hope was built on the destruction of others. The people followed him, willing to do whatever it took to get what Hitler had promised them.

"I got a letter yesterday from a man who calls himself the Heavenly Prince. He's written a book that they're selling in New Age stores and at New Age fairs. I met his followers at a show in New York last year. They were trying to get me to follow him back then, and now they're trying again. In the letter he wrote that I should 'put away my New Age ways' and 'learn to bow down to a higher power.' And, oh yes, he could help me stop 'my wayward practices.' Well, I hate that. I hate that in all religions. The intolerance. The 'my way is the only way.' I may not bow down to a higher power — you've always taught me that we are no less than God — but I believe there is a higher power and I communicate with that power. Why do I have to pretend to be less than I am? Why would any group encourage people to be less than they are?"

Õ

My mind flashed to a journey I had taken as a young child. I was walking in my special world, and I came to a circle of marble. In the center was a fountain. It sat there in a grassy clearing, tall trees around it. In the distance I could see a building, but it wasn't like any building I had ever seen before. It was soft; like everything around me, it seemed to pulse with life.

That night I met the man and woman I would see but not be able to touch in the lava world. They were stately, the very essence of royalty. Without thinking, I fell to my knees. Together they lifted me off the ground and then gently told me never to bow down to someone unless that someone was willing to bow down to me as well. They said that they were no greater than anyone else, that everything in the universe was equal.

"The trees, the insects, the animals, the people, the spirits — they are all one with what your world calls God," they said, their voices rich and elegant. "And don't allow anyone to bow to you, either," they went on. "Anyone who believes that he or she is holier than something or someone else is simply ignorant."

Õ

Rik had shared the memory with me. "So, why does the letter bother you?" he asked.

"Because that man is out there and he has followers, people who believe they are less because of him. Cults work because people don't believe they are as good as they really are. And organized religion seems to confirm that, which only makes the problem worse. I just wish I could make people understand that we are all equal, that we are all a part of God, that we don't have to demean ourselves to love God."

"Marci, you have a beautiful heart," Rik said. He smiled lovingly at me and then went on. "People follow others for many different reasons, but mostly because they're tired or hurt. They don't realize that change comes from within, that only they have the power to change themselves. And the people who feel they have to lead? They're weak; they need followers to make them feel powerful.

"There are people in your world who seem to feel good

about themselves only when they feel they are better than others. I've always been puzzled by the self-righteous — those who think a murderer or a rapist can't go to heaven, those who believe that their good deeds and sacrifices somehow make them better than a criminal.

"There is no better, no worse. There is just lost and found. Only you can lose yourself, and only you can find yourself. Everything else — like my being your guide or you teaching others — is simply a spark; only the individual can light the fire. You and I, we can't change things for others. I can't even change things for you. We can talk, yes, and I can give you advice; but only you can make your choices.

"Heavenly princes, gurus, dictators, all the people who say they can do it for you — even the pills and the exercise machines and the motivational programs — they can't really change your life; they can't make things better. There's only one cure, and it's inside you."

I nodded. This was a lesson of the lava. There is no right, no wrong. The paths we choose are simply different ways of learning. Still, I was puzzled.

"Rik," I said, "I understand what you're saying, that programs can't 'cure' people, but what about the meditation programs I teach? What about programs that help people learn more about themselves? And the program I teach on the phases of healing. Is it wrong to be doing that?"

"Do you put your students into a trance and then tell them, 'This is what's going to heal you'?" he asked.

"No. I just give them the space and the means to heal. I bring them to alpha and give them the suggestion that they might want to look for whatever is holding them back. I try to give them tools, but they have to use their own insight to heal."

"Then you're a spark, and what you're doing is fine. But if you ever find yourself saying, 'This is how to make your life perfect,' then you have to stop," he said.

"I will never say that what I teach or what I believe is the only truth. I don't ever want anyone to think of me as a guru or a leader," I said.

"There's nothing wrong with leading, Marci, as long as you encourage the people you lead to do better, to outshine you. Leading isn't telling people what to do. It's doing the things that are right for you, making your life an example. Real leaders don't look for followers; they inspire others by their example, by living their lives honestly.

"There's something else you should remember. Everyone is part of everyone else. If you've found a way to be happy, others may look to you to help them find their own happiness. There's nothing wrong with that. You're a messenger, and that's what your tapes are all about, carrying a message."

He took my hand. "And what is that message?" he asked.

"That people are beautiful, and that no matter what they've done or gone through or how much they hurt, they are perfect inside," I said.

"And what is a guru's message?" he asked.

"That the guru is perfect, and that as long as you are around the guru, you'll feel beautiful," I said.

"There's the difference. And as long as you remember that

difference, you'll be fine." Then Rik laughed and said, "Besides, you're not likely to forget. If you do, I'll be there ready to give you a good kick in the butt." Now the two of us were laughing.

"I love you Rik." I said.

"I love you too. He kissed my forehead and tousled my hair. Then he whispered to me, "It's time to be you. It's time to fly." I felt the power that was growing inside me soar with his words as we sat together talking and laughing until the sun went down.

Aura: *The energy emanating off of all objects, including the physical body. The energy surrounding the physical body appears as different colors, depending on the individual's emotions. Someone who is angry, for example, radiates a red glow; someone who's in love radiates a pink glow. The energy sometimes can be seen with the human eye, as well as with psychic perception. It is thought that the aura protects the human body.*

Butterfly
April 5, 1997

The next morning I woke up feeling tired and achy. Rik's words were echoing in my head: I was the only one who could make me well. All the diets and supplements in the world weren't going to cure me; only I could do that. I had learned so much in the world of lava — that I didn't have to fear the physical world, that I wasn't responsible for fixing the world's problems, that my job was to become my truth, and that for now David and I were on separate paths and that was okay. So why wasn't I better? What was holding me back?

"What do I need to do?" I called to the other side. "Why can't I let go?" The answer didn't come to me in words; instead, in my mind's eye, I saw the empowerment tapes I'd recorded over the past year.

Of course. When everyone had told me I would never recover from being raped as a child, I had created an empowerment program to help me heal. For years I had been helping others by teaching them the techniques I had used to heal myself, incorporating new learning along the way. It had worked before. Why wouldn't it work again? What I needed to do was empower myself.

I forced myself to get out of bed and went and found the tapes in a drawer, waiting to be edited. There were seven of them. I put the one called Creating Meditation into the tape recorder. I had made the tape to focus my energy on my true self, to help me create what I wanted in life. It was the last tape in the series because it asks that you know your true self before you use it. I had found that life sometimes makes us believe we want certain things when who we are inside really wants something very different. I knew what I wanted inside: I wanted to be healthy. I wanted to be with David and have the time and energy for our relationship. I wanted The Quest to be a success. And I wanted to travel and share the message of truth.

I crawled back into bed. As the music started, I put my hands on my abdomen and let the energy flow.

"Breathe into your feet, relaxing your feet. Breathe into your legs and hips, relaxing your hips and letting your legs release any tension that is there." My voice on the tape brought me deeper and deeper into myself, slowly soothing my body.

Then the tape led me to a waterfall and a bubbling pool of water. I sank down into the water, soaking myself in its warmth.

A woman came up behind me, knelt down, and began to rub my shoulders, gently working at the knots. I had never seen her before. Although she seemed caring, her touch was almost cold, as though she didn't want me to have to feel her energy. This was my time, time just for me.

After a while, the tape led me to an ornate full-length mirror. This was a special mirror: Reflected there was my higher self, my inner self. As I watched, my physical self began to take form. For the first time since I'd been sick, I was seeing the energy that surrounded my body.

I wanted to cry. My aura always had been a bright white tinged with pink. Now it was gray. I could see holes in it, places where my energy was spilling out. Without the protection of my energy, I was susceptible to the emotions of everyone around me. No wonder I'd been so tired and overwhelmed.

I forced myself to look beyond my aura, to see what I wanted in my life. In my mind, I created a health center. I saw it as a place where I could connect the physical world to the worlds I knew on the other side. I pictured my room there, and I dreamed of walking in beautiful gardens I had planted. I visualized my body — strong, healthy, and vibrant — my soul beaming out. I saw The Quest growing: me speaking all over the country while David was making his dreams of an empire come true. I could feel the excitement growing in me, an eagerness to make our dreams reality.

From a distance I heard voices. As they grew louder, I lost the vision. Over and over again, they were saying, "It's time to go. It's time to go away." I wanted to believe them. There was a huge world out there with so much to teach me. Now that I could see its beauty, I ached to go and explore it. But I knew I wasn't ready; I was still too tired, too weak.

But if my body was weak, my determination was strong and growing even stronger. I would make myself better, and then I would make all of my dreams come true. I would create a place where people could come and find their truth. I was going to get better.

Then there was silence. No voices, no tape. All of my senses were still: I couldn't see; I couldn't touch; I couldn't feel pain. I don't know how long I stayed that way. I came back to the sound of my voice saying, "Number Five, you're wide awake, feeling fine, and better than before."

"Good for Number Five," I thought, groaning. I certainly wasn't feeling fine. My whole body was aching.

"It's your soul," I heard Rik say as I fell back to sleep. "Your soul is tired, not your body. You have to stop fighting."

Õ

I dreamed about our trip to the West Coast. David and I left Yosemite and drove down along the coast to Carmel. We had spent a wonderful day at the beach. I remember feeling so alive and so safe, as though I belonged there.

We went to Monterey for supper and then spent an hour or two wandering through the town. Back at our hotel, we fell into bed. I was just drifting off to sleep when I felt Rik close by.

"Marci," he said, "let me talk to David. It's time."

I had known all day that Rik wanted to talk to David. We had talked about it, Rik and I, and agreed that he would speak to David through me. It was the only time Rik ever entered my body. Although David knew and had grown to like my guides — he'd even met some of his own through me— he couldn't seem to open up and talk to the spirits himself. I wanted to share their love with him. I wanted him to feel comfortable with the world that seemed to be sculpting our business and our lives. More than that, I wanted him to be able to turn to the spirits for help if he needed to.

I had talked to David about Rik's wanting to speak to him. When I told him it was time, he smiled and said he was ready. Slowly, as I felt Rik's presence enter me, I took myself — my soul — away. I could hear them talking, but I couldn't focus on what they were saying. The next day, David recounted their conversation.

"David," Rik said, "I need to talk to you about something."

"I'm here. I'm listening."

"At some point soon, I will have to take Marci away from you," Rik said.

"Take her where?" David asked sadly.

"There's a world that she needs to learn from, a world that will help her understand her power and who she is. She and I have to make a journey together. She won't be alone, so you don't have to be frightened for her, but you will have to let her go."

"I understand," David said. "But will we lose each other?"

"No," Rik said warmly. "You'll always be together in some way. You'll run the business, and you'll keep it alive and growing by using your marketing skills to sell Marci's ideas. Together, you're going to make The Quest a great success. Keeping the business going is important. More important, though, is letting her know that you're there for her, that she can call you or come home to you whenever she wants. It's going to be difficult for her to leave you, especially at first. She's going to miss you terribly; but it's something she has to do, and in her heart she knows that."

"I understand," David said. "At least I understand with my head. I just hope my heart understands when the time comes to let her go."

"I know it's going to be hard for both of you. But your destinies split here: You have to go separate ways. You are the ground, and she is the air. Remember, though, that the ground and the air always meet. You will both find your way through, I promise," Rik reassured him.

Õ

The next day, I listened to another tape, the one called Memory Block. I had created this tape to block out all memories of the physical world, to help the listener remember his or her soul.

I put the tape in the machine and lay back. In my mind, I was lying in grass, my back cool against the dampness of the earth. As I breathed the strong scent of wild flowers, I felt such wonder. Then it was night, and I was floating up into the stars. Above me I could see a tunnel, glowing with colors, their brilliance a kind of song. Something pulled me through the tunnel to a dark room lit only by a glowing sphere resting on a golden stand.

My ancient teacher was there. He asked me to place my hands on the sphere, and then he said, "All that you know of your world will disappear, and you will remember your truth."

Suddenly I heard Rik's voice: "To take this journey, you must give up everything you know."

As I touched the sphere, I began to fall. I couldn't see or feel anything, but I could hear the chant *"Home, home, home"* and the deep steady beat of a drum. In an instant I was back in the world of lava, looking at the molten sea; then, just as quickly, the sea was gone, transformed into a huge fire.

I began to dance before the fire. At first I couldn't feel its rhythm, and my steps were tentative. But soon its power overwhelmed me. The dance was new. I wasn't a young girl dancing for joy; I was a woman dancing to honor a great power. This was a dance of respect, a ceremony. I could feel my strength growing as the fire rose within me.

In time the fire burnt down to coals, and I felt the longing to touch them. I walked across the coals, pulling the energy they gave me into my heart, my abdomen, and my soul. I held the fire in my hands, and felt the power growing within me. This power — like my dancing — felt somehow older, fuller. I knew it was mine forever.

The scene changed. I was standing in a field, naked but not ashamed. My body was strong and toned. Suddenly I felt an ache to release my physical reality. I wanted to put away human worries — concerns about how much money we make or what others think or how our bodies are formed — and the boundaries they place on thought. I didn't understand why it was so important; but I knew that was the only way to live with the flow of power within me and to tap into real wealth, the richness of the universe.

I knew now that money and the search for it were hurting my soul. I had been so caught up in making The Quest grow that I had blocked out the sun. By reconnecting to my destiny, I would never want for riches — for life or love or beauty. They were already mine; I simply had forgotten how to touch them.

I could see flashes of the child who danced and laughed her

way into people's hearts and souls. But there was a difference now: Older, more powerful, I was the teacher. Girl and woman — fused by the fire. I was the fire, life, death, and rebirth. I was beauty and honesty.

Far too soon the tape brought me back. My mouth was dry, and I was hungry. I laughed to myself at the sudden shift from spiritual to physical. At the same time, I understood that all of it was spiritual, that everything is part of life and that everything holds power.

Õ

The next day I returned to the tapes. I knew I had to keep going. I felt as though I had two people inside me: one fighting to emerge and the other struggling to hold her back. There had to be a way they could live together. I had to keep remembering the truth.

I drifted into the Fortress Meditation, going deeper and deeper into myself. After two days of meditating, the soreness and tightness in my body were gone; I was feeling stronger and more secure.

Slowly the tape counted down, "Ten, nine, eight . . ." I floated into a field. In the distance I could see a forest and a stream. I felt the sun on my body, its warmth penetrating every muscle and bone.

I felt hands massaging me, relaxing my muscles. In my mind's eye I could see walls coming down, anger and confusion released, and the energy fields around me clearing. I didn't want to think; I simply lay there and rested.

When the massage ended, I opened my eyes and stood up. All around me was a thick stone wall. Everything looked gray; the only light was my own, the light of my truth. I had been here before, so I knew that the wall had come from me. This was a barrier I had built around my heart and soul. The last time I had seen a fortress like this, it had been built with painful memories of my life, memories that led me to close myself off from the world. But I had dealt with those memories. What was this fortress made of, I wondered.

In the center of the fortress I saw the symbol of my truth curled up like a baby, trying to rest. I heard Rik's words again: "Your soul is tired, not your body." Was that the problem? Had I been pushing for so long to become my truth that even though the way was clear, I just didn't have the strength to do it? I saw my future and realized that being a messenger for the other side wasn't going to be an easy life. The reality was I just didn't want to deal with it now. I needed to rest for a while.

The meditation ended, and I got up and walked onto my deck. I stared out at the water and the deep blue sky, and for a moment I felt the pull of my destiny. My arms pulsed with energy, like wings aching to fly. I knew that I had a wonderful destiny, and I longed for all of it. I hoped the future would include David and the friends I used to dream about, but I also knew I needed some time. What I didn't know was whether my destiny would allow me to have it.

Õ

I went into the Memory Meditation with no expectations. This journey had come to me after I remembered everything about the rape. It helped me deal with the memories in the wall of the fortress. That meant examining each memory, facing the pain of it, and then changing it — thinking about how the memory would have been different if love had been a factor in its making. That became my new memory, and that made remembering good. It also made forgiveness possible. This time there were no memories to change.

Instead I found myself floating along. I could see the health center I wanted to build. I saw David and me at a health exposition, our booth taking up an entire aisle with all the different services we were offering. I saw myself signing the book I had written, laughing and talking with the people waiting in line for a copy. And I could see the tour I was planning for next winter.

I was getting excited, thinking I had only eight months to finish up before I would be leaving. Then I caught myself. I needed a break, and here I was making plans for more work. Yes, the call of my destiny was strong, but I realized that my dreams for the future also were to blame for my exhaustion. In my passion to make the future happen, I had lost the present.

Rik's message about being a leader came back to me: "Real leaders don't look for followers; they inspire them by their example, by living their lives honestly." Well, I wasn't even living my life; all I was doing was achieving. And for what? I knew that when I died, I wouldn't be able to bring a health center or a book with me. All I would have is my truth. And here I was spending my life pushing instead of being.

I could see David and me together, running on a beach. I jumped and hugged him, and he swung me around like he used to. I saw friends I hadn't had time for in years sitting around my kitchen table, talking and laughing and sharing. I missed having fun. It had been so long. Somehow in trying to free myself from my commitments to the other side, I had stopped being my truth altogether.

But what value do I have, I wondered, if I'm not accomplishing something? And does it have to be all or nothing? Why can't I live my truth and help others? Why can't I let go once and for all? How many times would I need to be taught the same lessons — that I'm not responsible for the world, that the world is okay, and that the world has so much to offer me if I just let go.

"Maybe when you stop running from what you don't want to see," I heard Rik say. "The crossroads still are waiting."

"I went into the fortress, and nothing is bothering me," I said. "It's just my destiny."

I didn't want to hear what Rik had to say. I knew the crossroads were waiting, but I didn't want to take them. I didn't want to see what they would show me — a life that had never been and never would be my own.

I was saved by my voice on the tape counting me back out of the meditation. I stood up and went to shower. There were things I needed to take care of, and I was due at David's house.

The day was a blur. But when I went to bed that night, I lay awake thinking about the morning's journey. All my life, teachers and guidance counselors had told me that I was the "best of the best," "the cream of the crop." All my life, I had measured my worth by what I accomplished. Could I really stop trying to achieve and still become my truth?

In a flash of golden light I saw a room. A stained-glass window along one wall was reflecting rays of light. In front of the window was a long table, and seated all around the table were spirits. As they turned to look at me, one of them asked, "Are you ready to join us?"

Before I had time to answer, a second flash of light exploded through my soul and left me feeling a oneness with everything. I was alone in my bedroom, yet the room seemed full. I felt something burst inside me, my soul breaking free. It wasn't a spiritual letting go or a journey to another world: It was physical. As it grew inside me, power coursed through me in a stream of brilliant color. There was no pain, no fear. It was a joyous explosion of energy. And for a moment I saw myself — not working or teaching or doing — just my soul and my truth. It was glorious.

In that moment, I wasn't torn between worlds. I felt whole. I had found my truth, and I knew that it would help my body heal. I was free.

Or was I? Suddenly I was doubting again. What if this was like all the other times? What if I wasn't out of the woods yet? What if this was simply the dragon Rik had talked about? I pushed the thoughts away. I knew now that all experience — good and bad — was leading me forward. Yes, there was always the possibility of hurt. But as long as I faced that hurt with my truth, I would heal.

As I closed my eyes and drifted off to sleep, I felt another flash. Before me stood my teacher from the castle. In his hand he held the butterfly in the glass. I saw him smile, and then I saw the glass burst from the inside.

"Welcome home," he said.

And the butterfly? It flew from his hand into my heart. I really was free.

The Fall
April 12, 1997

"Why do you hate her so much?" David was yelling at one of his friends.

"Because she's a freak, that's why. She's simply a freak who can't fight her own battles, who sends her boyfriend to fight them for her," the girl screamed back at David. "Hey, Marci," she yelled to me, "why don't you come out here and fight me."

I couldn't believe this was happening. It had been a week since I had set myself free, and it had been a wonderful week. I had felt better than I had in a year.

Even that day had been wonderful. David and I had been at his brother's wedding. Seeing Steve and Sue get married was very special. They were so in love that they cried when they said their vows. I had never cried at a wedding before, but everyone shared their joy with tears. David was so handsome as he walked down the aisle in his tuxedo, his face beaming with happiness. And later as we danced, I thought how wonderful it was to be loved by him.

Now this was happening. Jody had been a friend of David's since childhood, and she had had it in for me almost from the start. I don't know why. She was living with a man and was talking about marriage herself. So I wasn't taking David away from her. She was nosy, and I didn't like that. So maybe that was it. All I know is that she didn't like me, and she made that perfectly clear.

It had been months since I'd seen Jody. But when we got to the church that morning, she started right in, throwing me dirty looks and rolling her eyes every time I spoke.

Later, at the reception, she finally spoke to me. No "Hello." No "How are you?" Just "So, did you make a profit last year with your business?" in a voice dripping with sarcasm.

"I don't think that's any of your business, Jody," I answered as calmly as possible.

She didn't like that one bit. "Well, then, I take that as a no," she laughed.

"No, it doesn't mean that we didn't make a profit. It means that it's none of your business. I'm not trying to be nasty; I just don't think it's an appropriate question," I said, my voice still calm.

"How dare you tell me what's appropriate?" she asked. "I just wanted to know when you're going to give up this ridiculous pipe dream."

Now I was getting angry, but she wouldn't let me talk. She held her hand up, a sign for me to stop speaking, and said, "No, Marci, don't try to worm your way out of this. No more words. You aren't allowed to speak another word to me."

"You've got to be kidding," I thought to myself. "I'm not allowed to speak another word to *her*."

David was furious when he heard what Jody had said. After the wedding, back at his parents' house, the two of them got into a fight. It was horrible and seemed so disrespectful on this special day.

"You know," David said as we drove home that night, "she's just jealous of you."

"I suppose," I said, lost in thought. After a moment, I went on: "David, this isn't the first time someone has attacked me for no reason; it's always happening. And usually whoever's doing the attacking homes in on the New Age connection, on my 'otherness.' But I don't think that's really what's making them angry. I think they're hurting inside, and lashing out is a way to deal with their pain. What I don't understand is why they attack me. I don't judge them. I don't pick on them. All I've ever tried to do was help people."

"You don't get it, do you?" he said.

"Get what?"

"People look at you, and they see your goodness, your sweetness. They aren't jealous because you're beautiful or have special power. They're jealous because your warmth and goodness make them feel unworthy. They're jealous because they want to be like you, and they can't," he said.

"Maybe you're right," I said, "but that doesn't make it any easier. I hate it when they call me a freak. And now I'm supposed to go out in the world and tell everyone about the things I see and do. Why? So that more people can hate me and call me a freak? What's the point?"

I could feel it, the self-pity. I would never be normal, I thought to myself, but at least I could keep my life a secret. I didn't have to go out and tell the world. Sure, the tapes were out there with my name on them, but that didn't mean I had to reach out beyond the New Age world. I was tired of being attacked.

The next day was Sunday, and by afternoon I had a fever and a sore throat. On Monday my head was stuffed up, and by Tuesday I could barely move. David and I were supposed to go away for the weekend, but at the rate I was going, I didn't think I would make it. When dinner didn't relieve my pounding headache, I fell into bed.

I was lying as still as possible, yet everything was moving. The day before the wedding I had said to David that I refused to be sick anymore, that I was going back to a regular schedule and would finish the projects I started a year and a half ago. He had been so proud of me. Now, just a few days later, here I was again, unable to function. It made no sense.

The next morning I woke up to sunshine streaming into the room. David came upstairs and kissed me lightly on the forehead. "I'm going to go back to my place and work. If you need me, call. Are you okay if I go?" he asked.

"Yes, I'll be fine. I'll talk to you later." I wanted him to go. The truth was I wasn't feeling better — I was feeling worse than the night before — but I didn't want to worry him, and I knew there was nothing he could do for me.

After he left, I tried to sit up, but I couldn't. The room was still spinning, and I felt a wave of nausea wash over me. "What's wrong with me? Please help me," I called to the spirits. I could feel them all around me.

The pain in my head seemed to lessen, and I fell back to sleep.

In my dream, the room was very bright. I could feel spirits looking down at me with love and concern, but they seemed so far away, as though something was holding them back.

Suddenly, Rich, the man who had given me the rose quartz, was standing by my bed. I wondered what he was doing there, in my room. Maybe he had come to take me somewhere to rest. I closed my eyes and pictured a place with beautiful gardens, a dance floor, massage therapists, and chiropractors; a place with a huge library, where I could read and study; a place where no one could hurt me.

"What's wrong with her?" he demanded to know from the spirits. As he spoke, he was running his hands over my body, feeling my energy. I was too sick to move. "She's very sick. Do you realize that?"

I could see the mass of colors that surrounded my body: bright reds, blues, purples, oranges, and yellows, all swirling in confusion.

"Her system is completely off. If she doesn't get help, she's going to be in big trouble. What's going on with her?" He was angry, and I could hear the urgency in his voice. Again I wondered why he was there.

"She's dying," one of the spirits announced matter-of-factly.

"What?" Rich asked.

"She's dying," the spirit repeated.

I remember thinking, "What is that spirit talking about. I have the flu." But I was too weak to give voice to the thought.

"Why is she dying?" Rich asked, more gently now. "Please,

can I help her?"

"She's the only one who can change this," another spirit said.

"Then why am I here? Why did you call me to her?"

"Because when she met you, she felt you were like her. And you're in her world. You can reach her, touch her; we can't. And even if we could, it wouldn't help. She needs to know there are other people in her world who are like her. She needs to know she can be herself in the physical world. We needed somebody who could help her through this time," a third spirit responded.

"You still haven't answered my question. Why is she dying? The last time I talked to her, she was a strong, vibrant young woman. Her soul sang out to me. Now, she's falling apart. Why?"

I listened closely. I, too, wanted to hear the answer. Why was I so weak? I thought I had been getting stronger. What was happening?

"The answer isn't simple," the spirit replied. "Marci has come so far. She's come to understand creation, life, and death. She's reached the deepest levels of hell and brought herself back to the heights of heaven. She's lived a lifetime and more in her twenty-three years. And most of those years have been filled with struggle. If she feels she's learned enough, struggled enough, then perhaps she feels it's time to leave.

"The sickness is her body's way of carrying out the decision her soul has made. Her soul has retreated; that's why she's dying. Most people die when they reach this point in their lives. And she'll die too unless she chooses to live the life of her soul in this body."

"Hasn't she already chosen that?" Rich asked. I knew the answer to that question: No, I hadn't.

"On the outside she has. But she's still afraid of being attacked; hurt still grows deeply within her. Someone attacked her the other day. It was a crossroads, and she chose to hide again. Until she chooses to live her truth, she'll just grow weaker. We thought that seeing you and realizing that you're able to live your truth in the physical world might help her choose what she really wants — life."

When I woke up, I crawled to the phone and called David. I'm not sure what I said, although I know I was crying. He came at once and took me to the doctor's office.

I remember sitting in Dr. Abbas's office, on the examination table, my back propped up against the wall.

"Your adrenals have gotten worse instead of better. Your blood pressure has barely come up at all. I don't understand why this is happening. You might have chronic fatigue syndrome. Have you ever had mononucleosis?"

"No. I've been really healthy all of my life," I said.

"Maybe it's candida," he said. "You could have an overgrowth of yeast in your system. I'll do a muscle test."

He set out several vials on the tray next to the examination table and then asked me to lie down. He started the test by bending my arm and then pulling it down, asking me to resist. I was able to do that until he placed one of the vials on my abdomen. Suddenly I had no strength. He repeated the test several times. Each time my resistance was fine until he put a vial on my abdomen; then all my strength would drain away.

"What is that?" I asked, pointing to the vial.

"It's a homeopathic sample of candida. You must have a complete overgrowth," he said. "I'm heading off for two weeks for a conference. When I get back, I'll start you on a diet for candida. I don't want to have you on it while I'm away because it probably will make you very sick in the beginning.

"One more thing. You should know that you're going to have to stay on this diet for the rest of your life. Candida can't be cured, just controlled."

At first I was elated. Finally, a logical explanation of why I was sick. I would just change my diet, and I would get better. Only later did I realize that I was grasping at something external again.

On the way home from the doctor's office, a song came on the radio. The words describe feeling as though you can fly. As I listened, I could feel my spirit lift and free itself from my body. I let go, leaving the pain of the day behind.

Suddenly, I was remembering my dream from the morning, the visit from Rich and the spirits' words. It seemed to me that my body was trying to make room for my soul. All I had to do was help my body by cleaning out the toxins, and then I would be fine. I wouldn't be sick anymore, and my soul would come back.

I turned to David and told him about the dream that morning.

"Do you think I'm crazy?" I asked. "I mean believing that I'm dying because my body has been through so much that it can't do all the changing it needs to do to house my soul. Does that sound nuts?"

"Marci, after everything you've been through, anything is possible."

Then I remembered a product I'd seen at a conference. The manufacturer guaranteed that it would cleanse the body. I described it to David. "Do you think I should order it?"

David barely hesitated: "It makes sense," he said, "that you healed your emotions and that now you have to heal your body. I think you should go ahead and place the order."

So I did. It was a long week and a half waiting for the product to arrive. I was so eager to start what I felt sure was the cure that I never really thought about what the spirits had said or that I already was feeling better, stronger, without the herbs.

When the herbs finally came, I changed my diet with a vengeance. On the program I could eat only fresh vegetables and fruits, and some grains. I had to cut out my usual source of protein, soy products. The program called for supplements every hour and a half and set times for eating. The first day I felt great. I ate something like two hundred calories the entire day, but my body felt incredible. My thinking was clear, and the swelling in my lymph nodes went down. The second day I was tired, but I slept soundly that afternoon and woke feeling rested — a sensation I hadn't had for more than a year. David and I were thrilled. We both thought the problem was solved. I would stay on the program for a month, slowly increasing my intake of herbs and decreasing my intake of food. I could do that; I'd fasted before and felt great.

But that night, everything changed. The thought of food nauseated me. By the next morning, I couldn't keep fruit juice down; for the first time since I was nine years old, I vomited. By afternoon, even water wouldn't stay down. The night was horrendous. Every hour I would wake with dry heaves. And now it was me, not the spirits, thinking I was dying.

David called the company that sold me the product. Someone there said I must have parasites in my system and that was why I was getting so sick, that I should start the program much slower. I was so depressed. In the first two days I had lost weight, my skin had cleared, and I was healthy. Now I was sicker than before. Everyone kept telling me that I had too many toxins in my body and that I had to release them.

"It doesn't make any sense, David," I said to him that night. "I've eaten healthy my entire life. This sickness doesn't make any sense."

He didn't have answers. I knew that he was as frustrated as I was.

So I cut back the quantity of herbs I was taking. I was sick for three more days. Finally, on the eighth day, I woke up feeling tired, but the nausea was gone. I was hungry and thirsty. David brought me a huge plate of watermelon and then kissed me on the forehead and left, promising to come back later.

I ate and then fell back to sleep, a deep sleep. When I woke up a couple of hours later, Rik was standing beside my bed.

"Do you really want the answers?" he asked.

I looked at him, my beautiful friend. I had done everything the spirits had told me to do, and look at me. I felt betrayed and hurt.

"I don't know," I said, deeply confused.

"Marci, we didn't mislead you. You only heard what you were ready to hear," he said.

"What does that mean?" I asked. "The spirit said that I had to heal my body or I would die."

"Where did you get the idea that the spirit was talking about your body?" he asked.

"He said that my body was tired, that my soul had gone

through enough for an entire lifetime in just twenty-three years. That sounds to me as though my body can't keep up with what's happening inside me."

"No, that wasn't it at all. What the spirit was saying was that you had to choose to live the life of your soul — to really live the life of your soul — for your body to be able to change; that if you didn't, you would die. Your organs are healthy: The problem is in the energy centers that control your body parts, not in your organs."

"But I've changed everything inside; there's nothing left to fix. How could it be something inside?" I asked.

"How could it be something outside?" he asked sadly. "We know that you've chosen to live, but you're still afraid and that's why you can't make your body healthy. Healing your body won't stop you from being afraid."

He stopped for a moment and then said, "Being sick is how you're protecting yourself. If you're sick, no one will attack you. If you're sick, you can't possibly take on responsibility for healing the world. If you're sick, David is going to be here taking care of you, not finding his truth. If you're sick, you don't have to go on."

He put his arms around me, but I pulled away.

"I don't understand. I've worked so hard to find myself, and I did. I found my soul. But I'm still sick. I know what you've told me about programs not working, and I know that I went and started one anyway, but I didn't know what else to do. Why did I get sick again?"

"Because it was so painful when Jody attacked you, and you just couldn't bear more pain. And there's another reason, a reason that lies within the crossroads. Marci, the only way out is through.

You have to look at your life."

"What does looking at my past have to do with anything?" I asked, frustrated by his words. I simply didn't want to go there.

Before Rik could answer, I saw my ancient teacher before me. In his hand was the butterfly, once again encased in glass. As I looked at the butterfly, I felt defeated.

"The answer lies within the crossroads," Rik said. "The dragon still exists. You have to go to its source."

I could feel the truth in what he said. I had to face this thing within me. I didn't know what it was that was frightening me so, but it was time to find out. I had asked for an answer; I hoped and prayed I would find it there.

Past-life Regression: *A form of meditation or hypnosis that taps into the subconscious knowledge of one's former incarnations. The knowledge is there — like early memories of childhood — but the conscious mind can't reach it. The subconscious — the mind of the soul — can recall any lifetime.*

Two Roads Taken
May 9, 1997

Rik was shimmering.

He held out his hand to me. He didn't say anything; he simply waited. After a moment, with a sigh, I put my hand in his. I didn't seem to have a choice. Together we journeyed back to the world of lava.

Once again, I saw the golden roads before me.

"Are you ready?" Rik asked.

I looked up at him, at his loving face, and told myself he would never ask me to do anything that would hurt me. Yet somehow I knew my life was about to change forever.

"Yes," I said. "Lead on."

"I can't. You have to take the first step."

And so I did.

As I took that first step, I saw my room again, the room I'd grown up in. The sun was shining, streaming in on my bed, the chest of drawers, and the desk — all painted a sky blue. There were my toys: the little table with the play stove under it, the doll's cradle next to the window, the small brown rocking chair filled with stuffed animals. And there I sat, just seven years old, at the desk writing in my diary:

> *When I grow up, God wants me to go and visit*
> *sick people. I'm to help them to remember that the*
> *other world isn't far away and to make them smile*
> *again. He also wants me to be a priest. I'm not*
> *sure how I can do that because the church won't*
> *allow me to be one because I'm a girl. But He*
> *says He'll take care of that.*
>
> *I have these friends and we go and play*
> *together in other worlds. I feel bad because when*
> *I'm there I don't have parents, but they just*
> *wouldn't understand. They think this world is*
> *make-believe, and I know that it isn't. Playing*
> *with my dolls is make-believe. This world I go to*
> *is real. When I'm there, I'm much older than I am*
> *right now. I don't try to be. It's just that I am.*
> *When I'm there I can be my real self, but when*
> *I'm here people are mean and they don't make*
> *much sense. They lie to one another and then get*
> *mad at me when I try to correct them. I can't help*
> *that I know when they are lying. They tell me I'm*
> *bad to correct them. That it is disrespectful. What*

I don't get is why grown-ups always want respect, but they don't respect kids.

From what I can see, this place I live in doesn't make any sense. Sometimes I think that I'm just dreaming this world that I live in, that the world I go to is the world that I'm really alive in. It gets very confusing to me. Like in my other world, I would never give up my own name to take on a man's name. In my other world I have decided that I will make up a new name with whomever I marry — if I ever marry at all. In my other world, boys being stronger and better than girls just doesn't happen. Everyone is equal. No one is made fun of for looking different or even acting different. No one hates. I don't want anyone here to know the person I am when I'm in my other world because they will try to take it away from me. In this world, people forget who they really are.

"Oh, God," I said to Rik. "I felt that way back then? I had forgotten I wrote that. I remember that I asked my mother for a diary because there were so many things that I couldn't talk about to any-one."

"That's when you chose two roads," Rik explained, "one to follow in the physical world, the other to follow in your special world."

And so we began to look at my life as a child. I am a Gemini, and that is obvious in every aspect of my life, even my young life.

My mind always was racing a mile a minute, from one thought to the next. I wanted to know everything, and that curiosity was coupled with an enormous capacity for learning — which often made me the teacher's pet. I was reading at an eighth-grade level by the time I was in the first grade. I loved school. I loved learning. Sometimes I felt as though nothing could fill my brain fast enough.

I loved the physical world, my family and my friends. I was very close to my mother, and I didn't like being apart from her. I also loved being with my grandmother. She lived downstairs from us, and she would watch my brother and me after school. Many days she would have her friends over to play cards — all of them speaking French. They would let me sit with them and would teach me the games.

On Sunday mornings we all would go to church. Then, in the afternoon, we would go to my other grandmother's house with my aunts and uncles and my eight cousins. With my long blond hair, big blue eyes, rosy cheeks, and propensity for talking up a storm, I was the center of attention. But even then I knew I was different; even then I knew not to let anyone know about my special world.

Religion was an important part of my family's life. My mother taught me how God created man, woman, and earth. She gave me the religion she was raised in, Catholicism, and I was very proud of being Catholic. As soon as I was able to read, I read the Bible constantly.

Sunday was my favorite day of the week because I could go to Sunday school and look for answers to all the questions I had. I loved going to church. For an hour I would sit there and talk. Not out loud, of course. I learned very early that no one could see the people around me, the people I could see. Adults used their eyes to see, but you couldn't see these people with your eyes; you had to feel them near you. And when you spoke with them, you spoke through your heart. During the service, the priest always told a story. Although those stories seemed to hold the answers to my questions, he never explained them to my satisfaction. I would listen to them, and my "friends" would tell me what they meant.

Still, it didn't matter if the church wasn't able to answer all my questions. I loved my faith. I loved Christ and the miracles he performed — walking on water, touching and healing. And when I read his words — "Greater things than this shall you do" — I believed them with all my soul.

I firmly believed that Christ was coming back. At night I would lie in bed and talk to him: "Please, you need to come back. People are confused here. I can see the hurt in their eyes. You need to come and help them." I used to dream that he would come back to earth, and I would take him to school with me. There, he would touch all the kids who were hurting because their parents didn't care or were drunk or didn't come home at night. Then, in my dreams, he would teach the kids that we all were supposed to be friends, that we weren't supposed to hurt other people or make fun of them.

My waking dreams, too, were about the church. I had memorized the Mass, and I would pretend to be a priest, leading the service. My sermons weren't of the fire-and-brimstone variety, though. Instead of telling my congregants how bad they were, I would tell them how beautiful they were and how God loved them just as they were. I would explain to them that there is no such thing as sin, and I would touch their hearts. Somehow I felt it was my responsibility to help them, at least until Christ came back. They needed so badly to know that they were loved.

I was seven years old.

Rik looked at me and nodded. "You took it on yourself at seven to start saving people."

There was more. At some point that year, desperate to understand God, I turned to my mother for help. After church, I would ask her every question I could think of. She answered those she could. More important, I think, she encouraged me to keep looking for the answers she couldn't supply, and she believed that I would find them.

"Marci," she would say, "there's nothing that you can't do."

Although I believed that God had somehow chosen me to help others, in time I realized that my god was not the god of original sin we prayed to in church on Sundays. My god wanted people to understand and know their fundamental goodness, their beauty. My god wanted people to know they were loved.

Over the next couple of years, we moved from a mill town into the country, a house on a quiet road, near a lake, with lots of woods to play in. I loved our new house, but my parents — feeling the stress of the move and home ownership — were fighting all the time. I began to retreat more and more into my beautiful world. There the spirits taught me to send dreams to other people and to heal my body with my hands. In the physical world, I discovered the power of nature and spent as much time as I could outside, by the lake and in the woods. The path I traveled those years was straight.

Up ahead, though, I saw a huge bump in the middle of the road. "What's that?" I asked Rik.

"It's a turning point," he said, "the first real turning point in your life. Already you had made some important choices: to help others and to understand God. But this is where your choices set you on the path that brought you to what you're facing now."

When I looked again, I saw myself on the day that I met Rik. There I was, small and innocent, up in the oak tree. I trembled with the cold and the wind; I was crying. I knew that if I jumped, if I just let myself slip from the branch, I would die. But despite my pain and my disappointment with the world, I couldn't do it. That little girl chose life.

Watching, I knew that I had made two choices that day. Yes, I would go on living in the physical world; but to survive there I would rely on my other world and my truth. I might live in the physical world, but I couldn't trust life there. Real life for me was on the other side.

Past the bump, the road evened out again. As we journeyed on, Rik and I, we saw flashes of my life. I was twelve now. It was night. I had gone to bed later than usual — I remember, it was school vacation. The house was dark and quiet; my parents were already asleep. As I did every night before I went to sleep, I had talked to the spirits around me. I was just dozing off when I heard someone walking — no, shuffling — in the kitchen. I knew it wasn't my mother or father; I knew it was a spirit. I could hear the air moving as it walked. Now the shuffling was getting closer. I jumped out of bed, grabbed all my stuffed animals, climbed back into bed, and wrapped them around me as tightly as I could. Through the open door to my bedroom I could see a blue light reflected in the picture window in the living room.

I could hear the spirit walking again. I buried my head deeper in the covers refusing to look out. I could feel it and hear it much closer now, in my room, near my desk. On the desk was a music box my godfather had given me for Christmas that year. It had a small on-off switch in the back, but you had to wind it up before it would work. I knew it wasn't wound, and I didn't hear anyone winding it up. Yet when the spirit flicked the switch on, music began to play. I was terrified and started screaming.

My parents finally heard me. I saw the lights go on in the living room. But by the time they got to my room, the music had stopped. I told them that the music box had turned on by itself, that I hadn't touched it. My father picked it up and checked: The switch was turned off.

"Maybe you jiggled it when you were getting ready for bed," my mother said. But I knew I hadn't touched it.

My parents took me into their bedroom and made a bed for me on the floor. In a few minutes, their breathing got deeper as they fell back to sleep. Then I heard it again, the shuffling. It went from my room to the living room to the doorway of my parents' room. I could feel it standing there. I was about to scream when I realized that my parents couldn't protect me; they couldn't see this world.

As I watched from the bed, the spirit took form. She was an old woman with gray-blue hair. I didn't know her. She walked past a cabinet in my parents' room. I heard the doors close gently and then reopen. Then she walked around their bed. Next to the bed was a big wicker basket in which my mother kept her sewing. I could hear the rustling of paper patterns as the spirit sat down in it. I was so scared, I couldn't breathe or swallow or even call to Rik. She looked at me and gently laughed, and then opened a book she'd been carrying and began to read me a story. I couldn't hear what she was reading, but in moments I was asleep.

The next night my parents sent me to sleep in my own room. This time I was ready: I was curled up with all my stuffed animals, and I called to Rik and every spirit I knew. But when the old woman shuffled through my door, neither animals nor spirits made me feel safer.

When she sat on the edge of my bed, I stuck out my leg and kicked her off. She landed on the floor. At first it felt good to know that I could defend myself, but then I was ashamed. She was just an old woman, and I could have hurt her. I called out to her and asked if she was okay.

She answered me as Rik does, in a voice I could hear in my soul. "Yes, I'm okay. You didn't hurt me." Her voice was sweet. Still, she sat on the floor not moving.

"Are you going to hurt me?" I asked.

"I'm not going to hurt you. I'm here to be with you," she said. Now I could hear a great deal of love in her voice.

I was feeling much safer. With all the self-confidence a twelve-year-old can muster, I told her she was allowed to sit down at the end of the bed but that she couldn't touch me. She agreed, lifted herself up off the floor, and gently sat down on the bed.

Just then, another spirit walked through my door. She was beautiful, dressed in a gorgeous iridescent gown. She told me that her name was Crystal and that she knew my mother very well, that she was sort of my mother's Rik. Crystal came and stood by my bed.

Then another spirit came into the room, a young dark-haired man who said his name was Tim. He, too, took a place next to my bed. Another young spirit, this one with blond hair, walked in. He said his name was Tom, and he went to stand next to Tim. A young woman joined them. Her name was Christine, she said, but I could call her Chris. Before she got to the bed, a little boy and girl came running through the door and jumped up on the bed. They told me that someday they would be my children, that they were waiting to come to me at the right time.

I was stunned. There always had been plenty of spirits around me, but except for Rik I had to travel to my special world to be with them. And none of them had had names. These spirits were right there beside me, in my room. They had names and personalities. I had no idea why they had come, but I wasn't scared anymore. In fact, I felt very safe.

Over time, other spirits came too. Sometimes, the sheer number of them was overwhelming. There were nights when I couldn't sleep for all the energy in my room — the spirits talking and laughing and dancing.

I know most people would call it imagination, but those spirits were very real to me. More than that, I couldn't control their comings and goings. No matter how hard I tried to ignore them or make them go away, I couldn't. Now and again, though, I could scare them into quiet. I remember one Saturday — I was in seventh grade — I had so much homework to do. I was home alone, trying to finish it, but cabinet doors kept banging and drawers kept opening and closing in the kitchen, and the sound of them shuffling back and forth from sink to cupboards made studying impossible. Finally, in desperation, I ran into the living room and screamed, "Shut up! I have to get some work done!" And there was silence. I could feel them there, all of them, but at least they were quiet.

Yes, there was noise and confusion, but there were also times when those spirits made me feel safe. Sometimes at night I would feel something dark, a force that wanted to hurt me. Rik and my guides taught me to fill my room with a white light — they called it "my intention to love." In the light I could see a dark form, the shape of a man, in the corner of the room. But I knew that as long as I surrounded myself with love, he couldn't harm me. Sometimes he would stand and watch me from across the room, but he never came close or touched me. When I asked about him, Rik explained that just as there are angry lost people in the physical world, so there are lost souls. Then he taught me that where love exists, evil can never enter.

I remember waking up one night about three o'clock. I heard banging in the kitchen and someone opening and closing the refrigerator door. I called out to my father, thinking it must be him, but there was no answer. Instead, through my open bedroom door, I could see a light — like the beam of a flashlight — hit the wall above the front door. The light stayed perfectly still. I was terrified. I was sure someone was in the house, and I was afraid he was going to kidnap me. I curled up in my blankets, wrapping them tightly around me. I heard the man come closer, but the beam of the flashlight never moved from the spot above the door. Then, all of a sudden, I heard laughing, a loud intense laugh. Whoever it was stood in the doorway to my room, but he didn't come in. My eyes were closed, but in my mind's eye I could see the man's form.

Finally, I couldn't stand the suspense anymore. Very quietly I pushed the blanket away from my face and peered out. My entire room was filled with a beautiful light; even the outside was bright, as though the sun were shining.

I felt Rik say, "You're safe, my child. You're safe."

Although the spirit still was laughing, he never came into my room. After a while, I fell asleep. When I woke up, just before dawn, my room was dark. I didn't understand what had happened. When I told my mother, she said my father probably had gotten up during the night.

"But I called to him," I said.

"Marci, I just don't know," my mother answered.

But I did. Something was there that night wanting to hurt me — why, I don't know — and there also was something there protecting me.

Some spirits were simply lost, literally. They didn't seem to realize they were dead. When they saw me, they talked to me matter-of-factly, as though I had happened into *their* lives. It fell to me to tell them they had died and to show them the way to the other side. It only happened a few times, and I kind of enjoyed it.

One time I woke up and felt someone in my room. It was a young man, and he came over and tried to kiss me. He told me his name, but I can't remember what it was. He explained to me that he didn't really know what he was doing in my room, but that he knew that he must have come for a reason. He sat down on my bed and tossed a football up in the air. I asked him where he was from, and he started telling me about his house and his life. He explained how the last thing he remembered was getting really drunk at a party.

I told him he was dead, but he didn't believe me. So I showed him the way. I relaxed and opened my mind to the other side. Through me he could see the gardens and all the beauty there. Then he was gone.

The golden road brought me to a morning during my April vacation in the seventh grade. It had been raining outside, and Liz, a friend, and I were in my bedroom, just talking and doing our nails, when we heard a crash in my parents' bedroom. We ran into the room, and there on the floor was a guitar my mother had hung on the wall three years before. I knew the guitar might have fallen off the wall, but it was lying in the middle of the room, as though someone had thrown it. Liz and I looked at each other nervously. Suddenly, behind us, the closet door slowly started to open, and we ran from the room screaming. When we got to my room, the rocking chair that usually was filled with my stuffed animals was moving back and forth. All the stuffed animals had been thrown on the floor.

Things like that always were happening. Whenever I was alone or with the two friends who knew about my other worlds, things would move or rock or make noise. Sometimes it happened when I was with friends who didn't know anything about my secret worlds.

In some ways I loved it: It made life interesting. But it also frightened me because I had no control. Wherever I was — in school, at the library, in a store — I would see and hear all the spirits around me, not just my own. I was always on guard, and sleeping wasn't easy. That's when I would journey to be with my other friends, the ones like me. Sharing with them made the bad things go away.

Looking back, I have to admit that I wouldn't change it for anything, not even being normal. The good far outweighed the bad. I never felt alone. I always had someone to talk to about my problems. I remember liking this boy or that one and being able to talk to the female spirits about what I was feeling. They always gave me great advice; now and then, they even let me see what a boy was thinking. And they helped me with my homework, and even helped me to remember what I had studied the night before when I had trouble with a test.

It's not that I didn't have people to talk to. My mother was still the best source of advice when it came to boys and life in general, and I had lots of friends. It was just that the spirits were with me all of the time; my mother and my friends couldn't be.

Of course, the spirits weren't with me physically. I saw them in my mind, almost like thoughts, and I could feel them, much like feeling love or happiness. When they spoke to me, I couldn't hear their words with my ears; instead I would sense what they were saying. Often I would ask them a question about the world or someone in my life, and I would know their answer before I "heard" their voices. Years ago, when I asked Rik why that happened, he explained to me that spirits don't really have voices or words; they speak in energy. When I asked a question, their answers came in pictures and vibrations.

"If you didn't use your head to interpret our words, you'd know instantly what we are saying. You would feel it," he told me. "And you can communicate the same way. You don't have to speak to talk to me or to the other spirits. But that takes some getting used to. You'll see. Soon you won't need words to understand what we're saying or to say what you want to say."

He was right, I realized, thinking back to our conversation. In the years since, I had learned to "speak" their language: We communicated now through our hearts, in the spirit of our love.

Õ

The golden road seemed to stretch on forever, marked here and there by flashes of my life, almost like film clips. The first one we came to marked my first journey into the possibilities of past-life regression. I was thirteen and in love with Matt, a gorgeous young man with striking blue eyes and an incredible body. The scene played out before me.

We were in a bowling alley, surrounded by his family and their friends. The friends had a newborn with them.

"Would you like to hold the baby, Matt?" the baby's mother asked.

Matt's mother smiled at him and nudged him to take the child. He gently took the baby in his arms and stared down at the sweet little face. I leaned up against him to look at the child. As I touched Matt's arm and saw the way he looked at that baby, my world tilted. Stunned, I knew that I had done this before, that somewhere, sometime, Matt and I had shared the bond of parenthood.

Two weeks later, I was home alone, doing homework in my room, when the phone rang. It was a girl I knew, calling to tell me that Matt was planning to break up with me, that he was going to start dating my best friend again. Once more my world wheeled out of focus. In the past month, Matt had become my life. When he touched my hair, I would just melt. When he held me in his arms, I felt like a princess. I wanted to marry him. At night we would talk on the phone for hours. He would tell me bedtime stories, describing the two of us in years to come at a cabin in the woods, swimming, playing in the water. Every night he would tell me a different story, but each one was filled with love and the promise of a beautiful life together.

As the girl rambled on about Matt and my best friend, the pain was overwhelming. It didn't matter that I knew he was scared of the intense feelings we had for each other. I had given him my love, my being, and he was turning away from me.

Without thinking, I hung up the phone, ran to the bathroom, and took a disposable razor out of the medicine chest. Something dark had come over me. I didn't feel anything — I was numb — as I started hacking at my left wrist. When I realized that the cuts I was making weren't deep enough to kill me, I ran to the kitchen and rummaged through a drawer until I found a serrated knife. Then, carefully, I started digging into the cuts I already had made. The numbness was gone; I welcomed the pain searing through my arm.

I stumbled back into the bathroom. Blood was running out of the wounds in a steady flow. I settled down on the floor, next to the hamper, to wait for death, my arm draped over the toilet.

As I sat there, preparing to die, I felt a presence with me in the darkness. I opened my eyes, but the room was empty. All I could see was my own face, stained with tears, in the full-length mirror that hung across from where I was sitting. But as I watched, the image in the mirror changed. I saw my mother finding me lying in a pool of blood. I could hear her screams and feel her pain. I couldn't bear it.

"You don't want to do this," I heard Rik say. I could feel him so strongly beside me, his love spreading through me.

But I did want to do it. I wanted to die.

"I want to go home with you. I want to be in your world. Please." Yet even as I said the words, I knew in my heart that I couldn't do this to my mother. I couldn't hurt her this way. I looked at my wrist, at the blood streaming from it, and then the strangest thing happened. I felt a soft touch there, as though someone was wrapping it in his hands, cupping my wrist so gently. It was Rik, filling me with his love.

"You don't have to do this," he said.

Crying now, as though his love had opened the floodgates of fear and pain, I tried to explain. "I'm so tired. And I hurt so much. I can't go on. Please, help me."

I had no sooner spoken the words than I felt a strong vibration in my wrist, a pulse, the beat of life. Within moments, the bleeding had stopped, and the cuts seemed to be healing. Rik let go of my wrist and pulled me into the warmth of his arms.

"I know you're tired," he said, caressing my face as he held me close. "I know," he murmured again and again.

We sat like that for an hour, Rik holding and comforting me, until the phone rang. As I stood up to answer it, I looked at my wrist. There were scabs on the wounds; there was no need to bandage them.

I picked up the phone and heard Matt's voice: "I miss you." He didn't mention breaking up with me, and I didn't ask. I was too tired to think about it.

A week later, Matt and I did break up. I cried in his arms when he told me that he loved me but that he just couldn't deal with it right now. He promised me we would be together again someday.

My mother took me shopping that night to cheer me up. I tried to explain to her why I was so sad. "On one level," I said, "I'm not sorry we broke up. I mean I was so attached to him that I was losing myself. If he just hadn't held that baby, I wouldn't care. But I feel as though we came together for a reason and never found out what it was."

My mother tried to console me, but she knew that I would have to figure it out for myself. She didn't know about the suicide attempt, and I didn't want her to know.

When we got home, I got another call from the girl who had told me that Matt was breaking up with me. She talked on about how my best friend and Matt were a couple again. When I got off the phone, I ran to my room, threw myself down on my bed, and sobbed for hours. My parents tried to comfort me, but there wasn't anything they could do.

I went to school the next day, determined to hold my head up. Matt was waiting for me by my locker. He put his arms around me and held me, whispering over and over that he was sorry, that he loved me, and that he wanted us to be together. He and my best friend had never planned to date again.

When I got home from school, I was so excited that I was dancing around the kitchen. My mother, however, was less than delighted to hear that Matt and I were back together.

"Marci," she said, "I'm worried about you. You're so wound

up with Matt that you're not eating. I'm worried that you're becoming anorexic."

I was shocked. Why couldn't she just be happy for me? So what if I was dieting again? I hated food, and I didn't want to eat. It had nothing to do with Matt. Besides, I was taking SlimFast, and that would keep me healthy. I wanted to go to my room and shut the door, but I knew that would mean a fight.

"Just listen to me," she said. "Your relationship with Matt is much more intense than it should be for a thirteen-year-old. Matt broke up with you because he's frightened by that intensity, and that's a normal response for a boy his age. Even before you told me what happened when he held the baby, even before you were dating — when you were just friends — I sensed that the two of you had lived a life together."

Seeing the puzzled look on my face, she started to explain past-life regression. "Some people believe that within the subconscious lie memories of our previous lifetimes. You believe in reincarnation. Well, this is just a way of seeing those other lives."

"Of course I believe in reincarnation. It doesn't make sense that we would live just one life and then be judged on the basis of that life. But I'm not sure about being able to see different lives," I said.

"Just give it a chance," she said. And I agreed.

Two weeks later, my mother took me to see a psychic reader who had promised to bring me to another life. The psychic took my hands. Together we took deep breaths as she counted us into the alpha state of consciousness. Then she walked me through a dark tunnel and out the other end. At first, all I could see was brilliant light. She asked me if I wanted to look for myself, but I said no; I was worried I would make it all up. So she started to tell me what she saw.

I was a young girl living in Holland on my father's farm. I don't know what year it was; some time in the 1800s I think. I had long braids and wore a simple dress.

"I see a young man with a very distinct walk," the psychic said. "He walks with great strength."

I couldn't believe it. Those were the very words I always used to describe Matt's powerful stride.

"Do you know who he is?" she asked.

"Yes," I said. "I have an idea."

Now I was beginning to see things for myself. At first she explained what we were seeing, but very quickly I stopped needing her help. The story was playing out in my own mind so fast I couldn't stop it. The young man worked on my father's farm, and we were in love. I saw us standing by a fence, flirting and laughing with each other.

The scene changed. We were inside a house. The furnishings were rustic and warm. There were flowers in a jar on a table. The young man was sitting on a low stool, holding a small baby in his arms; I was leaning over his shoulder. When I looked up into his face, I saw the enormous love he had for our child. As I watched from this life, tears were running down my face, and I was shaking. I knew that what I was seeing was real, that it had happened. With that thought, my eyes flashed open, and neither the psychic nor I could recapture the scene.

For hours after, I was exhausted but happy. I finally understood why Matt and I felt the way we did. We had come back together for a reason, because we wanted to love each other again. But parting was all right too. If we weren't meant to be together in this lifetime, we would be together again in some other lifetime.

I was back on the golden road. I turned to Rik and asked, "What did Matt have to do with the choices I've made in my life?"

"Matt helped you realize that people are here to learn, that life is a series of learning experiences, and that what you learn in one life stays with you in other lives. You are the sum of all your lives, not just this one. That's a very important lesson.

"He also taught you another important lesson: the value of independence. When you first thought Matt was breaking up with you, you were terribly hurt, but you were also very angry with yourself, that you'd allowed yourself to become so dependent on someone else. Matt taught you that you can't live your life for a relationship. He helped shape who you are today."

He stopped for a minute. Then he said, "You haven't said anything about the crossroads we came to the night you tried to take your life."

"I know," I said. "That night you saved my life for a second time. It seems as though you are always picking up my pieces."

"No," he said smiling. "Those aren't pieces; they're choices. Everyone faces them, and usually they indicate that your life is about to change dramatically."

"Well, my life didn't change dramatically after that, but it certainly wasn't the same. I became so curious about New Age, I dragged my mother to every store I could find. We would sit on her bed and she would ask me questions about life and I would tell her what the spirits told me. That's when I found a place in the physical world where I could be me."

Õ

Farther along the golden road, I could see myself sitting in a classroom surrounded by adults. They were asking me questions about their kids and how to get through to them. I was trying to frame an answer to a question one very nervous mother had asked, when, through the window, I noticed a bonfire blazing in the field outside.

It was my first time at the Healing Arts Festival. My mother and I had come to relax, to learn, and to find other people like me. It was like heaven, a place where I could be myself, where people simply accepted me. People here hugged one another and laughed and talked openly about the love they felt inside.

As I stared at the fire, I thought about the final event of the weekend — a fire walk. I wanted to do it so badly, but I was terrified. I kept hoping that the rain that had poured all the night before would come back and douse the fire. Then I wouldn't be embarrassed by backing out.

I had been afraid of fire since I was eight, since someone had set fire to my father's car. It was very late, almost three o'clock in the morning. My father was still at his nightly card game down the street. My mother woke to the sound of crackling, looked outside, and saw the car in flames in the driveway. She screamed to my brother and me and rushed us out of the house, in case the flames spread. Later I learned that the fire was a warning, that someone had threatened our lives. Ever since, fire and death had been linked in my mind.

Now I could see myself standing in front of the bed of coals, holding the hand of a girl my age. The fire tenders raked out the coals, creating a path in front of us. As I stood there, I prayed to the fire: "Please, I don't want to be afraid of you. I know you do more than destroy. Please show me your goodness."

Within moments, the people in front of us had crossed. It was our turn. My partner squeezed my hand. I was terrified. What if I burned my feet and could never dance again?

I hesitated but then realized I could do this. Over the past two years, I had come to believe that everything is energy, atoms and molecules moving at different speeds. If that was so, I reasoned, then we should be able to move through walls, fly, and even walk on fire. I took a deep breath and squeezed the girl's hand, and together we crossed the fire.

When we were across, I let out a cry of joy and jumped up and down. I did it. I had overcome my fear.

We walked the fire two more times. It was painless the first and second times. The third time, I got three small blisters on the bottom of one foot. But I knew why. That third time, I walked for the wrong reason: I didn't want to be shown up by my partner. That, too, was a valuable lesson: What others accomplish doesn't matter. Follow your own heart.

Heart Block
May 9, 1997

I could hear a noise at the edges of my being.

"What is that?" I wondered, not wanting to leave my journey with Rik. I needed to see all of this; I had put it off for too long. When I heard the answering machine turn on downstairs, I realized the phone had been ringing. I rolled over and picked up: "Hello," I said in a groggy distant voice.

"Hi. I'm calling from the company that manufactures the herbal program you've been taking. I hear you're having some problems with it, that you're vomiting." The voice on the line sounded cheerful and bubbly.

By now, I was fully conscious. "I'm glad you finally called," I said. It was Friday; David had called the company on Monday.

"Well, we've had so many people calling in with the same problem. I just want you to know that there's nothing to worry about. The product isn't poisonous or anything, and we're hard at work recalling that batch."

"Are you saying there's something wrong with the product?"

"It looks that way, yes. Now, you stopped taking the product on Monday, right?" she asked.

"Yes," I said, "but I went back on it yesterday afternoon, when I finally could get it to stay down. Someone from your company told my partner that I just had too many toxins in my system, that I should wait a few days and then go back on the product more slowly. I want these toxins out of my system," I said, keeping my voice calm.

"Oh, well, stop taking it immediately," she said. "Not that there's anything to worry about. In fact, we have one man who's on the very mild phase who's refusing to come off the product because he's seeing such great results.

"Now, just for our records, you've had vomiting, nausea, and dizziness."

I could hear her writing as she spoke. According to the manual that came with the herbs, those symptoms weren't unusual. So why she was she bothering to write them down? It didn't make sense.

"Now, I need the batch number from the bottle of herbs we sent you."

I asked her to hold on while I went downstairs to check the bottle. The product was a combination of herbs that was supposed to cleanse every system in the body. Before I took it, I had read the ingredients. At one time or another, I had taken every herb listed, so I'd been sure the product was safe.

I picked up the phone in the kitchen and read the numbers to the woman. She went on to tell me to drink some vegetable juice and plenty of water, to do an enema if I felt comfortable with it, and to take it easy until my body got over the dehydration.

"Should I do the parasite cleanse?" I asked.

"Oh, no," she said. "Don't do any cleansing for at least six weeks. You see, that batch of product was too strong: It pulled out too many toxins in your body way too quickly. It's probably overloaded your kidneys and your liver. That's probably why you got nauseated — it was a way for your body to rid itself of the toxins.

"We've never tested to be sure that all the batches are the right strength. But I can tell you that from now on, we'll be checking up one side and down the other to ensure the product is safe."

I couldn't believe it: The product had been too strong; I wasn't "overtoxic" after all. I should have been angry about the company's negligence, but I was thrilled to learn that there was nothing seriously wrong with me.

"God, I feel so much better," I said.

That's when she told me the scope of the problem, that everyone who had taken that batch of herbs had been sick, including the doctor who had created the program. Before she hung up she made it clear that all my symptoms would go away and that there was no need to see a doctor or to worry. Then she promised to send me a new batch of the product within six weeks.

Immediately I called my mother and David, and told them the good news: I wasn't overtoxic; it was just a bad batch of product. They were both happy to hear the news, but David still was worried. I told him not to be silly, that we should go out to dinner to celebrate. Reluctantly, he agreed.

When he came to pick me up a couple of hours later, I could see the worry in his face. I figured he was being overprotective. I wanted to go out; I didn't want to stay home and rest. That's all I'd been doing.

As soon as we got to the highway, I began to feel nauseated again. I rolled down the window to get air, and that seemed to settle my stomach. But now the muscles in my right arm had begun to ache, and there was a sharp pain in my lower back. And I was desperately thirsty. Something was very wrong with me, and I didn't know what.

"Marci, are you okay?" David asked.

I told him how I was feeling.

"Do you want to go to a hospital?" he asked, his concern growing.

"What could they do in a hospital? They can't flush my system any faster," I said.

So we went to the restaurant, where I drank as much water as I could and managed to keep my food down. Still, I was getting nervous; I didn't like the way I was feeling. Finally, I turned to David and said, "Okay, it wouldn't hurt to just call a hospital."

That's all he had to hear. In five minutes, he had paid the bill and we were back in the car on the way to the emergency room.

By the time we got to the hospital, I felt silly. I was sure I was fine, just overtoxic at the moment. The medical staff didn't think so; in short order, I was admitted to the cardiac intensive care unit and placed on a heart monitor. A nurse was shouting out numbers: "She's in a three. Now she's in a two. Now she's back in a three." I had no idea what was going on. Why was everyone so worried? I was fine. They had hooked me up to an IV, which was flushing out my system. Wasn't that enough?

Then I heard one of the nurses say, "I want you to bring in the external pacemaker and the medicine to start her heart just in case. I don't like how her arm and her back are aching. I think I want the cardiologist on the phone tonight."

"What's going on?" I asked.

"Honey," a nurse answered softly, "I don't want to scare you. Are you sure you want to know?"

"Yes, I want to know." Now I was very frightened.

"You're in heart block; your heart is beating very slowly. We don't know what's causing it, but we assume that it's the herbs you took. Right now, though, that doesn't matter. What matters is that you could go into cardiac arrest at any time, and we would have to hook you up to an external pacemaker to keep your heart going."

Then she pointed to a box of medicine by the bed. "This medicine also helps start the heart. If you need it, we'll inject it into your IV. We're going to watch you very closely, but we need you to lie still. You're a very lucky young woman, you know. You're in critical condition. If you hadn't come, your heart could have stopped and there would have been no way to get it going fast enough. You need to be here."

I couldn't believe this was happening. I'd walked into the hospital feeling silly; now I was in critical condition.

Although I knew my condition was serious, it was several days before I understood what had happened. According to the doctors, the bad batch of herbs had been contaminated with digitalis — they found deadly levels of the drug in my blood — and too much digitalis causes heart block. In second-degree heart block, some of the impulses from the atrium never reach the ventricles, causing an irregular pulse. In third-degree heart block, none of the impulses reach the ventricles, so the ventricles beat with their intrinsic rhythm. That rhythm often is so slow that the flow of blood to the brain and other parts of the body isn't sufficient. That's what happened to me. My heart was barely beating. (The normal resting rate is about 60 beats a minute; when I got to the hospital, my heartrate was somewhere between 20 and 30 beats a minute.) Yet somehow my other organs were healthy. My doctors kept repeating how lucky I was to be alive.

I was in the hospital for six days, most of them a blur. I remember trying to be brave, and I managed it during the day, following orders with just the right combination of curiosity and humor. But the nights were awful. That's when the weight of everything would hit me. I hated being prodded like a science project. I hated that everyone was using me as an example of the damage herbs could do. (The hospital had called in the Food and Drug Administration to examine the product I'd been using.) And I was afraid. I kept remembering what the spirit had said in my dream: "Most people die when they reach this point in their lives." What if this had happened because I hadn't chosen. I knew this wasn't my fault, but I was scared that I might die at any moment.

In the end, the doctors released me because there really wasn't anything more they could do. The FDA toxicology report had come back. It showed that the product had been contaminated with a digitalis-like substance. The product hadn't been too strong: It had been poisonous. And there was no antidote because this digitalis had come from a weed called squill, not from foxglove, and the antidote only works on the foxglove substance. I simply had to relax and let my body rid itself of the poison. I was to call if I had any problems.

I left the hospital with David, elated to be free and alive. It was a beautiful spring day, and I loved the feel of the sun on my face. I had been inside too long. But when we got back to my house, all the bottled-up emotions came pouring out. For a long time, David and I just held each other. The week had been tough on him, too. He had stayed with me almost constantly, leaving only to run errands or get clothes or food. But most of all, he, more than I, knew how sick I had been, and he was terrified that I would leave him.

By the next day, life was running full tilt. David and I needed to visit several of the stores that were selling my tapes. We would no sooner walk through the doors, when the owners would start firing questions at me: When are you going to start teaching again? When are you going to go on the empowerment tour you canceled? When is the next fire walk? When I got home, there was a message from a client who said she was in trouble and really needed to see me.

There were other messages on the machine that day, too. Somehow the press had gotten wind of the FDA report, and I found myself in the middle of a regulatory battle. On one side were the New Age people and nutritionists, who felt the FDA should keep its hands off the herbal industry; two years before, I'd fought alongside them. On the other, were doctors and government officials, arguing that my case made clear the need for immediate oversight. I was caught in the middle. Certainly my experience seemed to call out for regulation; but the problem hadn't stemmed from the herbs themselves, it was the fault of the manufacturing process.

I also was house hunting again. The house I was renting had been sold, and I had just a month to move. Everything seemed to be closing in on me. That's when it dawned on me: It was time for me to go away.

"David," I asked timidly, "can I talk to you about something?" It was the next day. I was making a huge decision, and I needed to be certain of it.

He looked at me and nodded.

"When I'm through with the tapes and the book I'm working on, I'm going to go away. I know I've said this before, but now I'm positive."

"It's okay," he said. "I want you to go. I understand."

I reached for his hand. "I know you do. The thing is that I kept saying I wanted to get away, but it was always more important for me to edit a new tape, write a book, build the health center, or do a promotional tour for The Quest. It was always more important to me to try to stop the pain I see in the world. But I woke up this morning feeling that tug on my soul to be somewhere else."

"Marci, I don't care if you never finish what you're working on. Just go," he said.

"No, I can't do that. I have to say to the world what I need to say; it's eating at me. I also need to find a permanent place to live, a place I always can come home to. But when those two things are done, I don't think I want to work at The Quest anymore."

"You do what you need to do." He was quiet for moment. Then, softly, he added: "I'm just afraid that I'll lose you."

"I'm afraid of that too, but I can't not go. I have to get away, or the stress will kill me. I've found myself now, and that person is a bird. I've been caged for too long — not by you, but by my life and my thoughts. I have to remember how to fly."

The next morning I woke to the tugging again. This time, though, I knew that I definitely was going. I didn't know where or how, but I was going. Thoughts of Europe were running through my mind; so were visions of the national parks here in the States. But I didn't let myself get caught up in decision making. I had time to decide.

As I was climbing out of bed, I suddenly knew what I had to do. Of course. I had to finish my journey with Rik. That was the only way to be sure I was making the right choice . . . and that the choice was mine to make. Today I had all kinds of appointments, but tomorrow I would continue to explore my life. Tomorrow I would know if I could really walk away.

Crossroads
May 18, 1997

I walked out the front door and stretched in the sunlight. It was a perfect spring day: The air was crisp; the birds were singing; the buds on the trees were bursting with life.

It had been a strange spring. March was warm; I remember being outside in shorts. Then in April we had one of the worst blizzards I'd ever seen. The next day was hot again, and all the snow melted. I found myself laughing at the thought that the weather and I had been behaving a lot alike. Hadn't I bloomed and then found myself digging out from a blizzard?

I started down the street at a slow pace. The doctors had warned me that I would be winded and tired until my heart returned to normal. But I couldn't stay in bed; I needed to move and feel my blood pumping.

I was at peace with my decision to go away. As soon as I was done with my walk, I planned to go home and return to the other side. I was looking forward to it. I was sure that I would find my answers there. For now, I was enjoying the steady beat of my heart and the pleasure of moving my body and feeling my muscles. It was good just to be alive.

As I walked along, the rhythm of my body — my breathing, my heartbeat — and the crunch of my shoes on the ground were relaxing me, lulling me. By the time I turned onto a back road, I was no longer feeling externally. The roads of my life were before me, and Rik was standing beside me.

"Are you ready?" he asked.

"Don't I have to lie down or something?" I asked.

"No," he said. "It's all here. It's been here all along, just waiting. It doesn't matter where your body is; it's your soul that takes the journey. Meditation isn't about being still; it's about listening."

But I had stopped listening. I could see myself at sixteen. I was standing in front of the mirror in my room, looking critically at my body. It didn't seem to matter how little I ate or how much I worked out, I was always ten pounds heavier than I wanted to be. This was the day I decided to use meditation to lose weight.

The process was simple. I would start by looking at myself in the mirror, seeing my body with that extra ten pounds, and then I'd slowly relax. As I went deeper and deeper into my subconscious, I would look in the mirror and see my body the way it was meant to be, the truth of my body. Then, slowly, I would count myself back up to consciousness, the image of my true weight in my mind.

I did that for several weeks, so intent on my body that I didn't realize the emotions that had begun rising to the surface. It started with feelings of inadequacy, memories of people telling me when I was little that I was fat . . . even though in photographs I look thin.

Then, one day I saw all the things that people had said and done that had taught me to look at myself through their eyes. I saw my brother's friends teasing me; I heard a boyfriend lashing out at me when I refused to have sex with him; I saw friends and family members commenting on my clothes, my hair, my skin, my weight.

I knew what I had to do. I took a pen and a pad of paper and started writing down all the painful words. Then I went out to the backyard, dug a hole, and burned it all — all the pages I had written that day and my old diaries. I was destroying my past so that I could start my future. When nothing was left but ashes, I filled in the hole with stones.

When I finished, I had an incredible sensation in my forehead, a pulsing that grew stronger and stronger, as though something was waking there. And my whole body felt lighter, freer. Two days later, the ten pounds were gone.

The scene changed. It was a month or two later. I had lost the weight, but I was still unhappy. I was living in several different worlds, and I was very confused. At school, I was a straight-A student, very quiet and withdrawn in class, answering the way I knew the teachers wanted me to. Although I had friends to laugh and joke with, I had only one friend I could confide in.

His name was Danny. He was the only person in the physical world — except for my mother — who really knew about my other worlds. Now Danny was moving, and already I was mourning the loss.

One day not long after Danny told me that his parents had sold their house, I ran into the woods upset and angry. "Don't you understand what it's like for me?" I screamed to Rik and the other spirits. "I need one person in this world who can understand me, someone I can talk to about anything without being afraid. I need a friend: I need a Danny."

Three hours later, my mother and I went to a New Age bookstore in the area. As we were checking out, we saw a small card on the counter. "Youth Group, Wednesday nights at six o'clock, starting June 7" it said. Then it listed several names and phone numbers to call for information. The first name on the list was Danny.

My mother and I looked at each other. She knew how upset I'd been about my friend Danny's moving away. I shook my head and said, "No, they couldn't have sent me a Danny."

The woman behind the counter overheard me. "Oh, you have to meet Danny. He started the youth group. He's so sweet and open. Why don't you come?"

"According to the card," I said, "the group started a few weeks ago. I'd be intruding."

"Oh no," she said. "No, you should join. They're looking for more members. They'd be happy to have you."

So I put my name on the list.

Three days later I started a summer job at a camp working as a counselor. The next Wednesday night, I went to the youth group meeting. Danny wasn't there that week, but the others were friendly. And although they were into things that I wasn't into and they were much older than I was, I felt comfortable with them.

The next Wednesday, all the counselors at camp met after

work to get to know one another. We were in a field playing silly games that were supposed to teach us teamwork. In one, we split up into groups and were supposed to create a machine. The kids in my group — we all knew and liked one another — were just starting to talk about the game, when this blond kid came running over and asked if he could join us. He was young, maybe eighteen, and I had never seen him before. When I asked him what he did at the camp, he said he worked with the oldest campers and that was why we had never met. We let him in the group, and he suggested that we make a washing machine. He knelt down on the grass — it was very wet; it had rained all afternoon — and started rotating back and forth. He told us to make a circle around him and swish back and forth, the motion of a washing machine. He was looking straight at me as he showed us how he wanted us to move, and I was trying really hard not to laugh.

Then he looked into my eyes and said, "Nice crystal."

I looked down at the crystal I was wearing around my neck. Everyone was wearing them that year — it was a fad — but I wore mine for the energy it held. Sure that he didn't know about the power of crystals, I simply thanked him. Later I found out that he was thinking, "She's just wearing it because everyone's wearing crystals. I bet she doesn't know anything about its power."

Fifteen minutes later, now sopping wet, we were on to a new game, and the head counselors were splitting us up into new teams. As we stood there, waiting to be chosen, I looked down at my wet clothes and laughed. I was supposed to go to the youth group meeting at the bookstore right from camp.

I turned to a friend standing next to me and said, "I can't

believe I'm going to a meeting like this."

The blond kid looked over at me and asked where my meeting was being held.

"In Fitchburg," I said.

"It wouldn't happen to be at Joya's Bookshop, would it?" he asked.

"Yes," I said.

"My name is Danny," he said, holding out his hand to shake mine. "I started that group."

Just a couple of hours later, Danny and I were at Joya's together. I led a meditation: "Close your eyes and take a deep breath, breathing in through your nose and out through your mouth. Let your body go deeper and deeper into a state of relaxation."

I counted them down from ten to one and asked them to picture a special place, a relaxing place, where they could feel who they were inside. I brought them there and then I had them lifting up, up, up, into the heavens, touching the stars all around them. I told them to leave the earth and all their worries behind. Then I asked them to find one another in the stars. They did, coming from different directions and places, to form a circle. We held hands and passed a light around the circle until it created a tremendous burst of love within the group that brought us to the world beyond. I let them go and explore the world I knew, and then slowly I brought them back.

Some had tears in their eyes. Others had big grins on their faces as they told me they had never experienced anything like what I had just shown them. No one had ever been able to get that far.

I was delighted. I finally had found a place where I belonged.

Õ

"You asked for someone to come into your life who would be able to understand the real you," Rik said. "That was Danny. And when you chose to start becoming the person you are inside, Danny was there to support you."

Ahead of us a road crossed my path. It marked a choice made, a life-changing choice. Memory flooded my consciousness in a wave.

About a month after I met the new Danny, I was meditating in my yard. It was a beautiful summer's day. That night there was going to be a lunar eclipse. The group from the bookstore was planning to watch the eclipse in a quarry in Fitchburg, high above the city's lights.

As I went deeper into my meditation, I saw the woman and the man who would stand just beyond my reach in the world of lava. They were so beautiful, and I could feel their energy, the life flowing through them.

The woman spoke to me. "Choose life or death," she said in a soft, almost musical voice. "You can't have both, Marci. You seem to want to die, to leave your body. This is a crossroad. Decide. Do you want to live or die?"

I thought carefully about what she said. For the longest time I had wanted to die. I had wanted to be with them on the other side; I seemed to belong there. But now, for the first time in my life, I had found friends who were like me, who could understand me. I wanted to live.

When I chose life, the woman wrapped a magnificent cloak around me. The outer part of the cloak was black; the inside was bright with every color imaginable. The colors swirled and radiated; they seemed to be alive. I felt an intense rush of energy through my body. Then she gave me a necklace, a chain with a small ring on it. Gently she closed the clasp for me.

When she'd finished, she lifted my chin so that I was looking directly into her eyes, and said, "I give you the circle of life, the gateway to worlds. Anything you wish for or ask for will come to you." Then they were both gone.

That night I told Danny what had happened. He marveled at the experience; I was in awe of my decision. For the first time in my life, I didn't want to die.

Õ

I turned to Rik.

"When you saved my life the day I cut my wrist, I didn't choose to live just for me. In fact, I didn't choose to live for me at all. I lived because I couldn't bear to hurt my mother. When the woman came to me, I chose to live because I wanted to," I said.

"That's only half true," Rik said. "You chose to live not because you loved life but because you didn't want to die. There's a difference." He stopped, and then seeing my confusion, went on: "You'll understand as we move on."

That fall, when I went back to school, I let myself be me. I carried my crystals with me. I wore shirts that bore the message of universal peace. I wrapped my books in covers Danny had helped me make, covers painted with New Age symbols. I wanted people to know who I was.

Gone was the quiet Marci, the shy Marci, the Marci in hiding. I had found my voice, and I was speaking words I always had wanted to say. When teachers asked me questions in classes or on tests, I answered them with my truth — I didn't simply feed them what they wanted to hear. Every paper I wrote, whatever the assigned subject, would touch on philosophy, ways of life I'd learned from the other side. My poor teachers. They didn't know what to make of me or my work. I would answer their questions but not the way they expected. Often my papers came back with two grades on them: an F that had been crossed off and then an A.

For me, this was a compromise. I had accepted that I lived in a world that didn't suit me, but I was determined to succeed. I might be talking out and dropping biology (I refused to dissect an animal) and writing what I wanted to write, but I also had plans. I was going to get straight As, run for student council, get accepted early at Smith, and be my class valedictorian. Most of all, I was going to win a National Merit Scholarship.

They were wonderful plans. In a matter of weeks, they were gone.

It was a few days before Halloween. I was getting ready for school when a conversation with my mother — I don't even remember what we were talking about — turned into a fight. I burst into tears and ran to my room. When she came in to talk to me, I started screaming that I just couldn't do it anymore, I couldn't keep living two different lives. I hated school. I hated the system that gave so much to strong students and so little to weak ones. I wanted to learn about the world — there was so much I wanted to understand — and I couldn't do that kind of learning in school.

My mother kept me home from school for two days. She worried that I was having a nervous breakdown. She kept saying, "Marci, just try to enjoy school; just do the best you can. Stop worrying about being the best. If you fail, you fail."

But I couldn't fail; I didn't know how to fail.

I went to the group meeting Wednesday night. By then I had decided that I wasn't going back to school. My mother and I talked it over and decided I could home-school with a tutor. She had spent a good part of the afternoon fighting with the school administration about it. When I told the members of the group what was going on, they were stunned. Here I was, the only one in the group who ever had cared about grades, and suddenly I was leaving school.

That night, we held hands and formed a circle, and then, together, we raised the energy in our bodies and allowed that energy to flow through us. I was my truth that night and bursting with energy, so much energy that the people on either side of me were sweating.

The next week I went back to school to take my pre-SATs. After the test, my guidance counselor and I talked about what was going on. She was convinced that I was upset about my parents' divorce — they had separated six months before — and urged me to come back to school. I told her my decision had nothing to do with the divorce. Then she told me that I had missed tryouts for the class-play competition, but that the teacher had said I still could get a part. I loved acting, and before I realized what was happening I had agreed to come back, get my assignments, and make up all the work I had missed before grades closed in two weeks.

By the time I got home, I was crying. I knew that I couldn't do it, that I couldn't go back to my old life. And the school had said no to a tutor. My mother had been hoping I'd transfer to a prep school anyway, so she got busy arranging interviews, trying to find a place for me in January, when the new term started. In the meantime, she said, I could stay home and study on my own.

I was free. I didn't have any idea what I was going to do with my life, but I was free.

I spent the next few weeks searching my soul. Finally, I made a decision. I didn't know what I wanted to do when I got older, but I did know who I wanted to be: I wanted to be the person I was in my third world; I wanted to be my truth. And I was sure that I couldn't be that person or learn what that person would have to know about the world in any high school.

My mother wasn't happy when I told her I wasn't going to go back to school, not even to prep school, but she stood by me. I couldn't have faced the onslaught of criticism from friends and family without her.

We both had a feeling that my leaving school had happened for a reason. And my mother's faith in her "special" daughter never wavered. She kept telling people, "My daughter has something special to bring to the world. I can't let her waste that talent by forcing her to be something she isn't."

"You could have taken the easy road," Rik said, meaning that I could have stayed in school.

"I know," I nodded, "but I'm glad I didn't. And it was my choice; I chose."

Õ

It was a few months later. I had started working at a brain-injury center nearby. My case child, a three-year-old named Dylan, was severely handicapped. A complication at birth had left him with only his brain stem. He was blind, deaf, and mute: He couldn't walk or even crawl; he couldn't feed himself. For three hours each day I worked with him, bringing him into the world as much as possible. I taught him to crawl in his own way; I did tactile-response exercises with him; I talked to him; and I helped with his physical therapy. I grew to love all the children at the center, but Dylan was my special joy. His smile was a gift. And I so badly wanted him to know the world he lived in.

One night Dylan came to me in a dream. He asked me why I wanted him to know the physical world when I so often had wanted to leave it. I realized that although this child's body lived in this world, he was living in the world beyond. When I woke up, I understood that I could communicate with Dylan through that other world.

As I worked with him the next day, I thought about the dream and what he had said. Why did I want him to join me in a world I didn't like? I knew why. I wanted him to know what it felt like to swing on a swing, to see a sunset, to dance to the beat of a drum. I wanted him to know what it felt like to go on a first date and fall in love, to dive off a diving board, to run through the woods, to watch a bird fly, to play with a dog. I wanted him to experience all of the things that I took for granted.

That little boy had given me a gift. He helped me appreciate the wonder of the world I lived in. Yes, there were amazing things to experience on the other side — love and power and peace and great beauty. But in the oneness there the individual was lost. In wanting Dylan to know the feeling of dance, of falling in love, of being kissed by someone you love, I came to cherish my physical life. How could I have been willing to throw that away? From that moment on, no matter how angry or hurt I am, I have never wanted to die.

Õ

I was back on the road with Rik. He was talking: "You didn't think you could do that job when they hired you. When you left school, you lost some of the things that used to make you feel confident. You weren't the best in the class anymore; your grades didn't count. But you did the job, and you did it really well. And in the process, you learned what you wanted to do next."

"That wasn't all I was learning," I said. "You said that when the woman asked me if I wanted to live or die, that I chose life by default. It was Dylan who made me want to live for the sake of living, to be alive for the wonder of it."

But I didn't want to talk. I wanted to go on to the next crossroads. I could see them just ahead of us.

It was the night I walked the fire for the second time. This walk was very different. It started with a ceremony to help us get in touch with our feelings and with the fire. I was seventeen, one of the youngest in the group.

I was standing in a ring of people around a huge fire. I could feel the heat on my face. As we held hands and circled the fire singing, I felt as if the flame reached into me and began to pull at my stomach, pulling out the shame I had been feeling. I shared my pain with the group — all those years of thinking I was fat, of bingeing and starving and dieting. I told the others how worthless I felt because I couldn't control the binge-and-starve cycles, how I wanted them to stop. I shared what I thought was my most shameful secret with those people, and when I'd finished, I felt free.

The instructor asked us to look deep within its flames and yell out what we heard. Within moments, others were talking about feeling free and the evolution of humanity. I stopped hearing them. I felt myself go further and further into the fire's soul. It spoke to me, and without realizing it I was repeating its words aloud: "I am you. Together, we are everything. How could I ever hurt what I am? I am the bringer of change. Whatever I touch can never remain the same."

I was thinking that the words were so true when I realized that everyone else had stopped talking. They were all looking at me, their eyes wide, their mouths open.

I walked the fire three times that night without burning myself. I danced with Rik and my friends across the coals. I felt my truth inside; the fire was bringing it out.

Later that night, as the tenders were banking the fire, I made two wishes on its embers: "Help me find a way to get rid of these eating disorders. Help me find a way to be me in the world."

I came back to the road for a moment. Visions of that year began flashing though my mind. I saw myself at Bancroft, where I learned Shiatsu, an ancient form of massage, and studied the mind-body connection. I saw myself dancing. I had joined a dance company and had begun serious training. And I dreamed again of meeting up with my friends and traveling with them, using dance and music and song to touch the hearts of young people and help ease their pain.

Freedom
May 18, 1997

I looked around. I was back in the physical world. I had no idea where I was or how far I had walked, but the surroundings were so beautiful and peaceful, I didn't care.

Rik was with me.

"It doesn't seem so now, but you felt lost that year, the year you were at Bancroft. You wanted so badly to know where you were heading. You kept begging, 'Where is my life going? Please send me a sign.'

"All the time you were learning, getting ready to choose your path. But you didn't understand that, so we sent you signs. Do you remember?"

I did. I had been struggling with a decision. My friends and family — even my mother — had been urging me to go to college. Finally, I agreed. I went for an interview and sent in the application.

I knew it was what everyone wanted me to do; I didn't know if I wanted to do it.

One morning I woke up so confused. I had mailed the forms to the college, but I felt sick inside for doing it. In my mind I spoke to Rik and the others: "Please give me a sign that you are with me and that I will know the right thing to do at the right time."

I was dressed and ready to leave for Bancroft, when I had an urge to go for a walk. I headed to the woods behind our house. I had gone just a short distance when I saw a huge black feather on the ground, one perfect feather lying there. Later that day, a woman told me it was a raven's feather. When a raven crosses your path, she explained, your life is being transformed, and you should be open to the magic the bird is trying to bring you.

For a while, the raven's feather helped. But after a month, still confused about going to college, I was asking again: "Please tell me which way I'm supposed to go. Are you here with me? Are you leading me forward?"

By now it was spring, and I was sitting in a grid of beautiful crystals I had set up in a ring of trees in the backyard. When I stood up, I found another feather, a blue jay's.

Several more months passed. It was summer, and I was finishing up my courses at Bancroft. College was fast approaching, and I still didn't know what to do. I knew I really didn't want to go, but I didn't feel I had other choices. I didn't know what I was supposed to do with my life. I kept wishing I would meet up with the friends in my dreams; I wanted my life to become what I had dreamed it would be. So again I asked, "Are you with me?"

I'd been getting up early every morning for a swim in the

lake down the road. One morning I had to struggle to get out of bed. I'd spent the night tossing and turning, questions running through my mind. As I walked toward the water, I was crying. I felt as though my life was out of my control. I could see a band of white in the middle of the lake, along the path I usually swam. I thought it must be pollen, although I remember thinking it was the wrong time of year for pollen. I jumped into the cold water and started swimming as fast as I could. I wanted to clear my head. Suddenly I found myself in a sea of feathers, thousands of beautiful white feathers floating on the surface of the lake.

I got the point: They were with me.

That September I went to college at Antioch, in Ohio. I knew from the start that it wasn't the right decision for me, but I didn't know how to get out of it. Everyone thought that I should go. More than that, everyone thought I wanted to go.

The ride out with my mother was difficult; I didn't want her to know how unhappy I was. After she got me settled in my room and left, it was even harder. I knew I was in the wrong place, and there was nothing I could do about it. The bill was paid; my scholarships were in place; and I didn't want to disappoint everyone at home.

My sense that I didn't belong at the school grew stronger over the next few days. I had chosen Antioch because it had a different philosophy of teaching, because it seemed to encourage discussion and diversity. What I found was widespread dissatisfaction with the status quo and with anyone who wasn't equally unhappy with the government or society.

There were some things that I enjoyed about being there. I

chose my classes, and they were filled with dance just the way I wanted. In the beginning I really liked my dance training, and I loved the dance parties on campus. I made lots of friends, and I was dating. I loved the town and the acres of conservation land that surrounded it.

It was dance that had brought me to the school; in the end it was dance that made me leave. With every class, the movements we were learning grew sadder. My body balked at the steps. For me, dance always had been a celebration; here it was a protest. And things were no better in my dance-appreciation class, where the students and the teacher found fault with any dance that "spoke" of love or beauty. I remember one day we were watching a videotape of Mikhail Baryshnikov, the great Russian dancer. It was a clip from a classical ballet, and he was astonishing. He danced with such strength and grace and beauty. And as I watched entranced, my classmates made fun of his performance.

When I got back from class that day, I sat on the bed in my dorm room and called to Rik and the other spirits. Again I asked for a sign. All of a sudden I heard birds chirping outside. I ran to the window. There were hundreds of chickadees on the tree outside.

As the birds burst into song outside, "Everything I Do I Do It for You" started playing on the radio. This, too, was a sign, I was sure of it. It was one of the songs I would dance to whenever I needed to touch my truth. So was the next song and the one after that.

I knew what I had to do: I had chosen the wrong path; I had to go home. Three days later, I had withdrawn from school, had packed up my car, and was driving home. I wasn't alone. As I drove, two huge ravens flew above me, seeing me safely on my way.

Õ

"You may have left college, but your learning wasn't over," Rik said. "You had begun this journey of the soul, and you needed to finish it. That was why you couldn't stay at Antioch."

I nodded, understanding it was time to go on.

Ahead of me were dark days. A month after I returned home from Antioch, I had started dating Danny. One night as we were kissing and holding each other, a feeling of shame flooded my body. It wasn't from anything Danny and I were doing; it came from deep inside me. I saw a man's face, the man who had haunted my dreams since I was a child. Suddenly, I knew that this man had raped me.

Over the next few weeks, I fell into a deep depression. I was trying to remember; at the same time, I was fighting the memories. I turned away from the other side; I was angry with the spirits for not protecting me, for not telling me. I turned to psychology to try to remember what had happened, and one therapist after another told me I probably would never remember. They tried to teach me skills to survive, but I didn't want to survive. I wanted to live. I had my entire life ahead of me, and no incident was going to keep me from it.

Eight months went by. My eating disorders resurfaced. Finally, I couldn't take it anymore, and I opened myself up to the other side. Rik was there, and I fell into his arms crying with the shame. He held me and told me it wasn't my shame. Then he looked into my eyes and there, reflected in his, I could see my truth. The memories came flooding back.

Over the next six months, with Rik's help, I journeyed into

my subconscious and dug out all of the memories in detail. I faced them head on, diving into the darkness and hell they created. I cried, tears of sorrow and anger and guilt and shame. I remember my mother and Danny holding me and rocking me and trying so hard to comfort me. I knew they were afraid I would kill myself, but I didn't want to die. I had chosen to live long before this, and I was going to get through it.

When I felt that all of the memories had surfaced, I held my truth like a beacon before me and touched the memories and felt their realness. Before I had tried to forget them; now I was determined to face them. All the rage and shame I had been feeling inside me I turned back on that man . . . and on my father. It was my father, I realized, who had forced me to spend time with that man. In my mind, I screamed at them that they had no right, and then I killed them both.

I felt the rage for several months, and then one day it was gone. It was as though the rape had never happened. I had used my mind to rewrite the past; it couldn't hurt me anymore. I began to live again, to work, to dance.

A few weeks later, I woke up one morning and in my mind I saw my father and that man standing before me. That morning, when I looked at them, I saw their souls and their pain. I couldn't be angry at them; all I felt was love for who they were inside. I knew I would never again sit down to a meal with my father or invite the man who raped me over to my house, but in that moment I forgave them.

A month or two later, I built a fire in the backyard, in the ring of trees with the crystals. There I burned all of the journals I'd kept during my healing. The fire seemed to burn forever. Finally, when nothing was left but ashes, I buried them. And in my mind I gave the shame back to its rightful owners, the men who had hurt me.

Then I built another fire. Within its flames I saw a new woman, one who carried no shame, who was alive and wanted to be her truth. I could start my life over again. The journey to hell and back had taken almost two years and every ounce of strength my soul had. But I had made it back. I was free.

Not long after, I discovered what I wanted to do with my life. Actually, Danny did the discovering. Although we had broken up almost a year before, he was still my best friend and supporter. We were in a New Age store that had opened nearby, when he suddenly turned to the owner and said, "Marci is the greatest meditation leader, and you really should have her teaching here."

I started teaching meditation. The response was great. Four months later, with the courage of that success, I decided to teach the methods I had used to change my memories of the rape. I called those methods Empowerment: A Journey of the Soul, and showed others how to use them to free themselves. It was a simple step from the classes to the tapes. Several of my students had asked me to make tapes of some of my meditations, and my friends convinced me it would be the easiest thing in the world to do. The Quest was born.

Rik laughed at the memory of my friends' saying it would be easy.

"From the time you remembered the rape until the time you started The Quest, you didn't think about what you were doing. You had decided to become your truth, and life simply led you in the right direction," he said.

Then he stopped and looked into my eyes. "We're almost there," he said.

In the distance I could see an enormous marker. This was it, the crossroads I needed to face.

"Are you ready?" Rik asked.

I took a deep breath and nodded. We walked on together.

Sweatlodge: *A Native American ceremony that uses heat to purify the body, mind, and spirit. Each tribe has its own design for the lodge itself, but the structure always represents the womb of Mother Earth. The participants enter that womb and sit in a circle around a fire or heated stones. The heat is intense: The belief is that sweating cleanses the body. And participants often have visions as the warmth overrides conscious thought.*

Flight
May 18, 1997

I went to California the year I turned twenty to learn to teach fire walking. The program was a week long, and it was the most amazing week of my life.

I was looking back at the first afternoon of training. There were thirty of us, sitting in a circle. We were going around the circle, each person in turn saying what held him or her back in life. For some, it was the fear of failing or being hurt; for others, it was a fear of not being good enough. As each person spoke, the group would repeat what he or she said.

Now it was my turn; everyone else had spoken. "It's so easy for them," I thought. "They rattled off whatever it was as though they enjoy carrying it around with them." I couldn't do it; the words wouldn't come.

They were looking at me, waiting for me to speak, encouraging me to go ahead. I started, "The thing that most holds me back in life is . . ." I couldn't say it. Then I blurted it out: "The thing that most holds me back in life is that I hold a very sacred gift inside me and I don't want it."

The others were silent. No one repeated my words. Then, one by one, they started talking: "You have to learn how to use that gift." "You have to help other people with it." "You have to learn to accept your gift."

I heard them, but their words meant little to me. None of them knew what it was like, how hard it had been to be different. My destiny had been forced on me, and I didn't want it.

For a second I was back in the physical world, still walking near my house. Then, just as quickly, I was in California again.

Breathe in, breathe out. Breathe in quickly, breathe it out. Breathe in, breathe out. I was hyperventilating, my body working as hard as it could. My hands were tingling, and I felt as though I was choking. I was exhausted. Colors flashed through my mind — first red, now green, now blue and black and bright yellow.

A man was sitting by my side massaging my muscles. "It's okay," he said, "I'm here for you." Everyone in the room had a partner: one breathing while the other supported. It was an exercise, a breathing technique to bring the mind and body into trance. Every breath in brought oxygen; every breath out took with it pain and stress. I knew I was supposed to relax, but I fought it. I was afraid of exposing myself to these people.

After forty-five minutes, I had no fight left, no reason to hold back, no reason even to breathe. I sensed blankets and hands on my body. At one point, I saw a shadow and felt someone's face close to mine. Then I heard the words, "Breathe Marci. Take a breath. Breathe. You need to breathe, Marci."

But I didn't need to breathe. I could fly. I was an eagle soaring higher and higher. The vastness of all that existed flowed within me.

Only when I was ready, when I was filled with wonder and joy, did I come back to my body and finally breathe. My partner and those who had tried to force me to breathe were looking at me. I could see the fear and puzzlement on their faces. They didn't understand what they had just witnessed.

Õ

Our instructions a couple of nights later were to get up in the morning and get dressed — "No showers, but *please* brush your teeth" — and then to meet in a large room in one of the buildings. Once we got there, one of the instructors stood up and told us today was the sweatlodge. We couldn't have breakfast, he said, but we had to drink five sixteen-ounce glasses of saltwater. After we drank the water, we were to pick up lava rocks and blankets, and bring them down the snowy hill to the sweatlodge. Then we were to go to our rooms and clean up our living space. While we were there, he said, we should make a list of the things we wanted to be rid of in our lives and in our bodies, shower, and change our clothing. After that, we should drink some juice and then report back.

This was the part of the training I was most nervous about. I don't like the heat of a sauna, and a sweatlodge is even hotter. But I had made up my mind to try. I was the first to start drinking the saltwater. The first few ounces weren't bad, but by the time I got to the bottom of the first glass, my stomach was turning. Drinking the second glass was torture. By the third glass, I knew I was going to be sick. By the fourth, I had decided I was in hell. And by the fifth, I wanted to hurt the instructors . . . badly. Everyone felt sick, and as we stumbled down the hill, carrying blankets and lava rocks, some people were throwing up. As for me, I held on tight to my friend Mark. Three times we went up and down that hill carrying supplies, all the while feeling desperately nauseated.

The last of my supplies delivered, I had to turn around, go back up the hill, and clean up the site of the fire walk the night before. A group of us shoveled what was left of the steaming ashes into buckets and then raked the area. I was feeling very sick, and the world was beginning to tilt as I headed back to my room and started straightening up. Suddenly the room was spinning, and I was on the floor.

Two people passing by the open door came running in. One helped me into the bed; the other went off to find the nurse. I thought I was going to die. The room was spinning; everything was moving. When the nurse came, she took my pulse and told me it was faint, that my blood pressure must be low. She gave me some juice with electrolytes, and in a few minutes I was feeling better. I thought the nurse would tell me to stay in bed for the day, but she didn't. She simply waited a while to be sure I was all right and then left.

After a bit, I forced myself to shower and dress, and dragged myself back to the group. I was determined to take part in the exercise; I wanted so badly to be an instructor.

I walked into the room as one of the instructors was finishing his explanation of the sweatlodge. He asked if we had any questions. There were none. We were anxious to get started.

The lodge was built by bowing young saplings and then weaving blankets around them to create walls to keep the warmth in. There was a hole in the center of the lodge for the rocks. Outside the lodge was a blazing fire where the rocks were heated.

We undressed outside and wrapped ourselves in towels. Inside the lodge it was dark. We formed a ceremonial circle and then spread our towels on the ground. I placed my towel between Mark's and my roommate's. As I sat down, helpers put the first lava rocks in the center of the pit, and the leader began pouring water over the rocks. I felt the first blast of heat. There wasn't much room in the lodge, and my neck, back, and knees hurt. I remember thinking, "There's no way I can get through this thing. I can't do this. It's too hot. My body hurts, and I'm so uncomfortable."

A "talking stick" was being passed around the circle. As it moved around the group, each person would say a prayer to be rid of something bad or to be given something good. I didn't know what I was going to say until I felt the stick in my hand. As I spoke, all the pain and discomfort disappeared.

"I want to join with the spirits and be with the other side. I want to feel my soul," I said.

The first round ended, and the helpers brought more rocks in. The stones glowed red as they poured water on them, and the heat rose. I could feel Mark and my roommate pull themselves back from the heat. But for some reason, I seemed to be drawn closer to it. I wanted to feel it. It seemed to fill me with its energy and life.

As the talking stick passed from hand to hand, we prayed for the people in our lives. When it was my turn, I had no idea whom I prayed for. I couldn't hear the others around me anymore. My heart and soul opened with a burst of light. Within the light, a brilliantly colored bird was flying.

I felt myself move closer to the heat, wishing they would make it hotter. For a moment I could hear others begging the leader to splash cool water on them. Then everything around me disappeared again; all that existed were the life and love that grew within me.

Suddenly the woman I would see later in the lava world was there with me, beautiful and glowing in the brilliant light. We came together, merging into one being.

When it was next my turn to pray, I found myself singing:

> *Amazing grace, how sweet the sound*
> *That saved a wretch like me.*
> *I once was lost, but now I'm found.*
> *Was blind, but now I see.*

As the others joined in, I could feel the words in the deepest part of me. I was hearing them, understanding them, for the first time. They were my story. I had been lost and ashamed; I had been blind. And now the light, the heat, had saved me, had shown me the way. I felt the woman's soul in mine, and together we danced in heaven.

Hours passed, but flying on the wings of grace, I had no sense of time. Once again I was asked for a prayer, but I couldn't think of one — I had everything I wanted. So again I sang, feeling the words throughout my being, a song to the Great Spirit, to the water, the air, the fire, and the earth.

I was the Great Spirit, and it was me.

It was over.

I walked out of the lodge into the brilliance of the sun with just a towel around my waist. I felt like a goddess. The others were bathing themselves in the snow, trying to cool off. I wasn't hot; nor was I cold. What I felt was a oneness with everything and everyone: the trees, the stream, the snow, my brothers and sisters. I was elated. Everything inside me had changed; everything felt so alive, so new.

Õ

It was two nights later, the night of the last fire walk — the forty-footer. I could see the scene, but at first it seemed to be playing in slow motion, hesitating. I, too, was hesitant. This was what I had come to face.

The beat of thirty drums burst through my being. It called to me, to my heartbeat, driving my body to dance. Beyond us I could see the fire, an enormous wall of flames. There was no fear, only the pounding of the music. I had entered a wonderful place where physical and spiritual worlds meet. Love poured over me from the other side, and I could feel it with my entire being, my soul and my flesh. This was my truth.

The night had started with a celebration. We had gathered — our group of soon-to-be instructors — and laughed and given one another gifts. Then we followed a path through the trees toward the fire. There were no lights; the flames guided us through the dusk.

Each of us was given a small drum. I remember standing

with the others, beating out the rhythm of my heartbeat. And then they were shadows — I could barely see them — and in their place, emerging from the veil, were spirits, hundreds of spirits.

Somewhere deep within me I heard an ancient call. As I stared into the flames, the fire beckoned, asking my soul to come home, to dance within its embrace. Tears streamed down my face as it spoke to me, not in words but in love. I could feel my truth struggling to break free of the walls I had built to protect me. The fire knew my truth and made the beauty of my soul its gift to me.

I stood before the flames, my soul naked, exposed — a young woman standing before her first lover, wanting to touch the unknown but shy and timid. The fire was my lover, and its spirit touched parts of me that I had forgotten. Gently, but with a passion I had never known, it pulled me in, touched me in my soul. I gasped in ecstasy as its power rushed through me. The awkwardness, the innocence, were gone. I was all that is glorious in life. I was the power of the trees joining the earth to the skies. I was the glow of the moon shining on snow-covered fields. I was the spirit of the wind carrying a flower's seed from garden to desert. I was life itself.

I danced as I had never danced before, with laughter and life and love filling the movements of my body. I looked up at the sky, in awe of the universe, and knew that I was so much more than a body or a place. I was God. I was heaven. Death and life were one.

The fire was my partner, filling me with desire. I wanted to be one with it, to feel it inside me, to know what it felt. I wanted to be the fire. The flames drew me closer and closer. I couldn't feel the heat; all I could feel was the fire's purity. It wasn't good or bad, it just was. It was its truth. I laughed again with the beautiful simplicity of it. Truth. No judging or being judged, just truth. And the only responsibility it had — the only responsibility I had — was to be that truth.

I couldn't wait for the coals to be raked into a path. I was aching to touch the fire with my body.

I danced harder and harder, the energy within me growing stronger, feeding my power and the power of the flames. For a moment I could see the others beating their drums for me. I had bared myself to the fire, and now I could see my soul in their eyes.

I moved closer to the fire, afraid they might take this glorious feeling away. The drummers pulled back. Did they know? Did they understand my fear? Were they afraid too? And in the fire I felt the answer. Truth. Like the fire, I must be my truth. Nothing else mattered.

With that understanding, my soul opened once more. The others moved closer to me again, as though they sensed a shift in energy. In that moment of acceptance I felt such overpowering love that I have no words to describe it. My ancient teacher once said to me, "The love the universe holds is so powerful that if you're not prepared for it, it could destroy you or make you mad." This was the love of the universe, and when it touched me, I felt so alive.

The coals were ready; the dancing was over. As I moved toward the place where the walk would begin, the others stepped away. They seemed to know that I would walk first, that I needed to touch the fire before it had been touched by anyone else, that I needed to feel only its truth. I asked the man leading the walk if I could go. He looked surprised, but I didn't care. I was so confident, so sure of myself, that I didn't need anyone's approval. He nodded yes.

Dancing and breathing in the essence of the flames, I stepped forward. As my feet touched the coals, everything went black, and I was filled with peace.

Õ

I was back on the road near my house. I took a deep breath and covered my eyes with my hands. Rik was there, but for a moment I shut him out. I needed to think about what I had just seen . . . without his help. I knew what this journey had been all about. I had been shown the beauty of my truth that night and had denied it. It had been calling to me ever since.

I remembered coming home from the training. I had changed so much in that week, but no one else had. And I had no one to talk to about the training, no one with whom to share that glorious experience. Even Danny couldn't understand. Within days, I was confused again, unsure about the direction of my life.

It's not that I didn't have friends. I did, but they just weren't interested in things otherworldly. They wanted to be twenty and go to clubs and dance and have fun. I had been spending a lot of time with Robbie. We met one night at a club, and he made me laugh as we tangoed around the dance floor. I liked that. And later, when I left him to dance with other men, he was fine about it. I liked that too.

I gave him my number, and he called the next night and we talked for a while. He was easy to talk to. But over the next few weeks, we kept missing each other, leaving messages and never being home for the calls back. A month passed before we ran into each other at the club again. We flirted and laughed, and when he pulled me to him in a hug as we were dancing, I felt as though I'd known him all my life.

I was so comfortable around Robbie. He didn't care about my other worlds, and I didn't mind that. He just wanted to have fun, to dance with me and sneak a kiss once in a while.

Then he came to a fire walk with me. It was the first walk I was leading, and friends and family had gathered to support me. Robbie decided to come along. The fire was raked out, and as I stood before the path I felt its glory and its call. I breathed it through my soul. The drums started beating, and I began to dance.

Then I looked up and saw Robbie standing at the edge of the fire. Although he smiled at me, I was sure he was asking himself what was happening to me. Suddenly I realized I didn't want him to see what comes over me when I walk the fire. Walls went up, and I shut down.

I crossed the fire four times that night, but not for me. I crossed to help the others. And when it was over, I felt empty and alone.

I made a choice that night to be normal, to turn my back on my truth. For two months I partied. I hung out with Robbie and his friend Charlie each night, dancing and just having fun. For a month, I stayed up until all hours, I ate whatever I wanted, I didn't work out, and I didn't worry about the state of the world.

Then it all changed. The army transferred Robbie and Charlie, and with them gone, I could feel a pulling at my soul. To quiet that call, I went back to work on the tapes I was planning to release that year through The Quest.

That's when I met David. He loved and accepted me — all

of me. Soon he became my business partner, and then something changed. I got so caught up in the business of marketing the magic, that I forgot the importance of the magic itself, of my connection.

I had forgotten something else. The crossroads grew brighter in my mind. The straight road had ended. My next step would take me onto a road that ran left and right. As I took that step, I saw myself in the living room with my mother, right after Robbie and Charlie had left, telling her that I was planning to go away for a while, that I needed to explore the world. Two months later, instead of traveling, I was getting the tapes ready to sell.

I turned to Rik. "I forgot that I had planned to go away. My god, I'm exactly where I started out three years ago, planning to travel, but what a roundabout road I've taken." I stopped for a minute as I realized what I had just said. "Rik, *'I've taken.'* I had a choice; I chose to start The Quest."

"That's right, Marci," Rik said. "And why did you choose to start The Quest?"

I laughed to myself. "Maybe because I didn't feel as though I had a choice. I had no money."

"No," he said, "it had nothing to do with money. If you'd really wanted to go, you would have found a way. You found the money to publish your tapes."

I thought long and hard. When I looked up, we were on the road walking toward my house. I had made a circle without even realizing it, just like the one I had made in my life. Two questions were running through my mind: Did I actually choose to stay three years ago? And if I did, was I sorry now about that choice?

I was crying as I turned to Rik again. "We need to talk," I

said. "Not just you and me. I need to talk with all of the teachers I have ever had."

I had barely thought the words, and they appeared. I could see them through the crystal wall. Rik was standing near the spirits from my bedroom. The beautiful man and woman were there, too. And there was my ancient teacher from the castle. There were hundreds of them. As I looked from face to face at these spirits who had taught me and watched over me and loved me, I heard the sound of glass breaking. The wall was coming down. I could feel their love as they waited for me to speak.

"All my life," I said, "I've only wanted to make you proud. I knew I had this gift, but I was sure it came with a responsibility, not just to help the world, but to help you. I felt I was your tool, the only way you could touch a hurting world.

"I was so torn. I wanted my freedom so badly, yet I felt a prisoner of my destiny. Rik asked me why I chose to create The Quest. There were two reasons. The first had to do with my knowledge. How could I see the pain in the world without helping to ease it? The Quest was a way to share that knowledge, to help others cope with their pain."

The man from the sky reached out and stroked my hair. "What is the other reason?" he asked.

"I felt I was your messenger, that everything you had taught me was for a single purpose, to take your message to the world."

I looked out on their faces. I saw the love there, and I knew I had to finish explaining. "I sound so dutiful," I said. "Since I was a young child you have guided me to be your voice. You taught me how to ease the world's pain. That was why I couldn't bear to look at my life or to face the experience I had at the forty-footer. It was just more proof that I couldn't have my own life. I felt as though you chose everything that happened so that I would be a better teacher.

"And whenever I walked away from teaching, I felt as though you were punishing me, forcing me back on the 'right' path. I started The Quest and have pushed ever since so that I could be free of this destiny once and for all."

I looked down. I was sure I had hurt them, and I couldn't bear to see that hurt. Then I went on: "Now I have a question. Will you let me walk away for as long as I choose?"

They didn't speak. Their message came to me in waves of energy.

"We're sorry." *Sorry?* I didn't understand.

"Can you forgive us?" *Forgive them?* I burst into tears. Of course I could forgive them. I loved them more than anything.

"We didn't push you so you could help others; we just missed you. We simply wanted to feel you with us again. Your destiny is to become your truth. *Your* power is just that, for *you.* Everything we did, we did for you, to help you accept who you are and to realize that being different doesn't mean you can't be loved. We just didn't understand how hard it is to be you in your world."

I was sitting on my deck, staring out over the water, but I still was connected to their world. I could feel their love, their warmth, all around me.

I felt another wave of energy: "We never chose for you. We may have nudged you and taught you enthusiastically, but we never chose for you. Every road you've taken has been a path you've chosen."

I was crying again. So I did have a life of my own. I did have choices. Whatever my reasons — right or wrong — the decisions had been mine.

I could feel them again. "Go and enjoy your life. Run free, and be the soul you are."

"But what about the others? If I go away, who will tell them?" I asked. "How will they know without me?"

"But you are telling them, Marci. Right now, in this book and on the tapes. And some of them already know. They've seen us in that place at the edge of their dreams. They know we're there listening to their prayers and wanting only to love them.

"You know your truth now. That's all we ever wanted for you. Go be who you want to be. If you decide to teach, that's wonderful. And if you decide not to teach, that too is wonderful. You are free."

With that message, I found myself back on the road of my life. Again I was at a crossroads, facing the same decision I had faced three years before. One road seemed to wind off; the other looked straight. I knew whichever road I took, I would travel with my truth. I would no longer be afraid of my gifts or hide them away. It was time for me to be me, to explore my world and take pleasure in it. With a smile, I stepped onto the straight path.

The sun danced across the water, and I felt them smile with me. This path had nothing to do with other people or spirits. It was mine. I had no idea where it would take me, but I was sure I would be okay.

From across the lake I heard music. I knew the words to the song; a friend had danced it with her father at her wedding. I was singing softly when Rik came up behind me and wrapped his arms around me.

"I'll be there, Marci," he whispered in my ear. "I'll be at your wedding and everything else that comes along. I'll be the one beaming with pride at my beautiful angel. You're free. Go fly."

And deep inside me, a butterfly broke free.

About the Author: Marci Archambeault has been teaching meditation and empowerment classes for 11 years. She is a certified fire walking instructor, a Swedish and Shiatsu massage therapist, and a Reiki practitioner. She is also the creator of The Quest — a company dedicated to helping people achieve their highest potential.

To Contact the Publisher: If you would like more information about this book, please write to the author in care of The Quest. We appreciate hearing from you and learning about your enjoyment of this book and how it has helped you. The Quest cannot guarantee that every letter will be responded to, but all will be reviewed. Please write to:

The Quest
P.O. Box 1321
Leominster, MA 01453

ph: (800) 777-9149
fax: (978) 466-1111

url: http://home.att.net/~TheQuest
e-mail: TheQuest@att.net

For a catalog, please enclose a self-addressed, stamped envelope for reply or $1.00 to cover costs.

ALSO BY MARCI ARCHAMBEAULT

Past Life Regression & After Life Journey: Past life regression can help you to understand more about yourself and how you react to this world. This tape will bring you to experience other life times where you will be able to gain knowledge that will help free your life.
ISBN: 1-888861-01-0   Retail: $14.95

Healing Journey: This tape will help you discover what is holding you back in life. It will help you to overcome fear and addictions. The Healing Journey will empower you to become the person you were meant to be.
ISBN: 1-888861-00-2   Retail: $14.95

Trance Channeling: Learn to speak to the spirit realm. With this tape you will meet your spirit guides and talk to loved ones that have passed on. You will get in touch with your own higher power and actually do a psychic reading with a partner.
ISBN: 1-888861-02-9   Retail: $14.95

Crystal Castle Journey: This tape will help your child to learn faster, to be more creative, to learn tools that will help them deal with their emotions, to feel free to express themselves, and to live healthier, happier lives.
ISBN: 1-888861-03-7   Retail: $14.95

Empowerment "A Journey of the Soul": Empowerment is an eight tape series that will help you to unlock your full potential. Empowerment will show you how to break through addictions and past programming, to heal the past, and to find the amazing person you truly are inside.
ISBN: 1-888861-04-5   Retail: $69.95

"The solutions to all problems lie within you — only the lack of knowledge keeps you stuck in the past."